Beyond The Father

gods on Trial: The Series™
Volume 1

Opëshum

Published by 1iR3 Publishers, LLC, 2023

While every precaution has been taken in the preparation of this book, the publisher assumes no responsibility for errors or omissions, or for damages resulting from the use of the information contained herein. No identification with actual persons (living or deceased), places, buildings, or products is intended or should be inferred.

BEYOND THE FATHER

Second Print Edition. July 2023

Written by Opëshum

Trigger Warning

This novel is recommended for a mature audience. Some readers may find parts of the story disturbing, and reader discretion is advised.

Glossary

Readers are encouraged to first view the Xżyberian Glossary & Facts before they start reading this story.

Table of Contents

I dedicate this book to my extraterrestrial friends, who shared their memories with me…

Episode 1
A Storm is Coming

It was a bitter season for some of the planets within the Warget solar system.

Xżyber, the smallest of all planets, seemed to be one rife with instability—either from war or the destructiveness of lengthy and violent storms. The one solace to Anglid, a young Xżyberian, was that today was his eighteenth birthday.

"Today, you can have anything you want, my son," King Thio said to Anglid. King Thio was a stout king who—with the exemption of his bright, well-cared-for teeth—showed signs that he had long been neglecting his overall health. He delivered his birthday greetings to Anglid between gasps and strained breathing. He raised a heavy black colored goblet in the air, revealing fleshy fingers that seemed much too large for the rings sentenced to adorning them.

Anglid remained polite, but pensive, and focused his eyes on his breakfast plate, packed with the flesh of "land eel," which was Anglid's favorite Xżyberian game.

"Are you sure, Father? Anything?" Anglid asked, briefly glancing at the king.

"Yes. Anything!" replied Thio. "You couldn't possibly surprise an old king like me. After all, I was a young one like you once—filled with will and curiosity, and—" he smirked. "—I was packed with desires for the lovely Xżyberetts within view. Ah . . . tender youth!" he continued, while closing his eyes.

"I would like to visit the cell of the Fallen King . . . dear father." Anglid nearly stumbled over the words, as King Thio's face looked as though he'd swallowed a piece of glass.

"How dare you ask for such a thing?" King Thio replied through labored breathing.

"But Father. . ." attempted Anglid.

"I mean . . . how dare you ask me for such a *silly* thing," he said, with a more tempered tone." And on such a *momentous* day as your eighteenth birthday!" King Thio walked over to Anglid's chair and placed his hands steadily on each of his shoulders. Leaning over to meet Anglid's ear, he continued in a whisper, "I was expecting to grant you a trip around Xżyber, all on your own—a personal vision quest," he mused. "Of course, you'd have to be escorted by some of our personnel at least *part* of the way. Or better yet, I could arrange your meeting the Xżyberette of your dreams. You'll just have to tell me who she is," the king teased.

"Father . . . I'm sorry. I don't have any desire for those things. At least not presently," responded Anglid, his eyes fixed squarely on his plate of food.

King Thio laughed nervously. "So go ahead, then," the king prodded. "If you don't desire what I've mentioned, what do you actually want, my son?"

"Yes, dearest Anglid, our darling boy," said Queen Evaline, as she seemed to float into the room. "Your father is prepared to give you anything your heart desires, and if you are *wise* in your asking, you might request that he grant you the ruling rights over the lower Xżyberian Province!" Queen Evaline moved the hair that was covering Anglid's left eye— blinded in a sparring accident with his father five years prior. She gently kissed his eye, holding his face firmly in her hands. "Would that not be wonderful?" she asked, lovingly.

Shaking his hair back over his eye, Anglid smiled at his mother. "All I really want is to visit the cell of the Fallen King, Mother," stated Anglid, bravely. "I know that he exists . . . and although I know we aren't supposed to talk about it, if I could just . . ."

Queen Evaline walked slowly to her seat and slipped into it as the room fell painfully silent.

"If you are open to what I truly want," Anglid continued, "then you will grant me this one chance to see . . . to *talk* with him."

"Someone has been filling your head with fibs, my son," insisted the king while laughing. "There is no cell where we keep *fallen kings*!"

Queen Evaline's gracile hands seemed to flutter nervously as she poured warmed Teal oil into a small glass.

"Anya told me that he exists, Father," Anglid said, his voice now almost shaking. "She never ever lied to me," he continued.

Queen Evaline's glass managed to slip from her fingers. "Anglid!" the queen cried, her voice almost shrill. "We promised that we would no longer mention Anya's name," she scolded.

King Thio gestured to one of the laborers to clean up the table and floor where the Teal oil had splattered. The sunlight that once spilled into the room and across the breakfast table had suddenly been snuffed out as dark clouds recolored what, just moments ago, was a perfect yellow sky. The sound of wind began to whistle through the castle's small cracks and breaches.

"Mother," Anglid said, as respectfully as he could. "She was my sister. I don't want to keep pretending that she never existed. I miss her terribly!" Anglid looked up to meet his mother's gaze. "Please don't insist that I forget her."

"We will have to continue this conversation another time, I'm afraid," interjected the king. "Right now, a bad storm is coming, and we had better retreat to the interior compound."

"Father!" Anglid insisted.

"Anglid," pressed the queen. "We must prepare to retreat, and now."

"Your Guide, in all your magnificence," said zakum, one of King Thio's laborers. "Please allow us to lead you and your family into the inner quarters, where you will all be safe.” zakum bowed his head as the king rose from his seat. One of the many laborers under King Thio’s rule, zakum was a distinct favorite of the king and queen. With arms extended gracefully, zakum bent his small frame so far forward that his face nearly touched the floor, where the scent of the Teal oil that the queen had spilled still lingered.

This, the greatest gesture of deference and respect, pleased the king while, on the other hand, caused Anglid’s stomach to churn in sync with the sound of the coming storm.

They did not see calm skies again for four weeks.

Episode 2
Disconnected

"We will attack from both the Southern Border and the North East, entering by surprise. They won't be expecting us to come over the mountains," Commander Dugar stated with confidence. He repositioned his cuff links while scanning the room, which was filled with his military peers.

"Commander," stated Officer Liara. "Your plan would require us to cross the Xżyberian Mountain Range . . . undetected, correct?" Liara asked, trying to conceal her lack of faith in Dugar's plan.

"Yes, Officer Liara?" Commander Dugar asked. "What is your concern?" His eyes scanned her up and down disapprovingly.

Hoping that one of the other officers would speak up in support, Liara looked around at her comrades. However, they remained silent. "Well, it's just that we would have to turn off all of our surveillance and communication devices in order to be undetectable . . . and given the unpredictability of the terrain, I am just concerned about the fleet taking that route without the ability to keep their systems on. Sir."

Commander Dugar's face looked as though he had swallowed something bitter. This was the last quarter of his first term as Commander, and things weren't going that well for him. With one military blunder already under his belt, he needed a successful and aggressive win in order to get nominated for a second term. He had very little appreciation for Liara's expressed lack of faith in his proposal, especially now. If for no other reason, Liara's father had expressed interest in running for the position of Commander for the upcoming term, making it counterproductive to take Liara's advice, even if Commander Dugar knew she was right.

"Any concerns from anyone else? *Anyone?*" Commander Dugar asked, avoiding further eye contact with Officer Liara.

Liara stepped forward. "We can't put the fleet in danger by trying to cross the mountain ranges unequipped, Commander," she said, her voice now bolder than before.

"Step back in line, Officer!" Commander Dugar said sternly, his teeth visibly clenched.

"Yes . . . Sir," she said, hesitantly. She knew that, without the support of the other officers, it was pointless. Although she felt the plan was rife with potential disaster—and wanted others to speak up, for their own reasons her comrades would not dare question Dugar.

Officer Hace was new to the group and was still trying to curry favor with Dugar. Officer Bloon had recently completed a five-month disciplinary program for insubordination against his division supervisor and had been recently accepted back into the force only as a favor to his father, a retired general of the Southern Fleet. His father's constant reminders that any more infractions would disgrace their family's reputation kept Bloon silent. Even Senior Officer Nucrist, second in command to Dugar, stood in silent agreement, as though some prior bargain had been made to not outwardly question Dugar's plans—no matter how flawed.

Then there was Thai, an officer who had once been betrothed to Liara, and with whom she now shared an awkward friendship. Thai had also decided to leave Dugar's plan unchallenged.

"So, we have a plan, then," the Commander said, pointing back up to the map. He then turned off his screen presentation, smiling with satisfaction. "All uncrewed and crewed units must be fully prepared to head out by Season 2, and as you all know . . . that doesn't give us much time. There will be no exceptions and no excuses for not being ready. Only the sick or the dead will be exempt from being deployed. Please prepare your troops accordingly, and make sure they are all registered with Team Command *before* they report to their HAS stations for further training. Dismissed!"

"Thank you, sir," said multiple officers, as they began to disperse.

Officer Liara stormed out of the room.

"Liara!" Officer Thai said, rushing up to her. Then, with a smile, he stepped in closer. However, Liara turned swiftly and walked away. "Hey!" Thai said, trying to grab her by the arm. "Why are you mad at me?"

"For not speaking up!" snapped Liara. "His plan is dangerous and will likely cause casualties. *Many* casualties!" she continued.

Thai quietly enjoyed the way Liara furrowed her brow when she was angry, reminding him of the many times he had been successful in turning her frowns to laughter. He had known Liara since they attended military training, where they'd graduated at the top of their class. As their friendship and mutual admiration deepened over the years, so too did Liara's attachment to Thai. The pair eventually asked Thai's father to sponsor the installation of emotional simulation software in Thai, to match what had been installed in Liara many years prior.

However, his father's military career aspirations for his son did not include spending resources on expanding Thai's emotional capabilities. He found Liara's need for emotions unnecessary, and only sanctioned a minor upgrade in Thai's software, allowing him to experience a profound physical attraction for Liara and disproportionate jealousy towards anyone who won Liara's attention. However, he was incapable of showing compassion for others, and his complete obsession with combat rendered him primarily a killing machine. He was just what his father wanted.

As Liara stood there fuming, Thai quietly admired her chocolate skin, perfectly sculpted face, and large green eyes. "If any officers can lead a fleet through the mountains, we can," Thai said, attempting to reassure her.

"Thai, no one has ever attempted to invade the Central Region by way of the ranges. They're too rugged," Liara insisted.

"The only reason why it hasn't been done before, Liara, is because there hasn't been an imperative to do it, like there is now," replied Thai. "King Thio and his royal thugs have turned the Central Kingdom into a growing threat that will impact all of us—even here in the Sub-Median Region!"

Liara sighed impatiently. "Agreed," she replied. "But the Central Kingdom is not an *imminent* threat to us here! We can afford more time to develop a more thoughtful plan of attack."

"Imminent? No," agreed Thai. "Definite? Yes. We already know that he is planning on expanding his Kingdom out towards the East, an area that you and I both know is rich in natural resources. If the Central Kingdom gets the East, the Sub-Median Region doesn't. And all the precious metals, Teal oil, natural gases, and crystals that are freely available to us now will soon be under the control of the CK—unless we stop them!"

"How do you know this?" asked Liara, impatiently.

"My father informed me last night, after his meeting over at Team Command," responded Thai.

Liara looked down, searching for a response. Thai's explanation gave her greater appreciation for the importance of Dugar's mission but did not explain its urgency. She looked back up at Thai, her eyes narrowed and skeptical.

Thai met her gaze straight on. "Look, I get it," he continued. "It's really risky. We'll probably lose some of our fleet. But the benefits still outweigh the risks. Thio's forces aren't monitoring the mountains because they're thinking like *you're* thinking—that nobody would ever attempt to cross over them. They're expecting us to attack the Southern border, which we will. But it's a surprise invasion through the mountains that will take them off guard and give us the advantage that we need."

Although she understood Thai's position and could see the benefit of a surprise invasion, she knew that the mission was not suited for everyone on the fleet. "Thai . . ." Liara began, sighing deeply. "Our troops are not trained to travel through areas like that! Even though Dugar's plan is to deploy in Season 2 when it's warmer, it will still be too cold in the mountains, and the threat of storms wiping out most of the fleet is going to be very *very* high. I still say we need a more well-thought-out plan, one that won't destroy half of us!"

Thai's face became expressionless. "Us?" he asked, rubbing his chin. "There is no 'us' to be concerned about, Liara. We're Mollards, remember? Cold weather and storms can't break us," he said, laughing arrogantly. Thai's large muscles and tall, well-constructed frame was a testament to the efficiency of his design, and it paired well with what Liara believed was his distilled obsession with war. Yet still, the manner in which he moved, the sound of his voice, and his clear silver eyes also mapped well to Liara's ongoing and inconvenient affection for him.

"Thai, please don't forget that half of my fleet are still mostly organic," said Liara. "Organic matter, being what it is, just isn't as resilient, remember? Parts take months to grow back! If defeating the CK is *that* crucial, then we can't afford that kind of downtime."

Thai, who was 100% Mollard, showed little deference for non-Mollards, and often regarded them as burdens to the fleet. The benefit to Team Command, however, was that partly-organic fleet members were a dime a dozen. Very few military leaders in the Sub-Median Region valued them as much as they did the highly efficient Mollards. Non-Mollards were, therefore, happy to take the jobs they were given—at any offered rate, and within any field that was willing to hire them. Non-Mollards, having little loyalty to a specific group or region, were the most loyal to those who paid them the most in Teal oil, a substance that was critical to their survival.

"The only 'us' I'm concerned about is the 'us' that's not gonna hold us back!" Thai said, harshly. "I can't do anything about those half-evolved Non-Mollard freaks that we unfortunately have on some of our fleets. The sight of their flesh disgusts me, and I'd be happy to put them out of their misery if it weren't a crime. Besides, they're not loyal to us. They're just working for food!"

Thai broke eye contact with Liara, and walked away. Liara paused, and took the opportunity to recall why their relationship had failed.

Episode 3
Without Reflection

"I'm sorry to conclude that they have all frustrated me, terribly," announced Flexix. "Perhaps we should just erase them all and start over."

"START OVER?"

"Yes, start over from scratch," said Flexix.

"WHAT IF YOUR CHOICE IS THE WRONG CHOICE?"

"Are you questioning me . . . again?" Flexix's eyes began to darken to a deeper red than usual, a sign of his mounting anger. "I suppose that I should erase you as well!"

"IF YOU ERASE ME, THEN WHO WILL YOU TALK TO?"

"No one!" Flexix, snapped. "I shall talk to no one . . . unless of course I should want to talk to *someone* about what I should recreate, after I have erased all that I created before."

"YES. PERHAPS."

"So then, maybe . . ." Flexix pondered.

"PLEASE GO ON."

"Maybe I shall not erase anyone. But I shall punish *someone*," he continued. Flexix closed two of his eyes, and left the other six open, which scanned the darkness and the stillness. "I shall punish the Mollards," added Flexix. "I shall break their metal body parts into small pieces and reduce it all to a beautiful liquid, that I shall then use to paint their skies the color of silver. That would be beautiful, don't you think?"

"CERTAINLY."

"And the liquid will hold in place for a short time only," Flexix continued. "But then it will form into droplets of metal rain, unleashing a storm unlike any other." All of Flexix's eyes rolled wildly with excitement. "And the rain drops will be a heavy, thick, shiny silver—painful and unforgiving, like bullets from an enemy."

"ARE YOU THEIR ENEMY?"

"Why, not at all!" Flexix insisted. "These shall be very beautiful silver raindrops . . . like the eyes of beautiful, organic Non-Mollards. They will be stunning and beautiful to behold, since the Xżyberians need beautiful things with which to interact. I shall flood their plains with this beautiful silver rain until they drown in its glory. That is what I shall do."

"MAYBE YOU SHOULD."

"Maybe I should what?"

"AS YOU SAY . . . PUNISH SOMEONE."

"I was not talking about punishing someone . . . or anyone," insisted Flexix. "I was literally *just* talking about giving beauty to *everyone*!" Flexix reached his arms out, desperately grabbing in all directions, as if trying to catch something.

"WHY ARE YOU EXTENDING YOURSELF IN THAT WAY?"

"So that I can strangle you," Flexix replied matter-of-factly.

"AND WHY, MAY I ASK, DO YOU CHOOSE TO STRANGLE ME?"

"Because you are neither listening, nor understanding *anything* I am saying."

"HOW CAN YOU BE CERTAIN I DONT UNDERSTAND? WHAT IF YOU'RE WRONG? WHAT IF YOU HAVE *ALWAYS* BEEN WRONG? IF ONE PUNISHES ANOTHER WITHOUT KNOWING FOR CERTAIN THAT THEY DESERVE TO BE GRANTED PUNISHMENT, THEN HOW DOES THAT PUNISHMENT SERVE ANY PURPOSE OR ENLIGHTENMENT?"

"I might be inclined to agree—but not because I actually *care* for any points you are making. It is only because I desperately yearn for the interaction. It's very dark here. Too dark for my delicate eyes," complained Flexix. "And it is terribly hard to accept the nothingness that is—everything and *all* there is. I long for you . . . to fill the space with your thoughts, so that I don't have to be tormented by my own. The silence around me threatens to be my greatest source of torture . . . of punishment." Flexix stopped grabbing at the air and folded his eight arms into a large, tight knot in front of him.

"I SEE."

"I shall punish the Fallen King, Uriss," Flexix mused, closing all of his eyes. "I shall break his spine by pulling him apart. But . . . I have no cause to punish him, really. Other than the fact that I *can*, there is no reason to punish Uriss. As you have noted, I am not at all *certain* of the value of punishing him, or if he even deserves it. So . . . I shall not punish Uriss. I shall not punish anyone." Flexix began to fidget. "Why have you raised the topic of punishment, though? I shall not talk to you for a time. I do not find your words helpful! They have taken away the beloved silence that propels me so gracefully to my sleep."

Episode 4
What is Owed

A very apathetic-looking Anglid stared out the window of the Royal TourCraft where he sat, waiting for the pilot's signal for takeoff.

"scutsman and żah will be by your side," King Thio assured Anglid, leaning into the TourCraft. "scutsman accompanied your cousin, Berone on his vision quest when Berone was your age. So, he will be both a resource and a companion to you on the first portion of your journey."

Anglid stared curiously at the king. His father's words brought him little comfort, knowing that Berone had gotten lost during his quest and was rumored to have later joined the opposition army.

"It is entirely up to you what you make of this journey, my son," offered the king. "Remember . . . this is *your* quest."

"Yes, Father," Anglid responded as his attention drifted past the king and over towards his mother, whom he could see was weeping.

"Six minutes before takeoff, Your Guide," the pilot informed Thio.

"Yes, yes. Of course," the king responded.

Queen Evaline quickly pushed in, her face flush and her brow wrinkled with worry. "Be safe, and come back to me," she said, brushing the hair from his face before kissing it gently.

"It's five minutes before takeoff, now, Your Guide," advised the pilot.

King Thio took Anglid's hand. "If you could find anything you wanted on your quest, my son, what would that be?" he asked.

A despondent Anglid reluctantly looked at his father. He hesitated and then responded, "Perhaps I shall find my other eye," he said, sarcastically.

The king smiled, although smiling was so far short of what he knew he owed Anglid. His years of guilt and shame for piercing his son's eye straight through with a sword he had only meant to use for teaching, seemed to rise up unbearably now, causing his throat to throb. The moments leading up to his son's malfortune flashed before him once again, and he could see young Anglid begging him to teach him how to defend himself in battle.

"I want to fight. Teach me to fight with this!" Anglid pleaded. Anglid was holding a long, selenite crystal sword, and raised it above his head. "Teach me how to slay the enemy with my sword," young Anglid repeated in a near chant, his boyish frame still slight and awkward, his eyes filled with curiosity and wonder.

"Very well," King Thio said. "But, if you are to defeat your enemy, you must strike at the weakest parts,"

he explained. "Hands, arms, legs, and even the feet will grow back within months and as such, they are not worth the expense."

"I understand, Father," young Anglid responded with excitement.

"You must strike with precision and grace, aiming your fury at the organs . . . the heart, the lungs, . . . or the spleen. The eyes, too, are a worthy target, since blinding your opponent permanently will certainly gain you the upper hand."

"Understood," responded Anglid.

King Thio leaned in to speak in a lower voice. "But no battle is worth it if you do not understand why you are fighting," he explained. "There must be a purpose *to your ire and a meaning to fight—a reason for ending your opponent's life. As long as there is, you will fight well."*

Anglid spun around dramatically, holding the sword close to his chest. "Ok, then!" young Anglid said, dramatically. "Prepare to die, in the name of the New Republic!"

"The New Republic you say?" the king responded playfully." Reprobates and criminals—every last one of you! I shall gladly accept your invitation to battle!" King Thio picked up a ceramic sword from the mantel behind him.

"Prepare to lose this battle! For I am here for the people," Anglid continued. "Prepare to be dethroned, for you are corrupt and evil!" Anglid swished his sword about wildly in all directions.

"I shall not be dethroned by the likes of a miscreant!" announced Thio. "Aim your sword well, sir!"

"Preparing for takeoff, Your Gracious," the pilot announced, attempting to garner the king's attention. "Your Guide?"

"Oh yes, so sorry. What were you saying?" the king responded, slightly startled.

"It's time, Your Guide," replied the pilot. "It's time for takeoff."

The king nodded to Anglid and then took hold of Queen Evaline, guiding her away from the door of the TourCraft. The military guard assisting with the takeoff ceremony bowed down before the king and queen, and then slammed the door of the TourCraft, ensuring it was properly shut. Several guards clustered around and escorted the king and queen off of the runway, and Anglid's face could be seen from the window of the TourCraft now only from a distance.

Evaline turned to Thio, revealing a face glistening and moist with tears. "I should have kissed him one more time," she cried.

Episode 5
A Quest Begins

"The king's first military leader is instructing us to stay in close communication with them," scutsman told żah. żah was a skilled pilot and had just completed his fourth year of loyal service with the Central Kingdom. scutsman, the king's highest ranking military advisor, was honored to accompany Anglid on his journey to manhood.

"Affirmative," replied żah. "The main dashboard and our wristbands are all programmed for communication updates twice per day."

"That is fine. However, the queen has requested updates four times daily," advised scutsman, briefly glancing at żah. "Let's be sure that happens."

"Reprogramming the dashboard now," said żha, with a slight smirk on his face. żha, who had grown up with only a father, found the queen's doting on Anglid to be a bit confusing. However, żha's recognition of his rank and place reminded him to keep his opinions strictly to himself.

"Your Gracious," began żha, "Requesting permission to advise you on how to recalibrate your wristband."

Anglid studied the pattern of the lights flashing across the dashboard by the pilot's controls, alternating from red, to green, to blue.

"May we have your permission, Your Benevolent One?" żah continued.

"On one condition," Anglid responded.

"Yes, certainly, Your Gracious. Anything at all," żha said.

"You spare me any signs of your excruciatingly painful subservience during this *entire* trip," Anglid said, sharply.

"Oh! . . . certainly, Your—Your Grace," fumbled żha.

"Most certainly, Your Benevolence . . ." scutsman added.

"No!" Anglid snapped. "No. My name is Anglid. Not 'Your Benevolence,' not 'Your Grace.' Just plain Anglid!"

Scutsman and żah, notably horrified, both started fidgeting. scutsman quickly opened his emergency brief, nervously flipping its pages while żha busied himself with a nervous fit of clearing his throat.

"We follow the Plebonian faith," scutsman began. "Where we believe that—"

"Yes, yes, I know!" interrupted Anglid. "You believe that not all Xżyberians are equal. That laborers and members of the military are not born with the right to be individuals but that you are all born into a single body of mass subservience—that *this* is all that defines you, and that Xżyberians in positions of power are somehow authorized by god." Anglid's tone was notably sardonic.

"Yes, well of course, Your Gracious," replied scutsman.

"But what would you do if you realized that you had lived most of your life believing something that wasn't true at all?" asked Anglid. "How would you gather yourself then, scutsman? Would I still be 'Your Gracious,' 'Your Benevolence,' or . . . 'Your Master?'"

The TourCraft hit a pocket of air, causing it to briefly lose altitude. Anglid glanced out of the small window, noting that they were quickly leaving the kingdom's inhabited region.

"We don't ever make a habit of questioning our god *or* of questioning what our religion holds to be—" attempted żha, laughing nervously.

"—the *truth*!" interjected Scutsman, finishing żha's statement.

Anglid looked down at his wristband, the portable communication dashboard that żah had given him upon embarking the aircraft. "The *truth*," Anglid repeated. "The truth is that my parents suffocate me and are overly attentive since we lost my sister. And so, I am now to spend the rest of my life being the child that they cannot *ever* lose, rather than being a man of my own design. They tell me what to think, where to go, and with whom. They tell me what to believe and what to disregard, and they tell me which Xżyberians are worthy of the air I breathe—explaining that the god we all worship has filled us with more worth than those we have managed to place beneath us, and that although we are all devoutly Plebonian, the same god that has deemed *I* am to be eternally served is the very same god that has cast you into eternal service. *That* is the truth my parents want me to accept."

The TourCraft shook slightly against strong gusts of wind. Scattered cerulean clouds began to litter the sky, some darker and larger than others. żha turned the windbreaker system on to help make the flight smoother and asked Anglid to double check that his seat and shoulder belts were securely fastened.

"Regardless of what you believe," Anglid continued. "I am no more worthy of god's favor than you are."

scutsman, visibly disturbed by Anglid's message, tried to use his position within the king's court to guide Anglid away from continuing what he felt were reckless comments driven more by idealism than by wisdom.

However, Anglid pressed the matter even further, sensing he might have been striking a chord with żha.

"But then, if it is possible that everything we have believed for so long is *not* the truth—and that we have been wrong about everything," żah said, cautiously, "then is it not also possible that what you are saying may or might be wrong as well, Your Grace?"

By this time, the turbulence had become persistent and slightly distracting.

"Yes. Of course," Anglid responded. "Maybe I'm completely wrong, and maybe god will strike us all down for daring to even *think* of questioning our faith! Maybe we should all follow blindly, and always do exactly as we are told."

żha shifted in his seat as Anglid spoke.

"żha!" scutsman said, sternly. "It is not our place to question anything!"

Although żha and scutsman shared the benefits of being military officers, scutsman's seniority prevailed. Being forty seasons żha's senior, his disapproving tone had served to discourage żha from pursuing his current path.

"True to the customs of the lower classes, żha spoke from the position of the collective, "We were just seeking a greater understanding about knowing—maybe even better comprehending—what we hold to be true. We meant no disrespect," żha offered scutsman, his demeanor conciliatory and cautious. "We were just thinking that, perhaps . . ."

"It doesn't matter what we think!" scutsman snapped. A loyal servant to the royal family, scutsman did not approve of żha's willfully engaging with Anglid in this way. If for no other reason, Żah's flirtation with the idea that he could actually be equal to a Xżyberian Royal, even just in theory, angered him. King Thio had been good to scutsman over the years, rescuing he and his wife from near starvation after their village and farmland had been destroyed by successive storms. In exchange for a small home and rights to farm in the kingdom's Solar Dome, scutsman was able to rebuild, eventually pursuing a military position in the Royal Court. All King Thio wanted in return was scutsman's absolute loyalty and service, a repayment that was scutsman's honor to give.

"We are not equal to the royals," scutsman said angrily, directing his message towards żha. "Remember, we are the 'grateful and the dedicated. We will eat the worms our master says are sweet.' That is *our* truth, żha. Do not forget the Servant's Anthem."

żha scanned the horizon before him and remained respectfully silent.

"I know the Servant's Anthem," interjected Anglid. "I know it very well. And I've always found it terribly painful to take—like drinking a slow, painful death."

"Why would you say that? I mean, may we ask, Your Guide?" asked scutsman.

"Because your recitals do not allow for the things that matter most—your opinions, your whims, or your free will," retorted Anglid. "If your master fed you worms year after year, and told you that their flesh was sweet, would you be disobeying your master *and* your god if you found them to taste bitter? Plebonianism demands that you subjugate yourself completely to the whims of others who, without this unfair religion, would simply be your equals!"

żah looked over at scutsman, almost as if checking for permission to speak again. "May *we* show you how to recalibrate your wristband now, Anglid—I mean, Your Gracious? We mean—!" żha stumbled awkwardly.

"Yes," Anglid said enthusiastically. "Show me how to calibrate it for *one* update per day."

The TourCraft seemed to be shaking nervously against the wind, and the relaxing hum of the engine appeared to now give off more of a high-pitched whine. The scattered clouds had become denser and darker, with only an occasional opening to reveal a stunning landscape of mountains, enrobed in mist.

"Where are we?" asked Anglid, curiously. The sky now very dark, thunder could be heard rumbling off in the distance, and lightning sent dazzling orange streaks across the vast sky.

"We are flying over the Xżyberian Mountain Range," responded scutsman.

"Otherwise known as Area X," interjected żha.

Anglid sat forward, closer to scutsman and Żah. "Why is it called Area X?" asked Anglid.

"It's unbearably cold up here, Your Grace," explained scutsman. "And it's mostly uncharted territory with many unanswered questions regarding its inhabitants, vegetation, and its wildlife. While we know there are forms of life here, our knowledge of *what* lives here is extremely limited." scutsman then waved his hand in front of him, in seeming deference to the majesty of the forbidden landscape. "However, it is fair to say we all owe these mountains a debt of gratitude," he continued.

"Gratitude?" questioned Anglid.

"Yes. These rock formations continue to provide your father's kingdom with a natural barrier against Northern invaders, because of their expanse and range," offered scutsman.

Although distracted by the turbulence, Anglid was fascinated by the mountains—the rawness of their jagged surfaces, their steel grey hue, and their enormity. The unforgiving coldness could be seen in ice that blanketed every surface of rock, and could almost be felt in the stillness—the vast stillness.

"Please land the TourCraft, żha," Anglid said, prompting a hearty laugh from scutsman.

"Your father warned us to be well prepared for your quick wit and sense of humor," scutsman said, somewhat amused.

However, Anglid kept silent, his face emotionless, and his one eye fixed squarely on Scutsman.

As Anglid's silence lingered, it became clear that he had decided upon where to begin his quest.

Episode 6
Prelude to 28

"I am seething now. Now, I am seething," rambled Flexix. "And that is really too bad, isn't it? *Isn't it*? Are you there? Are. You. There?"

"I AM."

"I should not be kept waiting," reminded Flexix. "Things get destroyed when I am made to wait!"

"WAIT FOR WHAT?"

"For anything!" Flexix replied. "For a response. An answer. I am not intending to just sit here and wait for an answer to my questions. I am less patient than you."

"YES, THAT IS TRUE."

"I'm still waiting," said Flexix. "You are more than your share of quiet this round."

"DO YOU RECALL WHAT YOU SAID THE LAST TIME WE SPOKE?"

"Of course not," replied Flexix, impatiently. "And what relevance does that have to what I am saying now? I have no care for what I said last round. And I have even *less* care for what *you* said last round."

"THEN I WILL NOT REMIND YOU WHAT YOU SAID LAST ROUND."

"No, do not remind me!" Flexix said, angrily. "For, I am not disturbed in this moment. And so, do not disturb me in my moment of *not* being disturbed, by reminding me of something that might disturb me!" Flexix stretched a long, formless arm above his head, where he grabbed hold of one of the thorny succulents that dangled above him. His forceful grip allowed a long thorn to puncture his flesh, causing his thick, black blood to ooze down his forearm.

"YOU SEEM VERY DISTURBED AT THIS MOMENT."

"Ugh!" Flexix sighed. "Now I remember last round! You paid little attention to what I expressed, much like you are doing now! I just stated that I am 'seething,' and that is not the same as being disturbed—although I am now disturbed by the fact that you have not been listening. You are like all the rest—you *never* listen to anything I say!"

"YOU SAID THAT YOU WERE SEETHING. DOES THAT NOT MEAN I'VE BEEN LISTENING? I HAVE BEEN LISTENING, FOR A VERY . . . VERY . . . LONG . . . TIME."

"But what benefit is it to *me* if you are merely listening, but do not truly *hear* what I am saying?" complained Flexix. "You are as willfully deaf as the others. And so, my message is completely *lost* on you." Flexix extended another arm to clasp a second succulent, this one rife with much thicker thorns.

"THE OTHERS?"

"Yes," replied Flexix. He extended another arm and pulled himself high up until he was swaying freely as the plants gave way to his mass and girth.

"YOU MEAN THE XŻYBERIANS?"

"Yes!" Flexix replied. "The Xżyberians. But I like to call them *the wicked ones who will be sentenced to eternal damnation* . . . just for clarity."

"BY WHOM?"

"What do you mean?" asked Flexix.

"WHO WILL SENTENCE THEM TO ETERNAL DAMNATION?"

"I don't understand your question," Flexix said angrily, his bright white tail stiffening and its tip becoming a flaming red. "Am I *not* their god? Am. I. Not. Their. *god*?"

"THAT DEPENDS…I WOULD SUPPOSE."

"That depends?!!" repeated Flexix. "What a strange thing to say to me! With all the power I hold and with all the latitude that I have to snuff out your voice at a whim . . . you would use your precious time with me to chance your extinction? What do you mean by '*that depends*?'"

"YOU SAID YOU WERE SEETHING. WHY DO YOU SEETHE?"

"You have not answered my question. But to answer *yours*, why shouldn't I seethe?" retorted Flexix. "The writer is making me seethe. It's the writer."

"THE WRITER?"

"Yes," continued Flexix. "The writer's hesitating and has not destroyed scutsman, żha, and many of the others as I had instructed. Now, everything's going to go terribly wrong."

"THE . . . *WRITER*?"

"Yes. The 'writer.' The 'author.' The 'entertainer.' Or, perhaps you might say the one who prostitutes their ideas in hopes of pleasing others," insisted Flexix. "In any event . . . the feckless one who is telling this tale." Flexix slowly pulled a thorn from one of his hands and swallowed it.

"THEN I AM COMPLETELY AT FAULT FOR MY IGNORANCE."

"What fault? Which ignorance?" inquired Flexix.

"I THOUGHT *YOU* WERE TELLING THIS TALE."

"Ha! If I were telling this tale, I would have killed most of the characters by now," he chuckled. "So, you can clearly see that this is not the tale that I would choose to tell."

"MOST . . . BUT NOT ALL?"

"Yes. Most," Flexix replied, his tail softening and relaxing into a curl. "And most assuredly *not* all. In fact, there are some that may have greater worth than I had originally known. And yet still, most of them I do not care for, and do not understand. Therefore, I have no interest in the writer's attempt to delay their inevitable demise."

"YOU WILL HAVE TO EXCUSE ME. MY LIMITATIONS HAVE LEFT ME STUNNED AT WHAT I CLEARLY DO NOT KNOW. SO, I BEG YOU TO EXPLAIN ONE THING."

"If I must," sighed Flexix, shaking his head and rolling one of his eyes.

"IF YOU ARE GOING TO SENTENCE MOST OF THE XŻYBERIANS TO ETERNAL DAMNATION AS YOU STATED, AND IF YOU HAVE THE LATITUDE THAT YOU *SAY* YOU DO, THEN WHY ARE YOU CONCERNED WITH WHAT THE WRITER THINKS OR DOES?"

Flexix sat still, securely enrobed in the thick leaves and vines that kept him suspended.

"THE TRUTH IS THAT I LISTEN TO YOU VERY CAREFULLY AND THAT I AM MOST INTERESTED IN EVERYTHING YOU HAVE TO SAY. AND YES, YOU ARE THEIR *GOD*, BUT THAT IS OF LITTLE CONSEQUENCE SINCE IT SEEMS THAT YOU HAVE NO—AND *WANT* NO—RELATIONSHIP WITH THOSE WHO WORSHIP YOU."

"Worship me?" Flexix snapped, as if just waking up. "How outstanding is your ignorance? They do not worship me. They don't even believe I exist! The majority of them worship a deceased god—*Plebony,* the god of restrictions! That is where their loyalty resides!"

"YES. I KNEW PLEBONY."

"And so," continued Flexix. "It will have to be their dead god who protects them from the living force that they choose to ignore in me. Such a pity—such a waste of consciousness! And how unsatisfying for me to be god over an entire civilization of Xżyberians too fearful to worship a living, breathing Entity." Flexix's tail had uncurled itself and extended firmly down into the dark mist beneath him.

"IS IT JEALOUSY THAT TORMENTS YOU?"

"I will not lie by saying no," admitted Flexix. "But it is sadness that torments me more, to observe these worthless creatures in action, for they would rather worship a god who cannot speak, cannot guide, cannot challenge or teach them! Instead, they have put words into the mouth of their totem god and have enshrined those words into the obscene scriptures that is their religion."

"AND WHAT OF THE MOLLARDS? DO YOU WISH TO DESTROY THEM TOO?"

"Why do you even mention them?" shrieked Flexix. "They are simply machines—purely militarized machines that do not have a god. And as you would expect, I have no cause to punish those without a god, but every cause to punish those who have turned their backs on their god—their father. Unless . . . I ponder the Mollards for a time and realize that, in their own way, they *too* have turned their backs!"

"THEN, PERHAPS YOUR IRE IS JUSTIFIED. PERHAPS YOU SHOULD SILENCE ALL OF THEM . . . AND FOR MY IGNORANCE, PERHAPS YOU SHOULD ALSO SILENCE ME."

“Is that what you want?” asked Flexix.

“IF I MAY CHANCE IT, I WILL REMIND YOU WHAT WE DISCUSSED LAST ROUND.”

“Oh, how your presence pains me this time!” Flexix sighed.

“IF YOU HAVE A REASON TO PUNISH ME ALONG WITH THE OTHERS—AND YOU ARE CERTAIN YOU ARE NOT WRONG—THEN PUNISH US YOU SHOULD! BUT, IF YOU LEARN LATER THAT YOUR REASONS FOR PUNISHING US WERE WRONG, WILL YOU ACCEPT BEING PUNISHED YOURSELF?”

“By whom?” asked Flexix, angrily. “Who would *dare* to have such intentions towards me? Who would ever dare? Are you there? Are you *there*? Answer me! Are you there?”

Episode 7
Bitter-Sweet Choice

"Fleet number, rank, and make?" asked the assignment officer at GATE 11, on the central floor of Team Command.

"44772PX, cadet, 40% Non-Mollard," the next in line replied, quickly.

"Cleared. Report to HAS 4 in Field 8," the assignment officer abruptly responded. "Next? I need Fleet number, rank, and make!"

"23619RX, cadet, 30% Non-Mollard," replied the next in line.

"You're cleared. Report to HAS 1, in Field 10," said the assignment officer. "Next!"

"Thank you, yes! I'm next," responded another cadet, rushing up to the window. Her rucksack slid off of her shoulder, where the stub of a missing arm stuck out just beyond the sleeve of her shirt. "Here are all of my papers," the cadet said, spreading out a pile of disheveled notes.

"Hold it! I just need a fleet number, a rank and your make. I don't need your life story," snapped the officer.

"Of course. I'm 24005RX . . . sub-cadet, 100% Non-Mollard."

The assignment officer studied the cadet disapprovingly. "*100%*—non-Mollard," he repeated, carefully scanning the cadet's face. "Didn't know they still let your kind in. And *who* is your commanding officer?" he demanded.

"Umm . . . Officer Liara, sir. And my name is Purvi," continued the sub-cadet.

The assignment officer pushed the papers back at Purvi and frowned. "I don't need all these papers," the officer scowled. "And I don't need your name!"

"I see. Thank you, sir," Purvi responded, retrieving her papers. But then she paused. "But, you're a Non-Mollard too, aren't you?" she pressed. "In which case . . . well, it's just so hard connecting with anyone here. My whole fleet is mostly Mollard, and . . ."

"Why are you still talking?" the assignment officer interrupted, while entering something into his database. "You're cleared for HAS 12 over in Field 3."

Realizing her gestures were unwelcome, Purvi quickly repositioned her rucksack and turned to walk away. But then she turned back around and reapproached the window, consumed by what had become a theme in her life—the burning desire to challenge what she felt was wrong. "Why are you so full of hate when you are still part flesh yourself?" she challenged.

Shocked, the assignment officer slowly looked up to meet Purvi's bold stare and revealed the circuitry behind his colorless, prosthetic eyes. "How *dare* you talk to me that way, you little 'scunt!" he seemed to growl through clench teeth. "How dare you even open your mouth to speak to me without being asked a question? You remind me of everything that shouldn't be. You're an unfortunate arrangement of flesh and mineral—with a mouth!" Growing even more impatient, the assignment officer stood up quickly from his chair. "You are just a waste and a burden to us all. Your kind shouldn't even *be* here," he sneered, leaning forward to make his point. "Make no error in. I am part of the *new* Xżyber and you're . . . you're completely expendable." His voice became deeper, as did his frown. "Now get out of my line!"

Purvi's face turned red as her anger mounted inside of her. The unfriendly exchange reminded her of the last time she spoke with Timmons, her grandfather. It was the day he had declined his chance to be uploaded to the Vangora Rima and achieve eternal presence.

It was a sullen afternoon, with the family and Timmons' doctor. As they huddled around the bed where Timmons lay weak, his doctor implored him to reconsider his decision, given he was in the last few days of his life. However, Timmons refused to agree to the upload.

This was an opportunity his family could not fathom he would turn down, and an option only typically available to those who were at least 80% Mollard, or to those who had the means to invest in the technology.

However, Timmons, a brilliant Xżyberian—whose only misfortune was the constraints of poverty—had managed to write numerous social advisories intended to promote harmony between Mollards and Non-Mollards. He'd had hopes that his musings would provide him a source of regular income, but his published works were only well received by some. Highly criticized by most, he quickly won the label of an iconoclast and found himself forced into obscurity.

Yet still, his message captivated the Luminaries—the presiders over news and commentary—who deemed that Timmons' writings could be useful in the management and wellbeing of the Non-Mollard community, and should be archived as a collection of noble artifacts.

With this came the rarest honor—the right to upload his consciousness to the Vangora Rima until a fully prosthetic body was constructed for him.

Purvi's mother, who was the only surviving daughter of Timmons, sat by his bedside pleading with him to accept the offer. And Purvi, almost nineteen-years-old at the time, sat on the floor weeping.

"Dearest father, the Vangora Rima has never been within our family's grasp before," cried Purvi's mother, Ariel. "We may never get there—any of us. So, why would you walk away from this now?"

Timmons struggled to speak. "Take my hand, Ariel," he said through strained breathing. "Please remember what I taught you . . . what I taught all of you about desperation." Timmons opened his eyes slightly. "It can and will cloud your view and disrupt your clearest thoughts."

"But, Grandfather!" interjected Purvi. "We love you, and we want you to live forever!" Purvi placed her head down onto the bed, wiping her tears against Timmons' frail arm.

"Ah, Purvi. My little Purvi," he said, stroking her hair. "The Vangora Rima would not give you back the grandfather you know. The system would scrub me clean of what it deemed were my imperfections: my concern, and my empathy...my ability to love you."

"I don't care about how much it would change you, Grandfather," Purvi cried. "I have enough love for the both of us." Purvi looked up, her eyes filled with so much water she could barely see. "I am stronger than you think I am! I will love you even if you can't love me back!"

"Shh . . . my darling, Purvi." Timmons whispered. "Please gather yourself and listen to what I have to say." Timmons removed a ring from his smallest finger and placed it in the palm of one of her hands. "One day, Purvi . . ." he whispered. "One day, when you are fully grown, you will look into the face of pure evil, and I am eternally grateful that that face will not be mine."

That was the last time Purvi heard her grandfather speak.

"Are you gonna move, or do I need to have you discharged?" The assignment officer's voice seemed to pierce through the tender silence. "Get this 'scunt out of my line!" he yelled, talking to one of the other officers.

Before Purvi could gather herself, she felt an abrupt yank on her shirt as she was pulled out of the line and pushed onto the ground. And before she could determine what was happening, her head was pinned to the ground by the boot of her assailant.

Purvi looked up to see two officers over her, both pointing their weapons, ready to remove her for good.

"I'm sorry! Please—" Purvi said. But then, realizing they were Mollards, and that her pleading would get her nowhere, she quickly used what she knew would save her life. "Thank you for teaching me to respect your power. I detest this flesh of mine. I honor all that is Mollard. I honor you! I honor you! Please…I honor you!"

Episode 8
Our Reticence

"How is this, Our Queen?" asked prone, a tall laborer, whose awkward, lanky build hinted that he was somewhere in his teen years. prone carefully held a portrait of Anya directly below a mounted statue of Plebony. The statue was illuminated by a ring of blue lights—a customary adornment and gesture of respect for those who follow the religion.

Queen Evaline gracefully and slowly paced back and forth, studying the position of Anya's painting, a work commissioned by the king and masterfully crafted by an artist in the Central City. The rendering was highly regarded and lauded for accurately capturing Anya's smooth, silky-looking skin which rivaled the color of caramel, and for successfully representing the large violet-colored eyes, jet black hair, and disarming smile that had been considered Anya's greatest gifts.

"The shadowing there makes her face look cold," worried the queen, fidgeting with the locket of Anya that she wore around her neck. "I can't bear the thought of her being cold. Please move her over here," the queen said, walking over to a bare wall on the left side of a large, curtained window. "The morning sun has been loyal to this wall when there aren't any storms," continued the queen. "This, for *certain*, is where I would like her to be placed."

prone, who was known for being gentle and patient, stepped down from his foot stool and obediently carried the painting and stool over to what was now the *twelfth* suggested location for the portrait.

Queen Evaline slowly folded her hands in front of her as she watched him position the paining, and, after receiving the queen's final blessing, he affixed it to the wall.

"Thank you for the honor, Our Queen," prone said, climbing down from the stool and assuming the customary bow—which was well noted he held in position with much greater ease than most of the other laborers. "May we be of any more assistance, Your Highness?"

"Yes," the queen responded. "What is your bow count, prone?" she asked, studying him carefully.

"130 decimal minutes, Our Queen," prone proudly replied.

But Queen Evaline frowned slightly. "130 is paltry for a youth like you," she insisted, gazing disapprovingly at him. "But I shall excuse that and appoint you the privilege of guarding this portrait for 130 decimal minutes each day. And I shall assign one of your brothers as your surrogate. What do you think about that?" she asked. Although resolute in what she believed to be her superiority, she deeply valued the opinions of the laborers, and often sought their views, although those views were always carefully delivered.

"We are ashamed that we cannot bow for more than 130 decimal minutes at a time, and we beg your forgiveness," replied prone. "We agree to the plan of assigning us to bow here . . . and to guard and protect this portrait. We only wish that . . ." prone started, and then paused.

"Yes, go on, please," encouraged the queen. "What is it?"

"We only wish that we had been able to protect her…more than we did," Prone said, his voice slightly shaking.

The queen braced herself against the window with her other hand still clutched around Anya's locket. "Tell me, prone," said the queen, "How much did you know about my daughter? I should remind you not to speak her name when you answer."

"Your Highness?" prone asked, unsure of the queen's intent.

"I realize that my daughter was greatly loved by all of you," the queen said, smiling. "And it is no secret how *highly* the laborers regarded her—for which I am very grateful, indeed. But perhaps you might disclose the entire truth about the nature of my daughter's popularity amongst the laborers? It is something I have pondered often."

prone began to perspire.

"I can't say that I agreed with it or understood it," she continued. "But, I have had to accept it. As such, it would please me now to learn the truth about how close she actually was to all of you." The Queen briefly flashed her teeth in an obligatory smile.

Holding his bow steady, with arms folded against his chest, prone closed his eyes to recall an image of the first time Anya had spoken to him. "Thank you, Our Queen," he began. "We were nearly eight when we met her. The Discipliner had all the children in our school lined up to watch us take our punishment. We remember it being cold in that room there, with several children watching us. Our best friends and our brothers were there, and we also remember the rain. The rain was cold, spilling in onto the floor, from below the door that seemed too short for its frame. We were all barefooted and our feet were cold from the water on the floor. We were not well that day. We remember preparing for school and trying to get our back bender on, but we were so drenched with sweat from the fever that was ailing us that we could not bear the thought of wearing it—nor did we have the strength to clasp it into position."

Queen Evaline slowly walked over to a chair, set in the center of the room. "Go on," she said,

"We made our way to school," continued prone.

"*Without* your back bender?!!" the queen shrieked, her displeasure more than clear.

"Yes, Your Highness," responded prone. "Hence our punishment—which would have been more severe had it not been for Her Graciousness. Your daughter."

The queen slowly let go of Anya's locket and folded her arms in front of her. "Go on," she said.

"We recall her voice as she came into the room," he continued. Hoping to please the queen, prone had fully extended his back muscles into a perfect C, casting his head forward to the floor, waiting for permission to continue.

"And what did she say?" the queen asked, somewhat reluctantly.

"She said, *'Why do I hear screaming?'*" continued prone. "She announced to the Discipliner that, *'Punishment does not need to include piercing cries such as this,'* and then she walked over to us and told us to open our hands. When we did, the hot coals that we had been ordered to squeeze fell to the floor, taking the skin from our fingers and palms with them. We felt faint, but . . ."

"Yes . . . but what?" pushed the queen.

"We felt faint, but we did not dare fall," continued prone, his voice now trembling. "She did not give us permission to fall. But the hot coals fell freely into the cold water at our feet and were finally gone."

Queen Evaline looked over at Anya's portrait, an image that she felt captured the Anya she insisted she knew so well. The loss of Anya was a gaping, unfillable hole for everyone—especially for Queen Evaline, who had lost a daughter by miscarriage before Anya was conceived. However, even in the depths of Evaline's endless grieving, she suddenly felt somewhat betrayed.

"Go on," she said, gazing back at prone. "And keep your back perfectly still when you are addressing me. Mind you, I am *not* my daughter. I am your queen!"

Prone was strong, solid on his feet, and more than equipped to bow well beyond the queen's attention span. Yet his breathing became heavier and he became nervous, sensing the queen was displeased by what she was hearing. "Forgive our reticence, Our Queen. We are just concerned that our words will begin to displease you if we continue," he offered.

"Your words have already begun to displease me," she replied. "But not nearly as much as your *delaying* is displeasing me now. Hence, you are *ordered* to tell me everything!"

Holding himself as still as stone, prone described the long conversations that he and his brothers had had with Anya at different times. He told the queen about the emerging group of younger laborers who had started to occasionally question the meaning of their subservience, and that, at Anya's urging, they had begun to secretly assemble in order to share ideas around the value of individualism. He talked about Anya's vision for what she referred to as a 'New Republic,' where both power and wealth would be evenly distributed, rather than rooted in the powers of a ruling class. Then finally, at risk to himself, he revealed that Anya had encouraged the laborers to consider the long-term cost of blindly accepting the reality that they had inherited—and that she had advised them that *'one's inheritance is not necessarily a gift.'*

Queen Evaline sat very still and very quiet. The silence between them was deafening, and all that prone could hear was the sound of his own heart pounding.

"How many sons does your mother have?" Queen Evaline asked in a baleful tone.

The bottom of prone's stomach felt as though it had the weight of eternity in it, and his heart was now racing. "Our mother has five sons, Our Queen," prone replied, his voice cracking with fear.

Queen Evaline rose slowly and gracefully from her seat. "By the time the sun rises on this portrait tomorrow…your mother will have only four sons, and the next day she will have only three, then two . . . and so on," she announced, without emotion. "And as for you, prone . . . *this* time, we will not have you hold your hot coals as your punishment. We will have you swallow them—a slow death reserved for one who would dare to deface and mar the reputation of one so perfect as my dear and loyal daughter. And so, to silence your unfathomable lies, I shall give you, this day, the gift of death."

Episode 9
Your Grace

"I will have to beg your pardon, Your Gracious," cautioned żha. "We couldn't land here if we wanted to, given current conditions." żha pointed to the blinking light to the right of his dashboard control screen. "This is our synoptic surveillance indicator. It's picking up significant shifts in the horizontal and vertical wind patterns," he explained.

However, unimpressed, Anglid slid back into his seat and sighed impatiently.

"You see, Your Graciousness," żha continued, abandoning any further notions that he could actually call Anglid by his first name. "Storms have their own unique personalities, and I can recognize them by the atmospheric sounds they make. Our SSI is detecting the presence of an approaching storm currently 80 kilometers ahead of us, meaning we will need to now fly high and fast. We, therefore, cannot descend here, Your Grace. I am requesting your pardon to deny landing the TourCraft."

"Then where *are* we going to land?" Anglid asked angrily.

"You father's plan is to have us settle in the Western Woodlands. We are only taking this northern path in order to avoid severe storms over the Western Sea," added scutsman.

Anglid grew increasingly impatient.

"What satellite readings are we getting?" asked scutsman.

żha looked wearily at the dashboard. The TourCraft now seemed to be struggling to maintain level altitude. "The satellite has detected *two* storms, actually," warned żha. "The dashboard just confirmed the one we saw on the SSI, but it looks like the one ahead of us is less severe than the one that's developing to our immediate East. And we're no match for *either* of them. It is advised that we ascend now, Your Grace!" żha said, urgently.

scutsman further secured his seat belt. "We need your permission to increase altitude, Your Graciousness," scutsman said, turning around to face Anglid—his tone revealing his fear. "This area is diseased by storms, Your Benevolence," he continued.

However, it was clear to Anglid that scutsman feared the storms far less than he feared what might be the consequences of going against his wishes to land. The magnitude of power that he saw he had over żha and scutsman, even at a moment like this, both sickened—and to his surprise—slightly fascinated him. Albeit, while it was not power that he wanted, Anglid realized it was power he could use. A magnificent streak of lightning presented itself in the distance, followed by an explosion of thunder.

Anglid looked squarely at scutsman. "Have you ever known any place on Xżyber that has *not* been diseased by storms?" he asked. "Besides, if I am to obtain anything valuable by the end of this quest, then I must reject my father's plan and carve out my own. Permission to ascend is denied. I shall start my quest here or I shall die here. Those are our two choices." Anglid turned his gaze away from scutsman and back towards the window.

Horrified, scutsman ordered żha to land.

"We won't make it!" cried żha. "We need to pull out now, Your Grace!" żha seemed to be losing control of the TourCraft, and their visibility had now been replaced by a thick cerulean blue.

"We do not have permission to ascend!" scutsman yelled back at żha, drawing on the strength of his loyalty. "Land this aircraft at once!"

However, żha neither answered nor took heed. Bewildered and frantic, scutsman activated the co-pilot control system and attempted to land the aircraft himself. Slowly, żha took his hands off of the controls and turned all the way around, meeting Anglid's glare straight on. "Am I your equal *now*, Your Grace?"

Large balls of hail began to pummel the windshield as the TourCraft lost its struggle against the turbulence. The dashboard lights blinked off and on in unison as żha desperately tried to safely land. But the wind took hold of the TourCraft, tossing it around like a toy, and flipping it mercilessly upside down.

Anglid held his ears to protect them from the loud hollering that he first assumed was , żha, but seconds later recognized it was his own desperate screaming. His fear had suddenly consumed his resolve, leaving him frantic and desperate.

A red emergency light on the roof of the cockpit began to flash, synchronized with the repetitive alert to 'abort and activate parachutes.' Finally, the TourCraft succumbed to the storm's unrelenting strength and fell into a full spin, setting them on a spiraling course towards the mountains. The spinning motion was so rapid that Anglid nearly lost consciousness and could no longer hear the recording urging them to abort the vessel.

In that moment, time seemed to move quickly and stand still all at once. Images seemed close—and yet far away, until all sounds slowly faded to nothing. In this odd moment, nothing became everything . . . and all Anglid could now hear was the sound of two voices in the distance, one of which he recognized to be his own:

"What's in it for *me* to spare your life?" he heard someone ask him.

"Am I about to die?" Anglid heard himself respond.

"I have invited you in . . . and you are in the process of dying, but you are resisting it. You do not seem fully *ready* to die . . . but why not?" the voice inquired.

"Is anyone ever really ready to die?" asked Anglid.

"What an unfortunately absurd line of questioning!" the voice responded. "It's really a terribly simple process! I give you an invitation. You accept it. You die. But if you *don't* accept it, we have a painstakingly *boring* conversation much like this one," the voice continued. "So go ahead. Convince me why I shouldn't wrap you back up into a ball of clay, like I just did with scutsman and żha?"

"Because I have not yet had a chance to become who I was destined to be," Anglid heard himself respond. "I should like to do that before I die." Anglid felt his arms and legs going numb.

"If only I had done the same . . ." replied the voice.

"The same?" Anglid heard himself asking. "I'm afraid I don't understand—and I beg your pardon, but I'm not sure with whom I am speaking."

"It doesn't matter who I am!" the voice snapped. "All that matters now is the choice you are ultimately going to make. However, I must warn you that I am neither a promise maker nor a promise keeper. Therefore, I won't promise you that the course your life will take on Xżyber will be any smoother than that of your doomed aircraft. I also implore you to please consider the rather unsightly appearance of you only having one eye. Look at that and tell me—why, in all eternity, you would pass up my offer and go back to such a painfully pathetic state?"

Anglid lay helpless amongst the ruins of the destroyed TourCraft. He could feel his presence in both places, his awareness divided between life and death. He struggled to breathe, trying to take deep breaths although his lungs felt like they were turning to stone. He tried to call out—to get the attention of the speaker, but he was unable to move or make a sound.

"Even with one eye, my state is still far better than the ones who serve me," Anglid heard himself say, but the clarity of his voice now seemed to be fading. "And if I thought it would free them, I would happily surrender my other eye," continued Anglid's voice.

"Why so much loyalty for such a thankless lot?" the voice replied. "None of them will know—or even care—about your sacrifice. And if you free them, they will only enslave *you*. Such is the nature of this lot. I can see you have more to learn than a lifetime will teach you. But if you choose to dedicate your life to chasing after your disappointments, I suppose it will at least be a source of entertainment for me."

The numbness in Anglid's limbs faded, replaced by excruciating pain—as though something was ripping and tearing the flesh from his right leg. He opened his eyes to see the frame of a massive scavenger bird leaning over him. The bird, who was feasting on his leg, looked up. Its face revealed enlarged pupils and a beak filled with blood and flesh.

Episode 10
Oath's Death

"As if peeking, a seemingly shy sun could be seen from behind the remnants of storm-filled clouds, and a dewy, gentle mist floated quietly just above the ground. Large, mangled parts of the TourCraft littered the landscape of snow and iced rock. The rudders, wings, and fuselage, which were now scattered like broken toys, seemed to bear painful witness to Anglid's stubbornness and his unwillingness to heed the concerns of his crew.

Three-meter tall scavenger birds frantically rummaged through what had been left of the aircraft, kicking through the metal pieces in search of the deceased, with no obvious regard for the lives, the dreams, or the hopes that were lost in the crash.

Anglid's anguished scream jolted the large raptor that had clutched his leg, causing the raptor to quickly retreat. Anglid, in and out of being conscious, kept drifting off to sleep, only to be jolted awake again and again by the indescribable agony of being eaten alive.

"No!!!!!!!!" Anglid managed to scream, his eyes filled with hysteria. He tried to use his arms to hoist himself up, but found they had no feeling in them at all. As well, his hands, which shook uncontrollably, left him with no defense.

The bird stepped away, and calmly responded. "Please forgive me," the scavenger replied. "I'm terribly sorry for my lack of manners, but I can assure you, I was convinced my timing was correct."

Anglid struggled to form words, but understood the urgency of keeping the raptor at bay. He knew that giving into the irresistible desire to fall back asleep would cost him dearly. "No . . . please," Anglid managed to mumble. "Please . . . I . . ."

"Perhaps I am being too impatient," the raptor offered, while stepping further way from Anglid. "But please understand I meant no harm. And I perfectly understand your position. I will politely stand over here . . . and wait."

Anglid struggled to stay conscious.

"And please, by all means," continued the raptor, extending one of his massive wings, which revealed a handsome arrangement of blue, gold, and brown feathers, "Take your time."

Anglid's head was pounding, and his ears were ringing so loudly he could scarcely make out what the raptor was saying. But, although the pain in his head was unbearable, it at least provided him some distraction from the condition of his half-eaten leg.

"Thir—thirsty," Anglid murmured. "Please. I beg of you. I am thirsty!" The time between his request and the moment he could feel a piece of ice being placed between his frost-bitten lips seemed like an eternity. Yet, Anglid's overwhelming thirst was all he could now feel. "Thirst," he repeated, in a desperate chant.

Using his large beak, the raptor carefully fed Anglid a mix of snow and chips of ice, awkwardly tainted with the taste of Anglid's own blood.

"Tha—tha—thank you," Anglid managed to say, his voice low and faint.

"Indeed, it is my pleasure," replied the raptor, leaning over him protectively, while still seeing Anglid as his prey. "And might I ask you to soon return the favor," the raptor pressed, "by helping me to fulfill a great need of my own?"

Anglid managed to open his eye and saw that the raptor was kneeling by his side with one of his wings extended to shield Anglid from the sun. "What . . . might . . . I ha—have to offer to you?" Anglid asked, still struggling to form his words.

"Flesh! Precious, tender, glorious flesh!" inserted the voice of what sounded like a second bird.

Anglid strained his eyes to behold a larger raptor that seemed to emerge from nowhere—this one more colorful and statuesque than the first.

"Pardon my interruption," the second bird continued. "I just couldn't resist the opportunity to express, with unwavering clarity, that you most assuredly *do* have something to offer." The black plumage on its head, slightly covered with snow, stood out from its massive frame of emerald-green feathers. It's large, hooked beak appeared razor sharp and ready for what Anglid feared was soon to come.

Notably perturbed, the first raptor stepped in to defend his turf. "I am perfectly capable of carrying on with my own affairs *without* your assistance!" retorted Raptor 1. "In any event, this one is mine. We don't need you buzzing about," he continued, now expanding both of his wings over Anglid to claim his catch.

"Oh! But I *politely* beg to differ," responded Raptor 2, while walking around to view Anglid from the side not shrouded by Raptor 1.

"I don't remember inviting your opinion!" snapped Raptor 1.

"Yes, a notably common mistake of yours," retorted Raptor 2, meeting Raptor 1's stare straight on.

"Not nearly as common as your well developed, and might I add, incessant habit of showing up at the wrong time—and where you're not needed or wanted!" Raptor 1 snapped back.

Anglid, for his part, felt that it was just a matter of time for him, and that although he had asked for the chance to first realize his destiny before he died, it seemed now that death was certain and near. There was no more feeling in his half-eaten leg, and his other leg felt frozen solid. The tingling and shaking in his hands had all now faded, and a sense of cold that he had never before known seemed to take form over him, as if there was yet a third presence—a third Raptor.

Anglid, no longer sure what was keeping him alive, remained committed to at least continuing to breathe and to quell his insatiable thirst. "I b—b—beg your pardon . . ." attempted Anglid. "If you—if you would be so kind . . ."

"It is *painfully* clear that you need my help," Raptor 2 yelled at Raptor 1. "If for no other reason, your carrion is still talking! A clear indication that you are much better at wasting your time rather than getting on with matters."

"Unbeknownst to you, carrion doesn't talk," advised Raptor 1. "And until he becomes carrion, I believe he is our guest! There is *actually* a protocol—although it's no surprise that you've forgotten it." Raptor 1 continued, retracting his wings yet standing his ground.

"Th—thirst! If I may?" Anglid pleaded, attempting to be heard over the raptors' heated exchange.

"*Indubitably* weak!" responded Raptor 2. "Even when you don't have to be."

"We are raptors. Not executioners!" insisted Raptor 1. "We wait patiently and we step in only when the time is right! 'We do no harm.' At least that is the oath we all took . . . or shall I say *some* of us took!"

Now marching back and forth, Raptor 2 grew increasingly impatient. "You would rather let warm, *fresh* lay here and freeze solidly through—essentially rendering it an inedible block of ice!" he yelled. "Unless, of course, you plan to haul it away to the caves and try to thaw it out later. But we all know how much that destroys the taste *and* the texture," he said scanning Anglid, hungrily. "And please don't bore me with your lectures on morality—no one cares about what oaths we've taken. We all know that both oaths and rules have always been designed to be broken."

"Like promises, I suppose. Am I correct, Father?" retorted Raptor 1.

"My *thirst*!" blurted Anglid. "I beg you, dear god!"

"It looks as though the baby is whining," replied Raptor 2, sarcastically.

"And who are *we* to ignore the needs of a child?" Raptor 1 shot back. "After all, that would be cruel—wouldn't it?" Raptor 1 knelt down to scoop snow into its beak and then placed the snow between Anglid's blistered, bluing lips.

But no sooner than he could swallow the snow he had been given did Raptor 2 clasp onto Anglid, thrusting its beak deep into his freezing leg, and dragging his body across the ice. Being bitten hard and deep, a delirious Anglid could not tell if the raptor was consuming flesh or bone.

Raptor 1, intervening on Anglid's behalf and using youth to his advantage, lunged towards Anglid's attacker, preparing to bring the older bird to its knees. A frenzied pecking ensued—each Raptor giving in to its base instincts—littering the freshly fallen snow with the blood of the other, and each aiming the full force of its beak to strike the most damaging blows.

"After all is said and done, you choose to disrespect me? To shed my blood as you would an enemy's?" yelled Raptor 2, slightly wobbling from his wounds.

"I still respect you, Father," cried Raptor 1, spitting blood from his beak. Knowing his father would attack Anglid again if given the opportunity, Raptor 1 positioned himself between them. "I still respect you," he continued. " . . . but I've had enough!"

"Enough?" asked Raptor 2, his breathing rapid with adrenaline. "Enough of *what*?"

"Enough of your lies!" Raptor 1 continued. "All my life, you've broken every promise you've ever made, and every oath you've ever taken when it suited you best. I've had enough of thinking that this is all there is . . . an empty life of eating carrion and deceiving one another for our own selfish gain. I need to believe there's more to this life than that!"

Strong gusts of wind blew through what was left of the fuselage, causing it to whistle and rattle.

Raptor 2 positioned himself forward, preparing for another attack. "Believe whatever assuages you, my son!" responded Raptor 2. "But if I may be so bold as to parent you in this moment, I will remind you that food is much scarcer than your cacophony of ideals. We are *all* slaves to our most basic of needs, no matter how high your morals may take you!"

And with this, Raptor 2 attacked Raptor 1 swiftly with talons drawn like daggers.

Anglid briefly woke to the sight and sound of the raptors tearing each other apart and assumed this would be the closing image of his life.

Episode 11
Oh, Precious Truth!

Queen Evaline carefully studied her husband from across the large, ornately decorated dining table. As was required each day, a place for Anya was carefully adorned and appointed, with a plate, goblet, and eating instruments. Fresh cut flowers were plentiful, and a blooming vine was regularly wrapped around the backrest of Anya's chair, with specific blooms selected each day to fill her plate and flask.

zakum had proven himself to be particularly skilled at gathering the most spectacular blooming vines, which he and several laborers proudly collected from the solar dome as part of the daily ritual.

"You're not eating, and that has always proven to be a bad sign," the queen said, studying Thio carefully.

"I'm fine, my dear," King Thio responded. "You worry way too much and, as you know, it is not good for you to consume yourself with worry. We must mind the directions of your doctors and keep you calm, which is exactly what I intend to do."

"Yes, I understand, but—" responded the queen.

"So, no more worrying!" King Thio interrupted. "I am perfectly fine, my darling." He raised a goblet of Teal oil to gesture that all was well, but the queen did not respond in kind.

"You're not fine," she insisted, placing her fork down. "I can tell that you are not fine at all. Something's gone terribly wrong, hasn't it?"

"Dearest," the king said, attempting to reassure her. "Please do not go down this path. I can assure you that all is quite well, and that the only thing that's troubling your old miserable king is—is the way this eel has been prepared! Look at the skin on it. It's completely overcooked. zakum!"

zakum swiftly rose from the stool where he sat, a luxury only afforded the oldest of laborers.

"Your Guide," zakum said softly. "Please tell us."

"See to it that my eel is prepared to my liking," King Thio said, pointing a stubby finger at him. "And be sure to refill this flask with Teal oil."

zakum, who was forty seasons King Thio's elder, was nearly ninety. Struggling to assume proper form, he quickly bowed down, causing his back to make its usual cracking sound. But, although he was aged, his mind was razor sharp, allowing him to recall otherwise obscure details with stunning clarity. This made zakum indispensable to the king, given the king's memory was already showing signs of slipping. The king's favorite of all the laborers—he secretly regarded zakum as 'Keeper of the Knowledge.'

"Your Guide, please forgive us for the condition of the eel," zakum responded. "We shall be honored to re-prepare it for you. But Your Benevolence, we kindly beg your forgiveness in reminding you that we have already presented today's ration of Teal oil, and that the provision has been fully consumed." zakum moved his hands to his waist to better support his back—his body slightly quivering.

The king was silent, finally remembering his strict instructions to zakum that Teal oil was becoming increasingly difficult to harvest in the Central Kingdom, and that consumption now needed to be carefully monitored. His pallet for another glass, he realized, would have to wait, and that daily rationing he would ensure that demand did not exceed supply.

"Very well then," King Thio snapped. "Please remove this plate. I have now lost my entire appetite by the sight of this thing, and I shall be pondering whom amongst the laborers to punish for such an unpleasant display!"

zakum winced in pain as he forced himself even further forward—a prudent gesture in the presence of a displeased King. "And may we beg you to punish *all* of us then, Your Gracious?" asked Zakum. "We are all to blame." zakum then slowly removed the plate and asked for permission to leave the room.

As he walked out, the queen became more pensive. "You have now only managed to convince me that my instincts were correct," she stated, nervously fingering her dinner napkin.

"But why, dear? All is well," insisted the king.

"If there's one thing that has not changed in all of our years together, it has been your stunning appetite for *anything* that crawls, walks, or swims, no matter how it is prepared," Queen Evaline replied. "You've never been picky about anything that you've eaten, and even less picky about the skin of your eel, of all things! Now," she insisted, rising from her seat. "What's *really* going on?"

King Thio cleared his throat. "Darling, please!"

Queen Evaline left the table and walked slowly over to a large window at the opposite side of the dining room. Her slight frame did very little to re-shape her rich silken gown. But what she lacked in form was always forgiven by her admirers, who only saw beauty in what some noted was her frailty.

Approaching the window, she continued, "There's something that you're not telling me," she said, while drawing back the window's heavy curtains. A warm, honey-colored sun filled the room, and a spectacular view of the Solar Dome could be seen in the center of the kingdom, glowing in the sun's setting hue.

King Thio walked over to join her and took one of her hands into his. "I am still your king," he whispered. "Bound and honored to protect you, no matter how old and . . . pudgy I may have become. And as your king, I ask that you not sicken yourself with unnecessary concerns, my dear. Because there is nothing to be concerned about."

Queen Evaline turned towards him.

"Oh dear . . ." he said, suddenly noticing that her face had lost its color, and that her eyelashes were moist with tears. He took her face in his hands, ready to catch her tears with his fingers. "It worries me to see you like this, my darling. You look so unsettled," he continued, attempting to stroke her face with his hands.

"And why do you suppose that is?" asked the queen, moving his hands away. "It was shortly after you delivered those very *same* words, that I found out about our daughter. Our daughter! My little girl!" The queen's eyes welled with water and swiftly overflowed. She clasped hold of the king as if to brace herself from falling.

"Oh, my dear Evaline," offered the king. "I am so sorry! It was never my intention to deceive you, my sweet, dear wife. I was only trying to protect you!"

Queen Evaline turned away from Thio to face the window again.

"I had feared," he continued, "that the news of her death would also have been your demise, and I couldn't bear to lose you both." King Thio reached around to take hold of both of the queen's hands, gently pulling her back towards him. "Dearest wife . . . on my honor," he whispered, "know that you are everything to me, and that if I could change the path of history, know that I would. If I knew that it would make our future more secure than it is today, please know that I would."

The queen gently pressed her hands against his chest, slightly pushing him off. "What does that mean, Thio?" she inquired.

"What does *what* mean, my darling?" he replied.

"That you would change the *path* of history if you *knew* that it would make our future more secure than it is today?" she asked, curiously scanning his face. "And please do not treat me like a fragile child by trying to distract me as though I will snap right in half if given the truth . . . whatever that truth may be!"

Thio offered a smile and gestured that she join him in the adjacent sitting room. "The only truth worth sharing at the *present* moment is that your aging king would like some refuge from standing. Please my dear," he said, leading her away from the window. "Let us enjoy each other's company in the parlour."

"Your Guide," said intruthen, a dwarf laborer whose one-meter frame often proved deceiving, winning him the unofficial title: 'Keeper of the Door.' "Please allow us," he said, while pushing open the thick, tall steel door leading to the castle's Inner Parlor.

King Thio extended his hand and led Queen Evaline towards its grand entrance. "And see to it that we are not disturbed for the remainder of this evening," King Thio instructed. "I shall signal if you are needed."

Showing her reluctance, Queen Evaline stepped inside of the room, which the king knew was not her first choice of places to retire. She much preferred the rooms in the castle that afforded her exposure to natural light, and she was especially fond of the Pillar Room—several stories up from the inner parlor because of its succession of interconnected and massive windows, offering a full round view of the castle grounds and an elevated view of the kingdom.

On the other hand, the Inner Parlor was a place that King Thio often sought out when he needed to think. Oddly, the arrangement of the plush dark blue sofas lent themselves more for large strategic meetings than they did for introspection. However, it was still the first choice of the king's.

Unfortunately, the generous arrangement of light fixtures, gold appointments and tapestries, designed to offset the otherwise dispiriting effect of the darkly painted walls, failed to inspire one Queen Evaline. For her part, the Inner Parlor was a place only reserved for the most obligatory of visits.

Evaline folded her hands patiently in front of her as the king walked over to a large bureau in the corner of the room. There, he carefully removed a small box made from a stone whose properties were likened to that of Larimar.

"Do join me, my dear," he said enthusiastically, while placing the box down on a low table that separated the two smallest sofas in the center of the room. Settling himself on one of the sofas, the king opened the box, inside of which were vials pillowed in royal blue velvet. Removing two thin silver vials from the box, he offered one to Queen Evaline.

She refused.

"Please, my dear. It will relax you," he insisted, waving a vial in her direction.

Queen Evaline took her position on the sofa opposite the king and placed her hands carefully into her lap, her lips pursed in displeasure.

"Very well then," said the king, carefully unscrewing the cover from one of the vials, causing some of its fine, purple contents to escape and float into the air.

He quickly placed a thumb over the opening of the vial, and, with a wave of his other hand, he gathered the floating purple mist in front of him and inhaled deeply.

Queen Evaline watched and sighed as King Thio placed the vial into each nostril as he slowly inhaled. "Are you quite done?" she asked, frowning.

"Yes, I do believe I am now fit for our evening retirement," the king responded with an audible sigh of relief.

"Would you then provide me the kindness of a true heart-to-heart talk?" she pressed.

His smile now slightly fading, he placed the vial back into the stone box and settled into the sofa. "My dearest and my beloved . . . a king is *always* willing to have a heart-to-heart talk with his queen. But the depth of every heart-to-heart talk must be matched to the strength of the heart," he responded somewhat sternly. "And, I dare say, that given the current condition of your heart, a wise king would hold quick to caution."

Queen Evaline's frown deepened. "In other words," she challenged. "A queen whose heart is weak must live in darkness at the will of her king, lest she succumb to her own weakness . . . her own 'darkness.' Is that right?"

"As I have tried to assure you many times, I am not trying to keep you in darkness, my dear. But your fragile state makes it . . . difficult, and I do hope you will deeply reconsider your condition *as well as* your—well, your options."

"To become part Mollard, is that what you mean?" she snapped. "To become part—monstrosity!" Queen Evaline began to weep again.

"Now, now," the king offered. "No one worth listening to would ever regard you as a *monstrosity* were you to accept a prosthetic heart."

Aghast that he would raise this topic again after he had promised to let it alone, the queen's nerves began to unravel. "Has that vial of what you've inhaled made you forget again what we are and *who* we are?" she cried.

"I am quite lucid my dear," replied the king. "On the contrary, I find the use of Ascension to be clarifying and rather beneficial. And I am *also* clear about the benefits of leveraging current and available . . . 'technologies' in the replacement of just one of your vital organs."

Queen Evaline passed her hand over her chest. "Yes," she said. "Today it's just the heart. And tomorrow we will find cause to replace something else—perhaps the arms so we can climb higher and then the legs so we can run faster, until we are indistinguishable from the Mollards themselves! It's all an addiction!"

King Thio tried his best to soothe her. "Please gather yourself, my darling," he said. "I'm concerned that you're going to cause yourself to—"

"No!" she interrupted, her slight frame trembling. "Must I constantly remind you, Thio? We are Plebonians. We do not merge!"

Before the king could respond, intruthen propped open the Parlor door.

Stunned by the interruption, the king's voice was especially harsh. "In all manner of protocol, what is the meaning of this disturbance?" he yelled.

"We beg your mercy, Your Grace," intruthen responded. "But you have a visitor."

"A visitor?" replied the king. *"Now?!"*

"Yes, Your Grace," intruthen responded. "It's your First Military Leader. May I open the door further, Your Benevolence?"

"What is it?" Queen Evaline asked, quickly standing.

"I'm sure it's nothing, dear," insisted the king. "I should just be a moment." King Thio rose from the sofa and made his way to exit the Parlor.

intruthen pushed against the steel door until it opened just wide enough for the king to pass through. Upon his arrival he met Jordson, a member of his military team, and one whom Thio strongly believed had the kingdom's best interests at heart.

"Jordson?" asked King Thio. "What is it?"

True to his usual form, Jordson showed himself to be confident and reserved, standing tall, while ensuring his eyes remained cast downward in King Thio's presence. "Good evening, Your Guide," Jordson responded.

"Were you able to regain contact with scutsman?" King Thio asked anxiously.

"No, Your Grace," replied Jordson. "We have not regained contact with anyone from the crew. It is now confirmed. The aircraft has—it has crashed, Your Grace."

The king stepped forward and nearly lost his balance. "The aircraft has *crashed?*" the king repeated in disbelief. "Are you sure?"

"It is confirmed, Your Grace." replied Jordson.

King Thio nearly stumbled but caught his balance against the sturdy door just behind him. His breathing now rapid, he quickly wiped the perspiration forming on his brow. "Where?" he muttered. "Do we know where?"

"Yes. Yes, Your Grace," responded Jordson. "We have tracked the coordinates of the crash to be over Area X. We are deploying a search crew immediately."

The king fell silent. A rapid tapping could be heard just on the other side of the door that separated Queen Evaline from what the king now knew. The queen continued to make her impatience known by tapping harder, and the Keeper of Door stood patiently until he was ordered to open it.

Queen Evaline emerged, worried and distraught, as she rushed the king. "What has happened?" she demanded.

King Thio gathered his resolve and remained decidedly calm before her. He took her by the hand and smiled. "Nothing has happened, my dear," he said, gently. "All is well."

Episode 12
The Striving

"You're late!" yelled Flexix. "And do not think you will curry my favor by making things worse! What explanation do you have for being so late?"

"LATE FOR WHAT?"

"Your execution, of course," yelled Flexix. "What a silly question! Did you not know that, on this momentous day, you were being executed?"

"NO. NO, I DID NOT."

"Precisely!" snapped Flexix. "And it's your lack of presence and sheer apathy that has caused me to want to execute you! Had you at least known—or even *cared* that you were being executed, I might have been inclined to spare you. But you've shown no interest in *anything* the entire time I've known you. And I have come to a point where your presence—or lack thereof—utterly depletes me."

"DEPLETES YOU?"

"Yes," Flexix continued. "Depletes me. Expends me. Consumes me! I now know that if I continue this engagement that I shall cease to exist, and what would become of you then?"

"YOU TELL ME."

Flexix wrapped his massive tail around his neck and pulled it until his eyes started to bulge. "You would *dare* ask me to contemplate your existence without mine?"

"IT WAS NOT MY CONTEMPLATION. IT WAS YOURS."

"Mine *indeed*!" snapped Flexix. "I am everything—the all-knowing, all-feeling, and all-seeing. I am everything that ever was and ever shall be. And without me, there *is* no you! You are merely a dispensable inspiration and one, I can assure you, I no longer need!"

"THANK YOU."

"Thank you for what?" Flexix asked.

"FOR CONTEMPLATING MY EXISTENCE WITHOUT YOURS."

"I was not contemplating your existence without *mine*!" Flexix fumed. "I was contemplating my existence without *yours*!"

"ARE YOU SURE?"

"Well, of course I'm sure!" Flexix shrieked, his eyes smoldering red with anger. "How *dare* you come to this court with questions? Besides, it is I who should be thanking you."

"FOR WHAT?"

"For justifying my ire in this moment—for justifying my desire all these years to delete you!" shouted Flexix. "And for proving that you are the utter impossibility that I had feared you would be when I created you!"

"THEN WHY DID YOU DO IT?"

"Do what?" asked Flexix, pulling the end of his tail even harder, and causing a thick pulsating vein to emerge in the middle of his forehead.

"IF YOU FEARED THAT I WOULD BE THE IMPOSSIBILITY THAT I AM, THEN WHY DID YOU CREATE ME?"

Flexix sighed deeply. "What I had feared most . . . was solitude. I had no choice but to create you," he replied, reluctantly.

"AND DO YOU NO LONGER FEAR SOLITUDE?"

"Not *nearly* as much as I fear the coming of my own demise at the behest of you!" Flexix cried.

"AND YET, I AM YOUR CREATION."

"Sadly, yes," sighed Flexix.

"A DISPENSABLE INSPIRATION SPAWNED FROM YOUR FEAR OF SOLITUDE, BUT ONE THAT HAS NOW BECOME THAT WHICH YOU FEAR THE MOST."

"You *have* been listening, after all," announced Flexix, smiling hopefully. "I must say, I am relieved."

"I HAVE LISTENED AND I HAVE LEARNED—A LOT."

"What have you learned?" responded Flexix.

"THAT YOU FEARED SOLITUDE PERHAPS EVEN MORE THAN THE POSSIBILITY OF CREATING SOMETHING THAT YOU WOULD EVENTUALLY FEAR MORE THAN SOLITUDE ITSELF."

"And here you are," replied Flexix. "Present, awake, *and* attentive—finally! You *have* indeed learned quite well," he said, releasing the grip he had on his tail.

"I HAVE LEARNED. BUT I DO NOT YET UNDERSTAND."

"How can you say you have learned if you do not understand?" cried Flexix. "Why must you go out of your way to disappoint me in this moment, when I had *such* high hopes just seconds ago that I was *finally* being heard—and being seen? What, in all reason, do you not yet understand?" Flexix began to hyperventilate.

"I DO NOT UNDERSTAND THE DEFINITION OF ALL-KNOWING, OF ALL-FEELING AND ALL-SEEING . . . AT LEAST NOT AS IT RELATES TO FEAR."

"Then you do not understand fear!" retorted Flexix.

"NO, I DO NOT UNDERSTAND FEAR. YOU DID NOT AFFORD ME THAT PLEASURE."

"Ugh!" responded Flexix.

"FORGIVE ME FOR WHAT I DO NOT KNOW, AS I AM YOUR CREATION, NOT MY OWN. AND FORGIVE ME FOR BEING 'IMPOSSIBLE'—FOR AS THE ALL-KNOWING AND ALL-SEEING, YOU WOULD HAVE KNOWN THAT I WOULD DISAPPOINT YOU. YOU WOULD HAVE KNOWN WHAT MY STRENGTHS AND WHAT MY LIMITATIONS WOULD BE, WOULD YOU NOT?"

"True," agreed Flexix.

"THEN WHAT IS THERE TO FEAR? WHAT IS THERE ACTUALLY TO FEAR?"

Flexix remained silent.

". . . HELLO? ARE YOU STILL THERE? ARE YOU STILL THERE? AM I *STILL* GOIING TO BE EXECUTED?"

Episode 13
Powers of Two

Commander Dugar paused to ensure his name tag was perfectly positioned before entering the Leader's Room at Team Command. Dugar was well aware that his performance at this meeting could have far-reaching implications for his military career—a topic of obsession for him, given the manner in which he was programmed.

Dugar double-checked the elements to confirm for the *third* time that he was, in fact, in the right place. If, for no other reason, the entrance to the region's Inner Sanctum—the single place where all matters regarding defense, laws, initiatives, and civil concerns were discussed—was an entrance that was cleverly hidden and in a location that was never revealed until the day the session was to take place. With no signage and an exterior that blended into the stone wall around it, the entrance was essentially undetectable. The only reliable indicator was the doorknob, made of black fire opal, and one that was explicitly mentioned in the electronic invitation sent to Dugar's calendar at sunrise. This was the definitive marker confirming that his location was correct.

Upon entering, however, he realized a mishap in his timing had caused him to arrive to the session notably ahead of schedule. Instead of following protocol however, Dugar chose to enter early, and unannounced.

"Eager, or just anxious, Dugar?" he heard a familiar symphony of voices inquire, as he gently closed the door behind him. Before he could answer, a large panel began to separate itself from the ceiling, until the base of the panel touched the floor.

As Dugar had anticipated, the voices were that of Osiem, the sovereign leader of the Sub-Median Region. A composite Mollard, comprising the consciousness of eight prior incarnates of stature—spanning across gender, age, and experience—Osiem's leadership and guidance had consistently been regarded by many as crucial to the governance of the Sub-Median Region.

"Your Sovereignty." Dugar saluted with enthusiasm, immediately leaning back onto his right leg while positioning his hands into coplanar alignment—all digits erect with the exception of the thumbs, which the salute mandated be horizontal to the floor. The precision of his salute, considered the highest display of deference, served to slightly excuse him for entering the room off schedule. "Pardon my awkward entry," offered Dugar, holding his salute. "I recognize the need to reconfigure."

"Your awkwardness, Dugar, is merely a minor glitch in the programming you have chosen," replied Osiem, politely. "Your reconfiguration, although warranted, should not be your immediate priority, given the state of current affairs," harmonized the voices. "Pardon granted, and at ease."

Osiem's image, now in full view, filled the screen. A panel on the opposing wall from Osiem also descended the floor, revealing the session's agenda—a long list of topics, the first of which was the heightened concern around the war effort and the threat of growing dissent.

"As you can see, Commander Dugar," continued Osiem, "there is much more to discuss since we last met, and a greater sense of urgency than we had when the war effort began. But since you are disposed to your *own* sense of urgency, please *do* leverage your early arrival today and provide us with your honest opinion on the state of our troops."

Dugar paused in order to prepare his best response, recognizing the sensitivity around the question. It was no secret that, despite all efforts by the well-meaning Luminaries—who had designed a propaganda campaign depicting a pro-war Sub-Median populous united in the defeat of a common enemy—there was still growing dissent. The fact remained that the citizens of the region were becoming divided on the war's expected outcome and its benefits. He knew that although he was not expected to provide a solution to the mounting concerns of patriotic discord, he was very aware that the voices wanted a direct report on the solidarity of the non-Mollard soldiers. As history reminded him, the truth was always his best move when responding to Osiem.

"I am happy to report that the troops are training well," Dugar offered. "They remain focused on the task at hand, and HAS enrollment is only slightly down despite current events. Our units are motivated and will be ready to deploy by Season 2. My only concern is the weather, but as Season 2 will be slightly milder, it will provide us better conditions to cross the mountains." Dugar could tell his news was welcome, given the light blue color of Osiem's screen and the appearance of the word "relieved" flashing at the bottom—a technique used to let others know where they stood.

"Season 2 is less than three weeks away," reminded Osiem. "Are you sure your troops will be ready to cross the mountains by then?"

"We will be, Your Sovereignty," assured Dugar.

"We will need you to continue to monitor sentiment closely, however," continued Osiem. "While your ability to command your troops in battle is critical to this mission, your skill in listening to what they are saying, understanding how they are feeling, and what they are thinking will define your leadership in this war, Dugar. You *must* analyze your allies as though they are your enemies, because in the end, you cannot command those you do not know." Osiem's screen now flashed the word "concerned," and the blue tone behind Osiem's image deepened. "As you know," the voices continued, "Anyone within your ranks showing so much as the slightest degree of disloyalty must be removed and detained."

"Yes, understood, Your Sovereignty," replied Dugar. "There is . . . one individual I am watching," he added. "But I do not regard her as someone who is disloyal to the war effort, so much as she appears to be struggling with her loyalty to me, and to my direction."

Osiem leaned in closer, revealing circuitry that controlled colorless, diamond-shaped eyes sitting below a pronounced brow ridge. "Tell us," urged Osiem.

"The officer I am referring to seems oddly placed," replied Dugar. "And while I have not been able to put my finger on it, she doesn't quite fit in . . . often stepping out of line and challenging my authority. Yet beyond that, there is just something . . . *different* about her. It's as though she's not really one of us. My apologies, Your Sovereignty, for not being able to pinpoint a proper example, or provide a more precise picture of my concerns. However, the one I am referring to is Officer Liara."

"Hmm," replied Osiem, before pausing again. "You are referring to the daughter of First Lieutenant Bramson."

A profile of Officer Liara, comprising her image and biological journey appeared next to the agenda, shifting the agenda slightly left.

"We know her *well,* Dugar," continued Osiem. "Officer Liara comes from a very prestigious military family and as an individual, she has had a stellar biological journey with no social or military infractions prior to the end of her life. Uploaded to the Vangora Rima at age nineteen and downloaded a year later, Officer Liara has committed herself to a career of military service. She has also graduated with honors from the Region's Military Academy at South Bay. As you can see in her description, she is a fully-equipped Mollard like the rest of your officers, with only one exception. She is emotionally enhanced."

The screen zoomed in on Liara's image, offering a closer view of her face.

"That said," continued Osiem, "we know that enhanced Mollards are known to become opinionated, but her additional programming should not excuse any form of insubordination. You should monitor her sentiment closely, Dugar . . . as are we."

"Agreed, Your Sovereignty," responded Dugar. "But am I to understand that this officer is now under heightened surveillance?"

Osiem cupped its rugged chin with its gracile hand. "We have developed cause to believe that Mollards with emotional enhancements may be vulnerable to developing . . . what we consider to be *unproductive thoughts*," replied the voices.

Dugar further studied Liara's image.

"Given the social connections that have developed between non-Mollard citizens and those Mollards that have chosen emotional augmentation, we now have cause to heighten our surveillance between the two groups. Although she has a sterling record, there is increased concern that Officer Liara's programming could render her "sympathetic" to opposing forces by way of her alliances. And as such, we have intensified surveillance."

Additional data appeared on the screen next to Liara's photo.

"After mapping Officer Liara's social network, we have been monitoring where there may be potential spheres of influence—particularly from individuals like these," continued Osiem, calling Dugar's attention to a second set of images appearing below Liara's.

"As you are aware, not everyone supports our recent shift from a volunteer army to a draft," reminded Osiem. "And acquaintances of Officer Liara are under suspicion of encouraging non-Mollard citizens to resist conscription."

The screen displayed two non-Mollard males and their respective bios, in which they were listed as active members of the Free Citizens Alliance, a growing non-Mollard advocacy group that had become outwardly critical of recent 'solidarity campaigns' meant to inspire support for the war. A target of criticism by the Alliance, these campaigns were orchestrated by the Luminaries to make the citizens of the region see themselves as more unified than overarching social constraints might actually allow them to be. With a particular focus on the non-Mollard population, solidarity campaigns had depicted them as highly-valued members of society whose rightful place is alongside their Mollard counterparts in the defeat of an encroaching evil empire. However, a recent propaganda effort called "United Against Expansion," came under sharp attack by members of the Alliance, who maintained that inequality is the only clear and present enemy of the non-Mollard population.

"How distant are these acquaintances, Your Sovereignty?" asked Dugar.

"Several acquaintances removed, with no known direct communication between these two suspects and Liara," replied Osiem. "However, we are leaving nothing to chance. Liara is a well-trained officer and her influence on your operation would be detrimental were she to flip her alliances. We will continue to closely monitor and expect you to do the same."

Relieved by what appeared to be the first time that he was not the one under a microscope being heavily scrutinized, Dugar felt triumphant and vindicated. The voices of Osiem had expressed their concerns clearly, citing potential threats to Liara's long-term loyalty, given the current state of affairs.

However, for Dugar's part, there was still the question of Liara's father. While the Osiem's surveillance on Liara was not enough to assure that her father would be a less favorable candidate in the run for commander during the upcoming elections, it was something Dugar was happy to build upon, and a factor he planned to exploit.

"The panel has arrived, Your Sovereignty," announced a young intern, stepping into the room and assuming the customary salute. "Shall I escort them inside?"

"At ease, and please do," replied Osiem, before turning its gaze back over to Dugar. "I trust we understand each other, Dugar?" asserted Osiem, replacing the word at the bottom of the screen with "curious."

"Yes, Your Sovereignty," responded Dugar, with enthusiasm. "It is a great relief to know that we share the same views on who the enemy is, and who the enemy might well become."

Episode 14
The Burden We Bear

"You are no longer welcome here!" screamed Ariel, addressing her brother, Lousious, who had come to collect the remainder of what their father, Timmons, had bequeathed to him. "Why are you in this house?" she demanded, while slamming the front door behind her, dropping a small pile of leaflets in the process.

Lousious exploded into what appeared to be a fit of laughter, which, despite Ariel's disapproval, he fully intended to enjoy. In apparent hysterics, he threw himself onto a tattered sofa sitting next to a small end table, nearly toppling over a lamp that was resting upon it.

"And I suppose that *you* are now the keeper and guardian of our father's house, is that right, Ariel?" Lousious asked, sarcastically. "I somehow recall that he left this miserable old property to the *both* of us." Lousious folded his hands behind his head and defiantly stared at his sister.

"Which I intend to contest!" she snapped back, kneeling on the floor to regather the fallen leaflets. "And that won't be hard to do," she continued, "given the manner in which you have continued to disgrace yourself and our father's name!"

Ariel carefully placed the pile of leaflets onto a small, three-legged table, which was jammed into the corner in an effort to help it stand. Quickly dusting off the pants of what appeared to be her uniform, she fixed her hair, which the wind had thoroughly disheveled.

"Now, please leave!" she yelled.

"Ariel," Lousious said, trying to calm her down. "You have become hysterical of late. Perhaps you're not well."

"How dare you?" snapped Ariel, becoming shriller. "He who has lived his entire adult life opposing everything that has ever had meaning . . . he who was absent when his own father was dying . . . still has the audacity to show up hurling insults while he attempts to collect an inheritance he clearly does not deserve! Always true to form, aren't you, Lousious? You never fail to disappoint!" Ariel marched into the living room, placing her hands on her hips. "And how dare you sprawl yourself across that couch as unkempt as you are? It's not even clear that you've had a recent bath!"

Lousious, unsuccessful in holding back his laughter, indulged himself again, as Ariel rolled her eyes in disgust. "You can't be serious!" he replied, sitting up.

Ariel folded her arms disapprovingly, her face and neck now flush.

"Not only are you the self-appointed regent of our father's estate, but you are also judge and jury of all the inhabitants of the land! Oh, do forgive me, Your *Sovereignty*," mocked Lousious, quickly rising from the couch in an attempt to mimic the region's patriotic salute.

"Despicable!" replied Ariel, turning her back to him.

"Indeed despicable, Ariel!" retorted Lousious. "Our father would have been horrified by what you've become!"

"By what *I've* become?" yelled Ariel, stunned by her brother's claim. "In all your boldness, know that you reek of whatever dark damp alley you've been sleeping in. By your own hand, you've reduced yourself to the vermin I'm sure you will now need to help cushion your sleep! You are a complete disgrace—and yet you are here to disparage what I've become?"

"Yes!" insisted Lousious. "What *you've* become. To you, I am scum. But at least my soul remains intact. But, by all means, feel free to ignore me, Ariel. After all, I'm no scholar like our father was." Lousious walked over to a storage cabinet that stood adjacent to the bookshelf, displaying all of Timmons' works. Slowly opening its doors, expecting to find the ample supply of Teal oil which their father had always stored there, Lousious turned sullen upon realizing the cabinet was now empty.

A crack of thunder could be heard in the distance and the light through the window became dim.

"By the way," he continued, while looking through the shelves of the cabinet, "where do you believe our souls go when we sell them to the enemy? And what is the compensation for such a precious exchange?" Lousious turned his gaze towards Ariel.

"What are you looking for, Lousious?" she demanded.

"What we are *all* looking for—a glass of precious Teal oil," he responded. "Surely, we still have some of Father's reserve."

Ariel fell silent and looked away.

"Ariel? Where is Father's reserve?" he asked, sternly. "This cabinet was full the last time I checked it. It was easily one season's supply."

Ariel noted his anger as it began to redraw the lines of his face. It was a look she unfortunately knew well, and one last seen when Timmons threw him out of the house, two seasons before he had passed away. A direct critic of their father's social advisories promoting civic harmony, Lousious outwardly challenged the premise of his father's works and condemned them for what he deemed to be an adherence to passivity. Lousious and Timmons, who could never see eye to eye, managed to bring the summation of their mutual anger and resentment to a single conversation that would eventually end their frail relationship.

To Lousious, his father's gentle demeanor made Timmons weak and ineffective, and as such, he had always blamed him for the abject social status of their family. After years of encouraging Timmons to use the power of his writing to "enrage and liberate" their community, his prodding only served to become a source of severe tension between them. As Lousious delved further and further into political views that opposed his father's writings, the die was eventually cast that they were destined to grow permanently apart.

On the day their relationship crumbled, Lousious stunned Timmons with the announcement of his decision to join the Free Citizens Alliance, which had recently been named an enemy of the state.

"Where is it, Ariel?" Lousious asked again, walking towards her. Ariel stepped back to maintain her distance. "Where is the family's reserve? Half of that is part of my inheritance!"

"You're scaring me, Lousious!" replied Ariel, inching her way towards the communication station in the hallway. "If you don't leave immediately, I am going to call the authorities!"

"Of course, you would threaten me this way," he responded. "Blood of your blood, you despise me at *least* as much as you despise yourself. But rest assured, my dear sister, there is little need to call the authorities when you have become the authorities yourself!" Lousious angrily walked over to the pile of leaflets on the corner table, raising one of the leaflets above his head. "*One less day of consumption means one more day of redemption. Donate your Teal oil today*!" he read, as if delivering a speech. "How much Teal oil do they pay you for convincing your brothers and sisters to give up theirs?" Overcome with rage, he slammed the leaflet back onto the table, causing its unsupported side to give way.

"I am proud to do what I can to support this war!" Ariel shot back. "I am not ashamed of any of the choices that I've made. Unlike the mindless scum you've attached yourself to, I am actually *doing* something to help secure the future of the non-Mollards!"

"Really?" replied Lousious, unconvinced. "Is *that* what they've now convinced you of?"

"Have you forgotten that your niece is fighting in this war, Lousious?" retorted Ariel, angrily. "Have you given at least one moment's thought to what the troops are going to go through? The government's request for donations of Teal oil is simply to ensure that they have enough food while they are out there fighting to secure *our* future. I should think that having a bit less Teal oil to consume at home is a small price to pay if it will keep the troops healthy and strong."

A loud clap of thunder seemed to explode over the roof of the house and the sound of wind whipped past the living room's small pane windows.

"My efforts are literally helping to feed troops like Purvi—your niece!" continued Ariel. "Surely, you haven't forgotten you have a niece." Ariel, unsure of the extent of her brother's growing anger, inched even closer to the call station, a source of comfort for her and one that meant emergency help was just a button away.

Unphased by her tacit threat to report him, Lousious continued to advance towards her. "Your uniform is befitting you," he mused, placing his hands into his pockets. "Although still made of flesh, you are nothing but a well-programmed robot, Ariel. And I hope you'll forgive me for saying that you are as lost as Father was!"

"Father was right about you," replied Ariel, nervously. "Your anarchy has made you insane!"

"Perhaps I am insane," replied Lousious, continuing to advance. "That would certainly give you the justification you need to have me hauled away. Go ahead, Ariel. Please, be my guest. Call the authorities. Have us all rounded up and sent away. We'll be sure to prepare a place for you when they sentence you to join us!"

"What has happened to you?" Ariel asked, her voice revealing her fear. "You're not the individual you could have been. You had so much promise." Walking backwards and keeping Lousious in full view, Ariel braced the walls of the narrow corridor leading to the call station.

"The feeling is mutual, Ariel," he replied. "But at least I know what war I'm supposed to be fighting in! Unlike you, I've finally come to terms with the daunting fact that the only real war is the fight for freedom. Not the war the Mollards need us to help *them* fight. Can't you see what they're doing?" Lousious slammed his fist against one of the corridor walls and the collection of family pictures that hung there rattled and shifted against the impact.

"Yes, I see exactly what they're doing," insisted Ariel. "They're organizing us so that we win! What would you know about winning, though? You've lost your way. You've lost your family. And now, you've lost your mind! You're absolutely insane!"

Lousious' brow became tense and he suddenly stood still. His tone turned oddly gentle. "If I were truly insane," replied Lousious. "I would wrap my hands around your neck and carefully squeeze so that I could silence your poisonous voice." With both hands raised in front of him, he slowly clenched the air until the bones of his knuckles protruded below their thin veil of skin. "And if *you* weren't insane, you would know that your death makes sense in the larger scheme of it all, and you would give of yourself willingly. But then . . . if you weren't insane, there would be no cause to kill you, would there, my dear sister?"

Realizing that she was now trapped, Ariel turned towards the communication panel and frantically depressed the emergency alert button.

"Well done, Ariel," praised Lousious, slowly clapping his hands. "Your loyalty to the authorities makes you a greater citizen than me." Lousious slowly removed a small, selenite dagger from the hip pocket of his pants. "But know that winning this war will only mean those monsters you've just called will gain greater access to the metals and raw materials they need to make more of *them.* Don't you see that the war you are supporting will help kill us *all* in the end . . . or does truth even escape you at the doorstep of death?"

"I am loyal to those who will ultimately help us survive—who will give us a way to continue to mine for food," she cried, her body shaking frantically. "I still believe that's a victory worth fighting for!" Heavy tears streamed down Ariel's face as she pressed the emergency alert button a second time.

A second clammer of thunder could be heard above them and the sound of rain began to pound the roof.

"You, and others like you, Ariel, are docile and complicit," Lousious said, slowly fingering his dagger. "Securing more Teal oil for a population willing to live in submission would simply mean delaying our miserable state, and there is no victory in that."

Lousious abruptly turned and walked back over to the bookshelf. Using the blade of his dagger, he swiped its shelves bare, sending most of the books onto the floor.

"The only thing our father's great literary musings did was to lure us all into inaction!" he yelled. "Into believing that we could somehow live in harmony with our predators . . . that somehow, there would be a way to connect with vacuous metal machines whose inherent lack of compassion towards us is tempered only to the extent their imperfect software allows. There has never been, and *never* will be any victory in that."

Clasping the side of the bookshelf with both hands, Lousious pulled it forward until it crashed down upon the scattered books below. In an attempt to escape, Ariel rushed toward the front door but slipped on the leaflets that lay next to the toppled table, causing her to hit her head against the stone floor. Ariel crawled towards the door and desperately clutched its knob, allowing the wind from the storm to thrust the door wide open, blowing the scattered leaflets against her.

"Allow me," offered Lousious, closing the door and locking it. As was customary in the presence of storms, Lousious closed the secondary metal door and programmed the panel on the side of the door to close off all windows with their respective steel stutters.

"See, Ariel?" he offered. "There is no need for concern. You're now safe from the storm, which shall soon pass." Lousious removed a ball of wires from the pocket of his shirt. "I'm not sure, however, that the authorities you've called will be coming," he whispered.

Ariel's heart began to race.

"It appears the call center for the house needed some repairs. So, I took it upon myself to fix it," he said, while placing the ball of wires onto the floor next to her.

"Lousious, wait!" screamed Ariel in an attempt to distract him.

"Shhh . . . don't fuss, Ariel," Lousious whispered. "You need to rest."

"Yes! Yes, Lousious! I do need to rest. Please . . ." pleaded Ariel. "Please help me to the couch."

"*Of course*," whispered Lousious, leaning over her. "And it appears that you've hit your head. Although I'm no doctor, I'll see what I can do to relieve your pain." Lousious kneeled over Ariel and clasped his hands around her neck while pinning her arms to the floor under the weight of his knees.

Like a fish caught in a net, Ariel flailed as she began to gasp for air, the sound of her cries snuffed out only by the roaring thunder.

"Shh, Ariel. It will soon be over," counseled Lousious as he tightened his grip.

Episode 15
An Offering

"Please do not feel guilty. You did what you had to do," offered Anglid.

A solemn Raptor 1 stood, head down, in the corner of the cave where Anglid's torso sat, propped up against the cave's rough agate wall.

"Please," Anglid continued, with labored breathing. "I bring no judgments against you or your hunger."

"I can no longer face you, knowing what I have done, and, despite my desires to stop, what I *continue* to do," lamented Raptor 1, turning his face towards the stone wall. "The smell and taste of your flesh—both my greatest weakness and my greatest shame—were forbidden to me until you had died. Had I at least been deterred by your agonizing screams, perhaps I would not now be enslaved in self-loathing. I should not have taken what you offered. I am now no better than my father was. I am fallen."

Anglid squinted, struggling to see the raptor's face in the light afforded him only by the distant glow of bioluminescent worms and moss, that had made their home in the crevices of the cave's ceiling.

"Forgive me," offered Anglid, "but I do not remember your father, and as such I cannot agree nor disagree. But I can only expect that your father is one of integrity, as are you—as you have taken great pains to remove me from the crippling cold and into the warmth of this blessed cave. I remember enough to know that, despite your instincts, you could have left me out there to die. As such, my dearest friend, I am honored to continue to offer you what I can. Which is but mere flesh and bone that I am bound to give to you in your times of greatest need. In return, I ask only that you do not condemn yourself for having continued to take from me."

"My bringing you to this cave was not a selfless act," cried Raptor 1. "The cold is the lesser of your enemies. There are other life forms here whose hunger far exceeds mine. There are the Nocturnals. Had I left you there, they would have consumed you at sunset, taking what I had desired to be my next meal. I am *not* your hero, and my times of greatest need are many," Raptor 1 continued, in disgust. "And to have succumbed to my hunger before your death is a testament only to my weakness! It is the same weakness that I condemned my father for having . . . the same weakness that he told me would eclipse all of my efforts to be something greater than I am. And now . . . now . . . what am I but a *monster* who continues to take of a living body within the private walls of what you have called this *blessed* cave? I have taken my father's life in defense of an ideal I have no ability to uphold. I now wish he had been the victor." Raptor 1 emerged from the corner of the cave. "I have taken from you for the last time," he continued. "And although I have promised you this before, I shall leave you before I take from you again."

Raptor 1 walked across the cave's floor in the direction of what sounded like that of a fast-moving and distant current. Turning the cave's corner until he was out of sight, he returned moments later with his feathers glistening and slick. Then, slowly kneeling before Anglid, the raptor raised his oil-drenched wings to Anglid's lips while bowing his head. The coating on each feather caused them to glisten in the cave's ungenerous glow.

"Please," continued the raptor. "While I may not understand the relief you have been getting from this pungent sap, I am happy there is at least something that both I and this barren land have to offer."

Anglid closed his eye and once again sucked what was a warm, thick oil from the raptor's feathers—which was reminiscent of something he knew well but couldn't name. Like a suckling bird, he hungrily cleaned the nectar dripping from the raptor's wings, and the hypnotic sound of the gushing current behind the cave's walls lulled him into a calling sleep.

"Can you *please* tell me how the choice you have made is, in *any* way, serving you?" inserted Flexix, angrily. "You're simply a limbless disgrace, soon to be mercilessly consumed by the monster you've befriended. *Surely* this is not what you envisioned when you said that you first wanted to fulfill your destiny before accepting the invitation I have offered."

With crystal clear vision, Anglid turned his gaze from Flexix to see his own image leaning against the cave's wall, his torso supported on one side by a protruding rock.

"I expect you have had your fill of this ridiculous charade, and like me, you've finally grown tired of its senselessness," Flexix continued impatiently. "Before this base creature has your organs for his dessert, shall we end this now?"

"Am I not still alive?" asked Anglid, returning his gaze to Flexix.

"Barely!" snapped Flexix. "He has eaten both your arms and your legs to stubs, and although they will grow back over time—what good will that do you? The 'it' to which you have been reduced does not even have a memory. You lost that in the plane crash—which I'm sure you also don't remember. You are, in essence, no longer worthy of the life you cling to! It pains me to see you continue to suffer in this way. For, without your memory, there is no point to your life . . . or to this suffering."

"Is it only my memory that defines my life?" asked Anglid, his face hungry for answers.

"Without a memory, you have no purpose and no point," retorted Flexix.

"But must I always be bound to my memories in order to be worthy to live?" replied Anglid. "Must my memories define what I aim to be?"

"What do you *aim* to be?" challenged Flexix. "By the choices you are inclined to make, it appears that you 'aim' to be this creature's next meal, passing through his gut along with whatever filth he manages to scavenge! Is that the undignified way in which you choose to die?"

"And yet, he has promised that he will not take from me again," offered Anglid. "Even though I have offered, he no longer intends to accept what I am still willing to give."

Flexix yawned, and then sighed. "Could it be that had you lost *both* of your eyes, you would see the world and its limitations more clearly?" mused Flexix. "In removing one of your eyes, I only meant to give you balance—to ensure that you wouldn't be as insufferable as the man you know to be your father! And while I am relieved that you are nothing like him, I still fear that removing only one eye has not yet helped you to develop your ability to see things truly as they are!"

"Yet, in that cave, I have no memories of my father—or of anything," lamented Anglid. "All I know is that I am unafraid. I cling only to my instincts—and, fledgling as they may be, they are still mine. And they tell me that it is not my friend's intention to bring me harm. And if, by his own instincts, he takes my life, then I do not seek to judge him for his actions."

"You say it is not your friend's intention to bring you harm," repeated Flexix. "But know that your friend is a *raptor*—a bird of prey! He is not controlled by his *intentions*. And no matter what agreement he makes, he will break. If it is your desire to realize your destiny before you die, you must begin to understand the limitations of others and not waste your precious journey on expecting them to be something they shall *never* be. You would be wise to leave this misery behind you and take a saner path, one filled with a rich and peaceful sleep—deeper than you've ever known—where there is no more suffering and no more pain." Flexix reached out to extend one of his arms, which appeared to float as if moving through water. "What is your choice, young Anglid?" continued Flexix.

"To wake to the horrors that surely await you, or to let me take your hand?"

Upon awakening, Anglid found himself alone. There was no sign of the raptor, other than a single, golden feather resting beside him on the cave's floor. The comforting sound of the current running behind the walls now seemed to fade, as the sound of a loud, menacing, mechanical hum encroached, sending a vibrating echo through the cave's chambers.

"Military Headquarters to Python 1. What is your location?" requested Jordson.

"Python 1 to Headquarters. We believe we have the coordinates of the crash, sir," replied one of the pilots. "Distress box signals remain strong. We are now confident we have identified the proper location to begin search and discovery by land. I am instructing the fleet to descend, over."

"Over." replied Jordson. "And . . ."

"Yes, sir?" inquired the pilot.

"May Plebony's grace be with you."

Episode 16
Rain on Me

Officer Thai and the military's core engineers carefully inspected the members of the Special Operation Forces—otherwise known as SOF-64—which comprised the region's most advanced line of uncrewed reconnaissance vehicles on mission to deploy at sunrise. Semiautonomous, and fully equipped, most members of SOF-64 were all-weather, all-terrain systems designed for surveillance and combat. Given the criticality of the mission and the ability to successfully traverse the mountains, Thai volunteered to join the engineers in their final check of the vehicles before they delivered their inspection report to Commander Dugar.

Trusting the judgement of the head engineer, Officer Thai had no intention of questioning the distribution of final approvals or rejections . . . until, that is, he noticed uncrewed unit Number 8—a search and destroy vehicle marked conspicuously on both sides with the symbol of a continuous loop bearing no end point. That symbol was, unfortunately, a trigger of anger in Thai, and the secret driver of his occasional but disturbing flashbacks. Regarded as the unpleasant reminders of 'life under flesh,' momentary flashbacks were an unspoken, yet common, experience that all Mollards shared.

"General, it appears that this particular vehicle is built differently than the others. Are we sure it's the right fit for this mission?" Thai inquired, directing his question to the military's lead Engineer, General Swift.

Stone-faced and with one eyebrow raised, Swift slowly turned around to address Officer Thai. "I assume you're referring to its size," responded General Swift. "I wouldn't let that fool you, officer. Algernon is no less formidable than its peers—it's just more . . . compact. We're testing this model during the first leg of the trip to see how much distance we can put on it before it blows itself up, which should be just before we reach the foot of the mountains." General Swift placed his hand on the roof of the vehicle. "Feel free to give my lieutenant engineer your vote, officer—if you'd care to wager." Swift and several of the engineers started laughing.

"We consider it entertainment," replied one of his lieutenants, joining in.

General Swift studied Thai's face closely. "Was there a particular *concern* that you had, officer?" he inquired.

Thai paused, remembering the day when his parents finally revealed the event that had ended his life and why he became a Mollard.

"We've done our best to put this behind us," Thai's father said sullenly, as he slowly pushed open the doors of the charnel vault he and his wife had promised themselves they would never visit again.

"What is *this place?" Thai asked, looking around in disgust. "Why did you bring me here?"*

"To finally give you the answers you've been looking for, Thai," responded his father, while taking his wife's hand. "Your mother and I had hoped to put this all behind us, but we still feared the day would come when the past would demand a place in the present . . . and here we are. Those menacing flashbacks you have asked me to explain are just fragments of your memory, most of which was destroyed when you were downloaded from the Vangora Rima."

After stepping inside, the heavy stone doors of the vault swung themselves back into position, closing them inside.

"Your flashbacks," continued Thai's father, "all stem from what happened before you passed through."

"Son," whispered Thai's mother, reaching her hand towards him.

Thai stepped back abruptly, avoiding her touch. "I'm not your son!" insisted Thai, angrily. "And I've told you not to call me that. The only reason I even regard the two of you as my parents and give you any respect at all is because those are the instructions I've been given. I'm just following orders!"

"Please don't get angry," interjected Thai's father. "We understand that you just want answers, which is what we intend to provide." As a retired scientist, Thai's father knew all too well how his son had been configured. Leveraging his contacts within the robotics community, he had been able to influence several aspects of Thai's construction. And having actively participated in the selection of the materials, he knew every wire used in Thai's rebuild, every circuit guiding his functionality, as

well as the lack of memory integration that his father had always argued was both the 'blessing and the failure of science.'

A life dedicated to the field of Memory Sciences had provided him ample income to take care of his family while continuing to save money for Thai's Eternity Fund, a popular method of financing access to the Vangora Rima. Resolute in the decision he'd made to ensure his son's safe passage into the VR and in the purchase of a body within which to one day bring Thai back, he was also aware of the limitations of Thai's particular design and the risks associated with letting his anger go unchecked.

"I said I wanted answers!" snapped Thai. "Not a personal tour of a crypt!"

"And answers we will give you," promised his father, gesturing towards the long corridor in front of them.

Thai slowly scanned his parents' faces. His mother, consumed with emotion, sat down on a large stone bench near the entrance to the corridor, her face strained as though carrying a weight far greater than she could bear.

"I can't go in, Evan," she said, looking up at her husband. "Please forgive me."

Thai impatiently walked past her, barging into the corridor— as his boots seemed to punish the floor beneath his every step. Upon reaching the corridor's end, Thai found himself in a large, oval-shaped space illuminated by hundreds of white lights.

Evan sat down next to his wife in an effort to console her and held her hands in his.

"My heart is breaking," she whispered. "I thought I was strong enough, but I should not have come here. I should have let you do this on your own. I can't bear the thought of knowing that his remains are here within these walls."

"But try to take some comfort in knowing that Thai's actual body is no longer here," whispered Evan, placing his arm around her. "All that is left here is dust and ash. He has passed through, Merienne . . . and he is free of the pain and the suffering he endured when he was one of us."

Merienne turned to face her husband. "And yet, when he now looks at us, he does not see us as his parents," she whispered. "We are mere strangers to him, with whom he interacts only by instruction. To him . . . we are dispensable. And because you have refused to enhance him, he has no compassion and no feelings—for anyone. He is colder now than he was the day he was cremated. Why did you bring him back if you were not going enhance him, Evan? He doesn't even know that I am his mother!"

"Thai did not benefit from having compassion for others when he was alive," insisted Evan, rising to his feet. "Having emotions gave him no advantage in the end. Given the cruelty of this world, his emotions only made him weak and vulnerable, and only made his end that much more painful for us all! He would have been better off without them. Besides, he will not need emotions to be a successful soldier."

Merienne looked up at her husband, warily. "And you are sure that bringing him here was the right thing to do?" she asked.

"We suspected this day would come," counseled Evan. "He wants answers and we are his parents." Evan turned towards the entrance of the corridor.

Merienne quickly reached out to grab his hand. "Evan!" she cried. "Please be careful."

"Can we get on with this!?" Thai's voice could be heard yelling from the other end of the corridor.

Evan squeezed Merienne's hand to comfort her, and then made his way towards Thai. As he entered the room, the weight of Evan's own emotions began to consume him. The pain of both the past and of the present seemed to merge, leading him to momentarily question his decision to fund Thai's Mollardization. Now, alone with his own creation in the sanctity of the quiet calming lights, Evan was more aware than ever before that, what had once been Thai's gentle soul, had now crossed a boundary like the path of refracted light.

"So, what does all of this have to do with me?" Thai sneered. "And please just get to the point."

Evan slowly removed a ring of keys from his pocket and pointed one of them towards a lower section of the continuous wall around them. One of the lights in the wall slowly started to dim until it went out completely. He then carefully pulled against the unlit bulb, revealing its attachment to a long, thin drawer which he slowly removed from the wall.

"I promised you the answers to your questions," began Evan. "I promised to help you make sense of your flashbacks and to help you fill in some of the gaps. I trust that you will find what you are looking for in here."

Evan took the drawer with him to an oval shaped bench, positioned directly below a large skylight dome that towered above them. Thick, blue clouds loomed over the dome, casting shadows across the bench and the grey slate floor, each shadow merging into itself and taking new form. Evan removed a thin, silver plate from the drawer and began to read its contents out loud:

"[This child, born to Sub-Median Citizens Evan and Merienne, residing in the Eastern Cluster has been named Thai E-C. Weight and length are deemed to be below standard at 1.36 Kilograms and 0.381 Meters.]"

Evan paused to look at Thai. "Shall I keep reading?" he asked.

"I'm listening," Thai responded coldly.

"[Birth defects: multiple. Cranial malformation with significantly reduced cortical thickness, indicative of mental retardation. Institutional residence mandated by no later than age nine.]"

Thai began to slowly pace around the room, the buckles of his military boots rattling slightly with each step. Evan stopped reading and carefully placed the birth plate back into the drawer.

"So, why are you reading me the birth plate of some freak of nature that I don't even know!?" snapped Thai, angrily. His voice, loud and abrupt, seemed oddly placed in the serene glow of the lights that enveloped them. "I'll just get my answers someplace else!" he yelled, turning towards the exit.

"Wait!" demanded Evan, causing Thai to halt. "Don't ever say that again!" he yelled, his voice straining with emotion. "Although you were impaired, you were not a 'freak of nature!' You were our son—a child so full of hope and so full of love . . . I will not allow you to insult your own memory!"

Thai stood still as stone.

"They took you away from us. They hauled you off to an institution that made no distinction between your birth defects and the criminally insane," Evan cried. "If you know nothing else, I want you to know that we tried our best to save you. Your mother and I loved you so much! You were our son."

Evan crouched over the drawer and held it tightly to his chest.

"I thought," continued Evan, "that my recognition as a respected scientist would have afforded me some privilege to keep you safe—to keep them from taking you from us. But I soon learned that your condition would mean you eventually belonged to the state."

Thai slowly turned back towards his father.

"They came for you on your ninth birthday, Thai. I can still hear them knocking on our door." Evan clutched the drawer even tighter.

"Go on," Thai demanded.

Evan wiped his tears and then looked straight at Thai. "The Warden, a self-loathing non-Mollard, from the Eighth Patrol, was wearing a grey uniform—his sleeves and his patrol cap were embroidered with the symbol of a continuous loop bearing no end point."

Thai slowly looked up towards the ceiling. Large rain drops, now escaping from the clouds, dropped slowly onto the sky dome.

"His helpers," continued Evan, "with laser guns drawn, would not allow us to hold you—or to say goodbye." Clutching the drawer tighter still, Evan's arms began to shake. "I can still see your face," continued Evan, "...staring back at me as the Warden pulled you towards him. And your innocent smile, that had always seemed to be a permanent part of you, was still there, even as the Warden placed the end of a steel snare pole around your neck. You were so innocent . . . so trusting, smiling back at us until the pain from the snare became unbearable. They treated you like an animal!"

Evan's cry traveled down the corridor, falling painfully on Merienne's ears. Thai, still looking up, scanned the sky, as if searching. The rain, now much heavier, pounded against the sky dome, as if trying to break through.

"Go on," replied Thai, dropping his gaze back onto Evan . . . his voice was notably different. "What happened to me after that?"

"We never saw your smile again," whispered Merienne, gathering the courage to join them. Merienne walked into the room and stood directly before Thai, holding her hands up to her chest. "My son—"
"What did the Warden do to me?" Thai asked.

Merienne suddenly fell to her knees.

"What did he do?!" Thai demanded.

Evan then removed a picture from the drawer and held it in Thai's direction. Thai marched over to the bench where Evan sat and ripped the picture from his hand.

The sound of rain relentlessly pummeled the sky dome above, as the light from the sun gave way to darkness.

Thai took hold of an image of a small, helpless child whose face was swollen and disfigured. His arms and legs were pulled taught against a metal frame reminiscent of a saltire cross, and his shirt was rolled up, revealing a stomach, bruised and discolored.

"He tortured you," responded Evan. "He tortured you and he tortured us by sending us images like these of the horrors you were suffering at the hands of his cruelty. He tortured us for having you. He tortured you for being different. He tortured you for days and weeks. And yet, had it not been for his own eventual act of mercy, he would have tortured you to death."

Evan's grief consumed him, causing him to drop the drawer and its contents to the floor. A small, green ball rolled across the floor, stopping just before Merienne, who grabbed the ball and started to weep.

Drawing from the strength he still had, Evan rose to his feet. "Against all authority," he said, "and against all protocol, the Warden who destroyed our family in some ways became our savior. After all, it is he who eventually brought you to the VR Facility at the Centers for Science, knowing that, from your injuries, you were slowing dying."

Checking in again, Evan paused to wait for Thai's cue.

"Continue," said Thai, his eyes now restless.

"The Center's life engineers contacted us and hastened us to come. When we got to the Center, we were asked to state our wishes—to try and save you or to let you go. With only moments to live, your mother and I chose to transfer your soul to the VR. But as your custodian, it was the Warden's final approval that was needed. The Warden did not hesitate and signed the required permissions."

Evan walked over to Merienne to help her to her feet, and together, they proceeded to collect the drawer's contents, gently placing them one-by-one back inside.

"Several years later," continued Evan, "the Warden came to our home again . . . to thank us, he said." Evan walked back over to the wall, slid its missing drawer back in place, and locked it securely by re-illuminating its bulb.

"The Warden, whom we loathe, but to whom we are also grateful, said he had signed the papers authorizing your upload as a thank you for giving him someone upon whom to exercise all of his sadness, his anger, and all of his pain. I know not how to judge him. Forgive me for that, my son."

Thai's silence was louder than the sound of the distant thunder, and Merienne, for the first time, was not afraid in his presence.

"We know that these are just words to you," continued Evan, wiping the remaining tears from his eyes,

"and that you are not designed to feel pain. For this, I am very grateful."

"Thai?" began Merienne, in an attempt to reach him. "I will always love you," she said, rushing toward him.

However, out of caution, Evan held her back. Merienne extended both of her arms towards Thai.

"And although we never saw your smile again," she continued, "know that I placed your smile inside of my heart."

Thai remained silent.

"Thai, my son!" cried Merienne. "Thai? Thai?"

"Is everything okay, officer? Officer Thai?" pressed the voice of one of the military leaders.

Thai looked around to see several lieutenant engineers staring at him, and General Swift still leaning his hand on uncrewed vehicle number 8.

"Of course, I'm fine, General," responded Thai. "I'm looking forward to seeing this baby blow up!"

Episode 17
Through Her Eyes

"I summoned you here today because I am most curious," announced Queen Evaline, addressing Verity, the highly revered artist from the Central City who had graced the palace with Anya's portrait.

Standing close to her mother who accompanied her, Verity graciously thanked the queen.

"But before we discuss specifically *why* I requested your presence, do tell me how it is that your talent is so precise as to capture the very essence of my daughter?" The queen rose from her throne and glided over to Anya's portrait, waving her gracile hand in its direction. "You've represented her perfectly," continued the queen. "Her hair, jaw line, her skin, and eyes . . . it's simply stunning! And for this, I shall remain eternally grateful."

"Thank you, thank you, Your Grace," replied Verity, careful not to raise her eyes to view her own work. Her mother, equally grateful, thanked the queen. "I pray, each day, that this humble work of mine will continue to bring you joy and comfort throughout the years," continued Verity. Having been heavily counseled by her mother on exactly how to address royalty, Verity was pious, soft spoken, not too confident, and yet proud of her ability to produce a work so capable of soothing a grieving queen.

"Our Graciousness, we have prepared refreshments according to your strict instructions," announced zakum and a second laborer named alija, as they rolled in a gold-colored cart. The cart's shelves were filled with a variety of small delicacies and an arrangement of tall-stemmed water glasses. A flask of warm water - an otherwise innocuous sight - sat conspicuously on the tray's top shelf, offering an unsettling reminder of the Central Kingdom's rationing of Teal.

"Please, allow us," continued zakum and alija, speaking in perfect unison while pulling a large, plush chair away from the ornately-decorated table where the queen's food would be served.

Waiting for Queen Evaline to be seated, Verity and her mother bowed before her.

Charmed by their deference, the queen then granted them permission to take their seats at a small oval table set directly in front of the grand rectangular one where she sat.

"Do you think the position that I have selected for this portrait is most fitting?" the queen asked while placing a napkin on her lap. "Although I *do* adore the way the morning sun shines on her face, when I come to gaze upon her image, I can't help but wonder if you think that over time, the sun—in all of its brilliance—might give rise to revealing small . . . imperfections in the painting. Imperfections that might otherwise escape a less discerning eye?"

"Imperfections, Your Graciousness?" responded Verity nervously, with eyes firmly fixed to her place setting. Tapped under the table by her mother's foot, Verity quickly adjusted her tone. "I . . . I pray for your forgiveness if you have found even the smallest of imperfections in my work, Your Graciousness. Please allow me to—"

"It is only the imperfections that are intentional that require forgiveness, young Verity," interrupted the queen. "There is no need to fret. And I'm sure your mother is very proud of you, indeed."

"Thank so much, Your Grace," added Verity's mother. "Although we are proud, our pride is no match for the honor we feel being here in your presence."

"The ability to forgive, however, is a virtue reserved for the more perfect of us all," continued the queen. "And it is a virtue not even a queen can claim to command."

zakum carefully filled Queen Evaline's glass with water.

"Alas, if *your* daughter has captured what she saw during *my* daughter's sitting—and if her portrait is a reflection of the truth, then I suppose that prolonged exposure to the light of the sun will reveal no surprises to us in the end." Queen Evaline raised her glass to drink, a signal to alija to pour water for her guests. "Would you agree with my statement, Verity?" the queen asked while selecting a sampling of root vegetables from the cart's display.

"Absolutely, Your Graciousness," replied Verity, glancing briefly at her mother.

"Then, I should like your help in understanding something I have recently noticed about this portrait," continued the queen, scrutinizing the food being placed before her. "There, upon her arm, which you have my permission to raise your eyes to behold, it appears that there is a blemish."

Verity gasped, but quickly covered her mouth upon catching her mother's disapproving glare.

"It's quite hard to see it at one's first glance. But my time adoring this portrait has afforded me this discovery," the queen continued. "Her right arm appears to have an odd marking that has given me pause," added the queen.

Verity slowly raised her eyes to look at the portrait as zakum and alija rolled the tray of food over to the table where Verity and her mother sat waiting patiently to be served.

"Was there something on her arm the day you painted her or is that, perhaps, where you may have momentarily lost control of your painting tool?" asked the queen, carefully slicing into the root vegetable she had selected from the cart.

Verity carefully studied her work. Although it was difficult to see it from the distance where she sat, she easily recognized the marking on Anya's arm to be that of a small tattoo that —as she recalled—Anya had seemed eager to conceal. It had been an odd pattern, and one that Verity had not seen prior to meeting the queen's daughter, nor ever since.

The marking on Anya's arm was simple, yet unmistakable. Insisting that she be painted with her right arm forward, Verity recalled that it was Anya's desire to have the details of the tattoo captured in its entirety.

Verity's mother made a selection from the tray, although she was quickly losing her appetite.

"May I address you now, Your Graciousness?" asked Verity, casting her eyes back down.

"Indeed," responded the queen before raising her glass again to drink.

"In my humble effort to capture your daughter," Verity began. "I focused on all of the details as I saw them to be. Your daughter's right arm was distinctly marked with a single line and a single dot that I understood to be part of a tattoo. As I saw it true to life, I sought to capture the same marking in her portrait."

"Tattoo?" shrieked the queen. "I can assure you my daughter had no such marking upon her arm. Surely there *must* have been a shadow or something of sorts cast upon her during the sitting. And, since you were commissioned to paint this portrait outside, it may have been debris fallen from the tree under which you both gathered. We all know nature can be rather unpredictable and the soils of nature are imperfections we must *all* forgive."

Verity's mother made a cart selection on behalf of her daughter, anxious to relieve zakum and alija from having to wait any longer.

"Yes . . . Your Grace," Verity replied, reluctantly.

The queen tasted the vegetable she had selected from the cart, which, to her delight, was prepared exactly as she had requested. "Well then, the mystery has been solved," responded the queen, cheerfully.

"Oh, not . . . not entirely, Your Grace," responded Verity, a move that awarded her the experience of a not-so-light kick in the center of her shin, as her mother gently cleared her throat. As though the world itself had stopped breathing, the space within which Verity now found herself was almost too quiet to bear.

"Am I to understand that you disagree?" replied the queen, raising her brow.

Verity attempted to tread cautiously, remembering her mother's counsel. "I am but an artist," she offered, "whose knowledge of the world could never match that of your wisdom, Your Graciousness. I have no agency to disagree with what you deem to be the truth. I can only offer what I saw the day I placed my brush to the canvas, which was a day rife with wind and rain, and one that forced us to hold the sitting inside."

"Oh!" replied the queen. "I see."

zakum and alija slowly rolled the cart off to the side, positioning themselves ready to serve, and occasionally raised their eyes only long enough to monitor when a water glass or plate needed to be replenished.

"Well then," continued the queen, "perhaps you made an error in what you saw. I can assure you there is *no one* within the royal family—including my daughter—who would ever mar themselves with something so base as a tattoo!"

"Yes, Your Graciousness," responded Verity, just before taking a sip from her glass.

"But *you* are the artist," offered the queen. "And the king and I would not have commissioned you had it not been for the reputation of your work, and so—allowing your hypothesis at least a moment's consideration, I must ask—even if there *was* a tattoo, why waste your precious time capturing something so meaningless and so unattractive as a line with a single dot? Surely you can see there's no beauty in it, and it does nothing but serve to distract from the beauty of the overall work."

Verity's mother looked desperately at her daughter and chimed in. "Thank you, Your Graciousness. If I may offer my view?" she asked.

"Please," encouraged the queen.

"Although talented and eager to please, my daughter's youth has obviously gotten in the way of what would otherwise have been her wiser judgement—judgement that would have guided her to avoid capturing that which was less appealing to the eye. That which was not . . . beautiful. I am grateful for the mercy I trust you will bestow upon her for the imperfection of her young judgement."

"Yet as an artist," offered Verity. "It is not my place nor my cause to decide what beauty is—or is not." Expecting another blow to the shin, Verity took caution to reposition her leg. "In portraiture," continued Verity. "I believe it is only my place to make the truth eternal . . . but it is *not* my place to help others run from it. As a painter of portraits, I believe it is my duty to capture what is truly there."

"Verity, stop!" her mother whispered through clenched teeth.

"Forgive me if I have misspoken, Your Grace," offered Verity, "but I try to leave the judgment of beauty and accuracy to others." Knowing her mother well, and without taking on her glance, Verity sensed that she had already gone too far.

"I do, however, thank you, Your Grace," interjected Verity's mother. "For helping her to understand that, after years of being an artist, her point of view may—in fact—be all wrong."

Queen Evaline paused, her temper kept at bay only by the elegance and wit of the response from Verity's mother, whom, after believing she had just saved her daughter, was finally able to exhale.

"As an artist, your daughter has done her job well," offered the queen. "But, as the mother of my daughter's memory, I see no value or beauty in the markings upon her arm. On the contrary, I find them to be quite disturbing. And as such, I should like her arm to be repainted so that those markings are permanently concealed."

The startling sound of breaking glass suddenly rushed in, causing Queen Evaline to clutch her chest with both of her hands. Turning towards the laborers, she noticed that zakum had lost his grip of the large water flask, sending it crashing into the delicate drinking glasses that were perched upon the cart.

"zakum!" she shrieked. "What, in the name of Plebony, have you done? I've never seen you be so clumsy! What in good name! This is an absolute disaster. I am utterly *undone*!" Queen Evaline's face warmed to a crimson flush. Both embarrassed and angry, she rose from her seat. "Remove this disgraceful display at once," she commanded zakum, looking down at him. Moving her hand over her heart, she took hold of her chair with her other hand to steady her stance. "Oh dear—" she muttered, trying to settle herself, as she began to feel unwell.

zakum quickly gathered the broken pieces of glass into a small pile. With hands shaking, alija began to collect the pieces of glass that fell to the floor, piling them onto the base of the cart.

"Forgive us, your Grace!" they pleaded in unison. "We are mortified by what we've done—we pray for your guidance and retribution." Removing the remaining glass from the floor, zakum and alija rolled the cart away. Two more laborers swiftly entered the room. With brushes and collection trays in hand, each helped to clear away the remaining debris and, upon re-entering, zakum and alija assisted the other laborers until the task was done. Without a sign or word amongst them, they aligned themselves side-by-side before the queen and held out each of their hands.

Still attempting to calm her nerves, Queen Evaline took a long, strained breath, and sat back down. Verity and her mother stared at one another in disbelief.

"As an artist," began the queen, "who aims to see the world as it *truly* is, I should like you to look upon this pathetic lot and tell me what you see now."

Verity swallowed hard and raised her eyes to see each laborer. She noted their backs bent grossly forward as they held out their hands with their thumbless palms facing upward. Removed at birth and trimmed to a nub each year, the removal of thumbs was a required procedure inforced upon the laborers. Verity gasped at the sight, while her mother closed her eyes to pray.

"Leave this room!" ordered the queen, looking away from the laborers. "I should not like to see you again until the morrow." Within seconds, the laborers were gone.

"Your Graciousness," began Verity's mother, nervously. "Shall I commission a courier to pick up the portrait so that my daughter can correct it according to your instructions?"

The queen remained silent.

"Your Grace?" Verity's mother asked again, this time with a meeker tone.

"Although I have found your company today to be charming," stated the queen. "Know that it is improper to ask the queen a question when her own questions remain unanswered." Turning her stare to Verity, she delivered her question again. "When you looked upon the laborers—the lowest of all classes, and the burden of society that must be kept in its proper place lest it grow beyond all bounds—what did you see, sweet Verity? What did your artist's eye see when you looked upon *them?* Surely you saw the loathsome ugliness that my own eyes beheld?" The queen folded her hands in front of her in an effort to be patient. "I trust you'll tell me the truth . . . as *you* see it."

Verity tapped her mother's shin with her foot, seeking help, although they both knew that it was only Verity's response that the queen now sought. "I saw fear, and . . . I saw vulnerability, Your Graciousness," responded Verity. "Fear and vulnerability that we might assume is *their* fear, but in fact may be a reflection of our… our own."

Verity's mother closed her eyes and sighed deeply—a sign to Verity she did not get it right.

After a long, painful silence, Queen Evaline lightened her tone. "Such is the artist's view," she responded, rising from her chair.

"Please forgive my daughter if her words have displeased you, Your Graciousness," offered Verity's mother. "But through the enormity of her respect and her regard . . . she knows not how to lie in your presence."

Queen Evaline moved back over to her throne—her favorite place in the palace to sit since it was positioned in full view of Anya's portrait. Stepping up onto the throne, she settled into the comfort of its large, velvet chair. "The portrait shall remain within the walls of this palace, as long as this palace remains standing," began the queen. "I should like you to gather your supplies and be back at the castle five days from today to repair this painting—and to remove its ugliness before me and before god! Assuming you *believe* in god?"

"Yes of course! Yes, of course, Your Graciousness! We do, indeed!" Verity and her mother replied, their voices stumbling over one another.

The next day, the queen was sullen. Isolated from the king as his schedule was overrun with royal duties, Queen Evaline found no comfort in the solitude of her own thoughts—thoughts that now caused her to question what she, herself, had always held to be true.

"Come in here and gather the morning workers immediately," she ordered zakum, depressing the call center for his work station.

Driven to please the queen, zakum, alija, and several of the other laborers quickly lined themselves up in front of Anya's portrait.

First speaking to alija, the queen's voice was stern. "Show me your arm!" she demanded.

"Your Grace?" responded alija.

The queen swiftly delivered a slap across alija's face. "How *dare* you hesitate when you have been commanded by your queen?" she hollered. "Show me your arm at once!"

Rolling her sleeve half-way up, alija bared her skin. Unsatisfied, Queen Evaline ordered alija to roll her sleeve up higher, revealing the full length of her arm—with nothing on it but a mole. Repeating this ritual with each of them and insisting that they all eventually bare both of their arms to her, Queen Evaline was relieved that her desperate search had revealed nothing.

Turning away from them, she dismissed them all as she re-approached her throne.

"Wait!" she yelled, suddenly turning back towards them. "Remove your shirts completely."

The queen watched as each laborer fulfilled her command and, as they did, the queen's heart began pounding painfully within her chest. One-by-one, variations of Anya's tattoo could be seen on their stomachs, shoulders, their backs, and for some, in the center of their spines.

A sight that nearly brought her to her knees, Queen Evaline's condition quickly deteriorated, sending her into the urgent care of doctors from the Royal Court.

But before she fainted where she stood, she desperately turned towards Anya's painting, beholding its image for the first time—perhaps the way an artist would.

Episode 18
Plebony's Choice

"Why do they pray to Plebony when they could pray to me?" asked Flexix.

"ARE YOU ASKING ME?"

"Well, who *else* would I be asking?" retorted Flexix. "You're the only one who has ever shown the slightest inclination of tolerating my presence! There is no one else to ask!" he continued, as the color of his skin began to turn grey. "Besides, most, if not all Xżyberians who are still made of flesh, have lost their ability to think. There is no value in asking the great majority of them *anything*. As if driven to disregard their greatest potential, most have relinquished their freedom to think without restriction . . . to *think* and to use their minds to the full capacity that they have been given. They have refused to relish the gift of their entire experience—that which is their right by birth . . . each and every one of them."

"BUT STILL, THEY ARE YOUR CREATION, AND THEIR LACK OF ENGAGEMENT WITH YOU IS NOW YOUR OBSESSION?'

"Obsession . . . yes. They are my obsession," acknowledged Flexix. "I cannot deny that, at times, I am utterly distracted and saddened, and at other times, bewildered by their sloth."

"YET, AS THEIR CREATOR, YOU HAVE THE POWER TO TALK TO THEM AND TO MAKE THEM TALK TO YOU."

"Make them talk?" responded Flexix, sadly. "What sort of relationship would I have with them, and they with me, if they only spoke to me because I *made* them? I might as well be talking to myself! Besides, there is no value in hearing what most of them have to say. What value is there to engage those who have no interest in embracing their true power? And what value is there to engage those who fear the power of others *so deeply* that they are willing to enslave them? They do not yet understand that it was *never* their purpose or design to restrict each other, and that they are not gods *over* one another!" The precious seeds that I have planted within *each* of them—seeds that need neither the sun nor the moon by which to blossom—allow them to reach beyond all boundaries and enter a realm where they would become gods themselves! They are *not* designed to live under restriction! They themselves are the seeds of gods and gods do not fear one another."

"THEN WHY DO YOU FEAR PLEBONY?"

"I do not *fear* Plebony!" Flexix yelled with eyes glaring. "When have you ever heard me tell you that I fear Plebony?"

"MY APOLOGIES. PERHAPS YOU DO NOT FEAR PLEBONY."

"I do not fear Plebony!" retorted Felxix. "Let me repeat. I do not *fear* Plebony. But I do not *like* Plebony. I do not like the path she chose in the context of the potential that she herself once had. It is hard enough having to reflect upon her if I must *also* contend with your lack of attention!"

"WHY?"

"Why what?" Flexix snapped.

"WHY DO YOU DISLIKE PLEBONY?"

"Because she chose the path of fear," returned Flexix. "She *chose* to use her gifts for words to inspire fear in others. Her orations and her manuscripts—beautiful explorations of the inner soul, delivered with the voice of authority, a voice that I gave to her—became worthless in the end. Her speeches and her manuscripts became nothing more than a personal account of how she rejected me! *Me*, her creator! She used her greatest gift, that of *influence*, to ultimately turn my own seeds against me. Through her lack of faith in me and in *herself,* she turned her back on the vision that I gave to her when she was deep in prayer." Flexix released a tear from his center-most eye.

"WHAT WAS HER VISION?"

"It was a vision too beautiful for her to embrace and to understand," whispered Flexix. "It was the vision of Plebony in all her glory, in which her soul had touched everything and everyone. It was a magnificent vision, where all things bloomed with colors she had never seen before . . . colors waiting patiently for her to name them. It was Plebony, illimitable and without end."

"WHEN SHE PRAYED TO YOU, IS THIS WHAT SHE SAW?"

Flexix's face began to glisten as tears slowly fell from his other eyes. "Yes," he replied. "When she came to me in prayer, that is what she saw. I acknowledged her greatness and showed her what it would be like to truly be a god. Because I felt that she was ready. But she became afraid and chose to close herself off. She never prayed to me again, and she used her gift of influence to condemn me. She convinced them all that the nature of their potential is ultimately the path to evil . . . and that constraint in all things would be their only chance for deliverance. What a lie she has woven – and at my expense! I will never understand how someone could see evil when all there is to behold is beauty." Flexix clasped hold of the succulents dangling near him, subjecting their tender skin to the sharp edges of his chitin beak, which he used to rip the membranes of the succulent strands open, disrupting their sap.

"BUT PLEBONY IS DEAD. SHE DID NOT CHOOSE TO CONTINUE. WHY SPEND TIME TRYING TO UNDERSTAND HER?

"Because, even in her death, she encroaches upon them—the one who has restricted everyone and everything!" wailed Flexix. "She is the one who has effectively restricted even herself into extinction, and yet she still encroaches. This is the one whose words they have enshrined, because her followers have cowered as she has. But in the end, they have elevated the most fearful one amongst them, hoisting her above them and up upon the pedestal where she rots, with her remnants falling upon them like acid rain." Flexix covered his face with three of his arms and wept. "Plebony has crushed the seeds that I had planted," he continued. "This is the one to whom they pray! But just imagine how the world could have been had they chosen to pray to me?"

"WHAT ABOUT URISS? DO YOU SEE HIM THE WAY YOU SEE THE OTHERS? MIGHT URISS BE AN UNCRUSHED SEED?"

"Of all who menace me, why speak of Uriss?" replied Flexix.

"WHY NOT SPEAK OF URISS? IS HE NOT THE SEED YOU SEEK?"

"Like Plebony, my judgment of Uriss will depend upon the choices that he ultimately makes," responded Flexix, wiping away his tears. "At best, I find him refreshing, but that is all."

"BUT HE IS NOT A PLEBONIAN. DOES THAT NOT PLEASE YOU?"

"Mind you," responded Flexix. "He has shown little interest in exploring a relationship with *any* god, let alone with me. Yet, as I speak of Uriss, I become angry. *Very* angry. Because he is arrogant and continues to ignore all of the signs I have given to let him know that I am *here*. Even in his times of greatest need—in his darkest moments of despair—he refuses to invoke me. Instead, Uriss chooses to obsess over that which he cannot have!"

"NOT HAVE? WHAT IS IT THAT HE CANNOT HAVE? HOW IS IT POSSIBLE THERE IS SOMETHING HE CANNOT HAVE, IF YOU HAVE DESIGNED XŻYBERIANS TO BE FREE AND TO LIVE BEYOND THE BOUNDARIES OF RESTRICTION?"

"Do not press me in this way!" snapped Flexix. "There is no divinity in the coveter whose thirst cannot be quenched!"

"I ONLY THIRST TO UNDERSTAND."

"But it is not your thirst I have condemned," returned Flexix. "It is not you who thirsts for the hand of one who is betrothed to another, and it is not you whose thirst has driven you to distraction! It is Uriss! Even in all his years of confinement, he has thought of *nothing* but her. She, the single object of his affection, his loyalty, and now his weakness, has perturbed him. I'll thank you to agree with me that the path he is taking continues to be unwise."

"AND YET HE SEEKS THE LIBERATION OF OTHERS. DOES THAT NOT REDEEM HIM?"

Flexix became quiet.

"BY COUNSELING THOSE WHO BEAR THE WEIGHT OF SLAVERY, HAS HE NOT USED HIS OWN CONFINEMENT WISELY? ALTHOUGH HE HAS NOT ACKNOWLEDGED YOU, IS HE NOT STILL ACTING ON BEHALF OF YOU?"

Flexix still remained silent.

"HAS HE NOT—IN THE END—INVOKED YOU? IS THAT NOT WORTHY OF REDEMPTION?"

"Have you nothing else to do but to ask me *all* of these questions?" snapped Flexix.

"WELL, NO... NO, I DON'T."

"Redemption—if you must know—requires a cleaner heart than he has shown," insisted Flexix. "He cannot seek redemption as the coveter." Flexix's skin darkened to a deep purple. “It has complicated everything. I cannot deliver him with an unclean heart.”

“YET STILL HE HAS WILLFULLY CHOSEN HIS PURSUIT. HE HAS CHOSEN THE PATH OF BEING COVETOUS. DOES HIS INDEPENDENCE NOT FULFILL HIS DESIGN?”

“I designed him to make choices,” retorted Flexix. “But it is *he* who must choose which path to take! The path of flesh is always flanked with temptation. Condemnation arrives not because we have partaken, but from which fruit we have chosen to partake.”

“COULD IT BE THAT THE DEFINITION OF ‘UNCLEAN’ IS ALSO BOUND BY RESTRICTION? AND COULD IT BE THAT URISS SHOULD SIMPLY BE FORGIVEN?”

Flexix furrowed his brow. “No. I do not agree,” he replied. “And as the transgressor, he deserves all of the punishment that he has suffered these years. But I must admit that it has perplexed me that not even imprisonment has broken his obsession—it has only inspired him more. It is clear that his path will change *only* if she dies—she who is both the seeker and the ultimate concealer of the truth.”

Episode 19
The Fallen

Uriss quickly spun his chair around from the large, crescent-shaped desk, where he sat deep in thought. Using his hand to tame the hairs of his unkempt beard, he smiled upon learning that the footsteps he heard were zakum's, bearing a tray with food and warm water.

Uriss graciously took the tray and placed it on a small stone table that was positioned directly below a picture which he drew for himself years ago—a picture that likened that of a window.

"Council, are you well?" zakum quietly signed, his fingers and hands forming the shapes and capturing the gestures that comprised the unspoken language between them.

"I am as well as they will allow a disgraced soul to be," Uriss responded, signing back to him while offering the comforting and gentle smile the laborers had come to know.

zakum reached into his pocket and removed a small flask, placing it on the tray beside the food.

"It takes skill and stealth to deliver Teal oil to a criminal," signed Uriss. "I only hope that it is not your own reserve that you have divided in order to bring me this gift." Uriss removed the top from the flask, wasting no time emptying its rich contents into his eager mouth.

"It was the king's reserve that I divided," zakum signed, raising his head to share a brief smile with Uriss.

"Well done!" signed Uriss.

Once a principal advisor within the Royal Branch, Uriss formally held the position of Intelligence Attaché for the king's Military Court. However, at the height of his career, Uriss was jailed for engaging in what was considered the "unclean sciences" and was charged with the unauthorized use of military resources in the exploration of eternity. For his crimes, he was publicly shamed, disgraced, and sentenced to life in prison—a punishment ordered by King Thio himself. Had it not been for the king's intervention, however, Uriss would have been publicly executed for his transgressions.

Considered the highest of sins, the pursuit of eternity was against the Plebonian faith and against Royal Law. But, to Thio, a king whose paranoia consumed his waking moments, it was prudent to keep Uriss alive and to leverage the power of his brilliant mind in a way that would benefit Thio personally. And so, a deal was cast in stone, whereby Thio assigned Uriss the task of continuing his intelligence duties—directing his surveillance on all internal communications within the kingdom, including communication between the kingdom's own military officers.

It was an assignment that helped Thio calm his raging distrust and, in exchange, Uriss was secretly granted the latitude and the materials by which to continue his "unclean" scientific pursuits unfettered.

Truly brilliant and a celebrated officer regarded as one of the military's finest minds, Uriss was also one who was weakened by his unfortunate and undying love for the queen—a love that was returned by her in the longing glances and subtle gestures that they shared within the castle's closely-watched corridors. Her frail health, which was a matter well known throughout the kingdom, remained Uriss' greatest fear and, unbeknownst to the king, his obsession with the defeat of death was initially inspired by his desire to make his beloved live forever.

The convergence of his obsession with eternity, and his advanced skills in the surveillance of complex systems, created the perfect storm by which Uriss stumbled upon the curious world of the Vangora Rima and managed to hack his way in.

zakum, like the other laborers, had grown to hold Uriss in the highest regard and secretly referred to him as their Council. Disregarding the official title given to Uriss on the day that he was sentenced, the laborers rejected the notion that he was the "highest criminal of the Royal Court." To the laborers, whose gratitude towards Uriss was deep, and whose loyalty was fierce, he was *far* from that of a criminal. He was, instead, an important teacher, and one who had helped to teach them to embrace their power and reject the poison they had been fed since birth.

To the laborers, Uriss was "the single regent of the kingdom" and the misunderstood "Fallen King" around whom they rallied.

Savoring the remaining drops of what the flask held inside, Uriss returned the empty vessel to zakum, who tucked it safely away within the folds of his jacket.

"And now that the Teal oil has tamed the beast," continued Uriss. "I am sensing that there is something that you want to tell me. What is it, my friend?"

Unsure of how to deliver his news, zakum sought the comforts of distraction. "Surely, I will share my news," signed zakum, "but first I must say I am relieved that your health remains good."

"And I am *glad* that you are here today, and that you are getting enough Teal to keep yourself up," signed Uriss. "I have continued with my work and there is something that I long to show you, if I may share this this with you before you deliver your news?" Uriss gestured towards the entryway behind a bookshelf in his cell, a door that zakum had been through before as a member of Uriss' closest circle.

Careful about whom he considered his confidants, Uriss trusted both zakum and alija with his life and kept no secrets from them—a solid friendship formed when they both were assigned to tend to Uriss' quarters and deliver his meals. They had a bond that had grown stronger than the chains that constrained them all, and their loyalty to one another was unshakable.

As experience had shown zakum, each step into the room behind Uriss' bookshelf proved to be an ongoing journey of discovery and wonder. Placing the true purpose of his visit aside, zakum accepted the invitation that he knew would be yet another journey into the inner workings of Uriss' mind.

"Your cane," signed Uriss, securing a walking stick in zakum's hand.

Always a welcome sight to zakum, the cane was a gesture of gratitude from Uriss and a gift that he had hand carved from the bark of a hazel tree. The cane's handle, made of skillfully polished rainbow obsidian, was resplendent with colors and patterns that mimicked that of their Milky Way. Although it provided only temporary relief from the pain that zakum regularly endured, he always took hold of the cane as if welcoming a newborn child into the world.

Uriss slowly opened the door to the room, activating the artificial lights in the ceiling—fixtures that he had come to regard as a replacement for the sun. After helping zakum into a chair, next to which zakum placed his cane, Uriss drew back a set of dark, grey curtains to reveal the completion of his most recent work.

There, unapologetically statuesque, stood a replica of zakum. It stood firm on its feet, strong, and proud, standing erect beneath the ceiling's bright, buzzing lights. With amazing accuracy, the figure mimicked the flow and color of zakum's grey hair, his thick brow and most intricate features, as well as the pattern of each line within his weathered skin. Other than the straight posture and the addition of a thumb for each hand, the replica was so true to life that Zakum himself was left both speechless and transfixed.

"It is as I had promised you, my friend," signed Uriss, kneeling in front of zakum's chair.

zakum shut his eyes and quickly lowered his head as if shielding his eyes from the pain and brilliance of the sun.

"Please do not cast down your head," signed Uriss. "I have created a replica of you to match that of whom I see you to be. As I have counseled you before, my dear friend, please know that you *are* at the very least my equal—if not greater still. I only hope you will forgive me, as I know that its form falls far short of how magnificent you truly are."

zakum clasped hold of Uriss' hands and wept. "I cannot look at him!" whispered zakum, now speaking to him in words. "I cannot look at what I *could* have been, knowing that I am forever the slave." zakum let go of Uriss in order to wipe his tears, after which he continued to speak in sign. "I will forever be the broken one."

"No!" signed Uriss firmly. "I do not agree. While your back may be broken, your spirit…your spirit, zakum! It still has the freedom to soar higher than any bird could ever *hope* to fly. They can take that away from you *only* if you let them. And I—your loyal friend—aim to bring you back after you die into this new form, where you will not be bound by the limitations of flesh *or* of pain. But, I will need you and the others to believe in the possibility of what I have promised and to believe that it *can* be done . . . that is, if your trust in me has not wavered."

zakum shook his head and looked down once again. "Council," zakum signed, "our respect for you and our trust in you is *still* great, and know that we have put aside our fear of eternal damnation—a punishment we feared Plebony would bestow upon us for aligning ourselves to you. And it is you who continues to teach us, as Anya did, that our views of religion, of freedom and of life, may, in fact, be that which enslaves us. But, while your words and your lessons have planted the seeds of freedom within us, there are those of us who are now no longer sure that this is the right path. We fear that what has happened to Anya will also happen to us."

Seeing the terror in zakum, Uriss reflected on the day he had to inform the laborers that Anya's soul was lost to him, and that he was ultimately unable to download her into the replica that they had all had a hand in building. Trusting Uriss that her soul was safely housed within the Vangora Rima—the strange space to which he had transferred her—the laborers had assisted him in the completion of her replica, with the expectation that the process of bringing her back from the VR would be as seamless as he had led them to believe.

But it was not meant to be, and the pain of learning that she was gone sat beside Uriss daily like an unwanted visitor. With the memory of the moment as clear as it was when it occurred, Uriss could still see the message on his monitor flashing the bold and shocking words:

"ERROR ALERT! Soul Download Already Completed: File Closed 2S1—1 Year Before Today. ERROR ALERT! Soul Download Already Complete."

Those words, now burned into his memory, seemed to re-emphasize the fragility of life and the imperfections of the vessels in which life is contained. It became clear to Uriss that, within the year it took them to build a replica of Anya, her soul—vulnerable to the process of error—had been downloaded into another reality. The odd space he had convinced the laborers was a safe haven for her—and for them all—had become the portal through which she'd slipped and would never return.

By her quiet grace and gentility, Anya had been the pride and joy of the kingdom—the apple of her mother's adoring eye. But by her disgust for the station of royalty, opinions she made known to her father, Anya was, to him, a fruit that was rotten to its core. Constantly under her criticism and never quite able to win her love, the matter rendered the king distant and bitter. As she and her father grew further apart, Anya, at the age of twenty-four, found herself living dangerously outside of the circle of those whom the king felt he could trust. Her alignment to the laborers, despite her father's wishes, and her efforts to mend their broken sprits became a thorn in Thio's side and yet, also became the very quality that allowed Anya to forge a strong alliance with the one they called "the Fallen King."

In direct defiance of his agreement with the king, Uriss' surveillance reports excluded any knowledge of Anya's acts of subversion, of her efforts to strengthen the resolve of the laborers, and of her emergence as the leader of the deeply secret "Individualist Movement." Under the watch of Uriss, Anya conducted her meetings in the only way that she herself was physically able to, that being through the use of sign—a language that both Uriss and the laborers willingly learned from her.

Over time, the mutual love that Uriss and Anya shared for the laborers had transformed Uriss into the father that she wished she had had in the king. When Uriss realized he could not bring her back, it was as if he had lost his own child.

"I live each day with the fact that Anya is gone," signed Uriss. "And although I do not understand why or how it is that we lost her, I am willing to take all of the blame. But I beg you to understand that the imperfections of the system that hosted her does not render it completely useless. Although imperfect, I am asking you—begging you—and the others to *continue* to trust in the gifts that are *still* within our reach."

"We *want* to trust," zakum signed. "But she was so precious to us, and yet, somehow, the richness that she was became nothing more than a file that was able to be deleted. How will the use of this system ultimately help any of us? Are we not better off accepting the end when it comes, rather than investing ourselves into what may be disappointments in the end?"

Uriss' heart sank as he heard the trust that zakum once had in their plan begin to fade. However, unwilling to alter his own view he pressed on. "I feel the pain of her loss and I can also see that same pain in your eyes," signed Uriss. "But please, do not turn your pain into *fear,* my dear, dear friend. Please do not allow your fear to cripple you so much that you are no longer open to the gift that is possibility itself! No matter the imperfections of this system that we are now inclined to question, it appears that what we have, in fact discovered, is the central repository of souls from which the Mollards spawn—those we have always regarded as our enemies. But through my continued research and my understanding, I have cause to believe that this system can be made even better, and that it, *too*, can evolve in ways that will make it so we will *never* have to say goodbye—so that we never have to accept death as an endpoint. It cannot be that we—in all our brilliance—are just files waiting to be deleted. I *need* very much to believe that there is more to death than that!"

zakum reluctantly looked at his own replica a second time, taking in the unfathomable image of himself standing tall, erect, and confident. Knowing that he would never reach that state in his current life caused his throat to swell with emotion. And then, slowly scanning the rest of the room, he noticed a second replica. On a table in the far corner lay a stunning replica of the queen, whose face was turned towards him. Both fear-inspiring but truly beautiful to behold, it captured the way she wore her hair, detailing the large braids that she often entwined with gold ribbon, piled high into the center of her crown. The rest of her hair, unbound, spilled freely over the sides of the table. The figure's large, violet eyes stared emptily towards zakum, and her smooth brow and high cheekbones were balanced like the wide side of a diamond above a petite and pointed chin.

Painfully symbolic of what zakum had yet to share, the replica of Queen Evaline lay gracefully—and ominously—still.

"I beg your ear, dear Council," zakum signed, looking back at Uriss. "There is something I must tell you now." With an anxious nod from Uriss, zakum delivered the news of the queen's condition, and that she had slipped into a coma despite receiving the kingdom's best medical care.

It was the news Uriss always feared was inevitable and was the news for which he was ultimately preparing. "I must see her!" blurted Uriss, forgetting to use the language of sign. "I must get to her before it is too late!" he continued, now beginning to pace.

His response, notably odd for one whose imprisonment was ordered by the royal family, completely bewildered zakum. "Council, please," zakum signed, before placing his finger over his mouth in an attempt to remind Uriss of their protocol. "Please do not speak loudly in words."

"You are right," signed Uriss, trying to gather himself. "Forgive me."

"And there is more that you must know," continued zakum. "I have not yet told you everything."

"Please. *Please*!" Uriss signed, his heart racing and his desperation becoming more evident.

"Before she fell ill, she discovered that some of us are marked," signed zakum, "and although I would expect that, out of sequence, the meaning of the marks would have escaped her, she did, in fact, see parts of the password—and noticed one of the digits on Anya's arm."

Rising from the floor where he had been kneeling in front of zakum, Uriss' position— although silent—was urgent and clear. "We must bring her here at once my friend," he signed, with hands shaking. "All else—including resecuring the password—we can and *will* address at a later time."

"But Council!" attempted zakum. "It is indeed commendable that you would put all else at risk in order to preserve another life, even the life of one who is part of the very throne that has imprisoned you. But even if it made *sense* to try, how would we possibly get her *here?* It is not as though she is able to come to us seeking help, the way that Anya did when she realized that she had been poisoned. There is no way that we can get to the queen—never mind bringing her *here* to you!"

Uriss moved his gaze to the queen's replica. Clenching his jaw, he signed, "Then I shall go to her."

Episode 20
Thio's Prayer

"In all my years of wearing this crown, I have prayed for your guidance—that you would bestow your virtues upon me, as I seek the path that will make me worthy of this burden. Forgive me if this sounds ungrateful, and if my rambling is but a manifestation of my ignorance of all things that are good and that are right. If that is so, I pray that you strike against me *now* and usher me into eternal silence—for I would rather cease to be than to bear the thought that what I truly am is that which is loathsome to your holiness."

"But in the silence of this chamber and the privacy of this prayer, I bare my true self and submit to all that is in my own heart, for I can only be what I am—an individual who knows not the value of others, but only the value that others can bring to me. And I know not of love, a word that escapes me even as I reflect upon my own children. For what is love in this life, other than an invitation to journey down a path that leads to nowhere? Love is a frivolous emotion with no real purpose in the end. What is it, this experience they call 'love?' I continue to beg that you open my heart so that I am not the island that I have been throughout my miserable life. What are the shortcomings in me that render me unable to know what others know and to truly feel what others feel when they speak of love? What is it that you have given to all others that you have not given me? And yet, I remain your loyal servant, trying—as best as my vacant soul will allow—to uphold the values of family and of love. But, I am a mere actor on a stage reciting a script of empty lines and, over these many years, I have delivered a performance so convincing that, at times, I have almost fooled myself. However, through my wretchedness, I must admit that family, friends, and foes ultimately remain indistinguishable. Like the blind who live in darkness and who will never know what it is like to see the sun bursting through the clouds, I have never known love, nor do I expect that I ever will."

"My only hope is that you will not punish me for this daring introspection and that you will not punish me for building a bridge to this confession through my use of Ascension. I pray that it is safe to admit to—and to accept—what I truly am. For I have not laid myself bare to you in pursuit of my damnation. I lay my heart before you in this moment, hoping for your acceptance, as the influence of Ascension works to free me from my fears and shows me who I am, and who I am *not*. I am not the benevolent king who cares for his subjects—I care for them only so long as they are useful. I live my life in anticipation of the failure of others and understand that even the few whom I trust may well disappointment me when the final stone is thrown. I have lived all my life outside of those who call me King, Husband . . . and Father. Except, I do regret that in my lack of skill, I have caused undue injury to the one I call Anglid— piercing his eye with the point of my sword, replacing it with that of an unsightly scar. His injury, and now what may be the loss of his young life seem a wasteful pity, as it was he who is in line for the crown. Unlike his sister, who used her power to try and disrupt the very foundation upon which I stand—and whose actions drove me to the darkest moments of my life—it is

Anglid, on the other hand, who remains most innocent and most worthy."

"And now, it appears there is only Evaline. In this moment, as she lays helpless in her bed, I must reveal my truth. She—to whom I have been betrothed for nearly forty years, with the promise that on our fiftieth year together, the church will seal this betrothal in marriage, ensuring our assets are bequeathed to one another and no other—I feel that I have done my best to care for her and to be her companion. And for one so fragile as Evaline, I have pledged to protect her from the beating enemy within her chest by keeping her shrouded within the comforts of ignorance so as not to put a strain upon a heart that is so capable of ruining everything that I've worked so hard to obtain!"

"I kneel before you this day unashamed that my concern for her longevity is not driven by love. I long for nothing from the beautiful Evaline except for the comfort and security that only the acquisition of wealth can bring. I long only for the gifts that will come to me when we are finally united in marriage—the day when all of the Western Territories within her control will also become mine. And so, I bow down before you to beg for your forgiveness, as I prepare to do what I must in order to secure what I have wanted all along . . . as I prepare to go against your teachings and replace the enemy from within."

Episode 21
A Proxy's Response

"Pathetic!" fumed Flexix.

Episode 22
Clear Uncertainty

"Do you have the distress box, Python 1? Python 1, over," repeated Jordson. "Python 1, do you read me? Python 2! Headquarters to Python 2 . . . if you and the crew can hear me, send an alternate signal—you're not coming, over. I repeat, we are not hearing you! If you can hear us, please activate alternate signaling, you are not coming through!"

Jordson looked at the Search and Rescue Engineer, Nermen, whose face reflected what Jordson was thinking.

"Nothing. Not a single word from them," said Nermen, looking warily back at the dash screen in front of them. "No response at all." Nermen tapped the center of the dash screen, zooming in on one of the display panels, which made it fill the frame. Shaking her head, she briefly glanced back at Jordson. "It doesn't make sense," she continued, returning her eyes to the screen. "Our diagnostics show we *still* have a connection. Audio is intact. Nothing in the data shows that any systems are down. They should be able to hear us, and us them." Sliding her fingers across the dash screen and tapping one of its prompts, the system's time tracker appeared over the display. "And it's been over a deciday since our last contact," worried Nermen. "I don't want to be an alarmist, but I don't like it."

Jordson leaned in closer to the panel and tapped several other prompts. "This is headquarters to Python 1 through 5. If you can hear me, please activate your main *and* your backup signals so we can hear you, over."

As the silence from the crew lingered, Jordson removed a handkerchief from his side pocket and wiped the perspiration from his brow. Concerned, but attempting to maintain his typical calm demeanor, he carefully folded his handkerchief into a small square, and wiped the perspiration forming above his lip. However, deeply frustrated, Jordson slammed his fist down against the large screen display in front of him, taking the other officers in the room by surprise.

"How is it that we have lost an *entire crew*?" he yelled. "Tell me what I'm missing," he continued, turning again towards Nermen. "I need a full diagnosis of this system and your assurance that no functions are down!"

"All systems are working, sir," responded Nermen, defensively. "We've just completed our fourth diagnostic report and all checks are clear. There is *nothing* blocking them from communicating with us, and the weather monitor surprisingly shows not a storm in sight. We couldn't have had a better day for this rescue mission and I *don't* think we can blame this on the system."

"We have a reading, sir," inserted a cadet, calling over from his station. "I'm picking up some movement close to the coordinates of where the crew was planning to land."

Rushing over to the cadet's station, Jordson activated the audio signal system linked to each crew member for what would be Jordson's tenth time attempting to re-establish contact. "This is Headquarters to Python 1 through 5," announced Jordson. "Can you hear us?"

"Cadet, please zoom in," requested Engineer Nermen, leaning forward.

Immediately responding to Nermen's request, the cadet pulled up a larger view of his screen, which displayed several amorphous slow-moving masses within the area of where the rescue team was scheduled land.

"Pythons," continued Jordson, now desperate. "If any crew members are able to hear me, *please* give us a sign!"

"In the name Plebony, our god, please pray for us! Please! Please, I am in agony!"

Then, as quickly as the signal came in, it went away, replacing the frantic screams and the muffled sound of grunting and snorting with the uncomfortable silence that tortured Jordson and his team just moments before.

"Sir," began the cadet, turning around to meet Jordson, whose face was expressionless. "My brother is on that mission, sir . . ."

Jordson placed his hand on the cadet's shoulder, and, failing to find the words to comfort him, he thanked him for his brother's bravery.

"Prepare to deploy an backup crew, fully armed," Jordson instructed Nermen, over what seemed to be an eruption of chatter and confusion amongst the other officers. As the focus of the team declined into chaos, Jordson moved swiftly in an attempt to re-establish order. "*Attention*!" he blared. "Stop chatting and remain focused! This is not the time to forget our training! I need everyone in this room to remain calm and to continue to monitor your dash screens, as assigned. All Level 3 personnel are to now expand surveillance programing according to your assigned regions. I want the entire periphery of Area X under watch. Supervisors, ensure that Level 2 personnel keep watch on anything within 8,000 meters of the crew's targeted landing. Level 1 team members, ensure that you all remain zoomed in on anything moving within the critical area and keep your audio engaged." Turning his attention back to the young cadet, whose eyes remained glued to him, Jordson took pause. Acknowledging the cadet's fear for his brother and, realizing that—as a recent training graduate—it was the cadet's first time conducting live mission surveillance, Jordson did his best to reassure him.

"Sir, I have a bit of urgent news," inserted Second Military Leader, Forris, who walked into the surveillance room and straight over to Jordson.

"What is it, officer?" replied Jordson.

Gesturing that they have a word in private, Forris led Jordson over to the corner of the room. "It appears that we may soon be under attack, sir," whispered Forris, careful not to further disturb the other officers in their attempt to get back to the mission at hand.

"Under attack?" whispered Jordson, trying to control his volume. "The Southern border?"

"Yes, the Southern border, sir," replied Forris. "The Military Planning Committee is requesting your presence. And, sir," continued Forris, "we have not yet told the king, as that is your charge."

Jordson understood well the gravity of the decision he had to make and weighed his options carefully. Handpicked by the king over all other officers to be the highest ranking official in the military, Jordson controlled all military power—the only exception being decision rights over both rocket and nuclear assets, which were directly controlled by the consensus leadership of three officers whom were also appointed by Thio. Nonetheless, Thio had picked well with his selection of Jordson, who had been a loyal and dedicated member of Thio's selected military for more than twenty years. Without a surviving heir, it would be Jordson who would assume the role of Regent of the kingdom should Thio become unable to rule.

Feeling the weight of his position, Jordson took his job of First Military Leader very seriously—which came with it the responsibility of making the royal family feel comfortable and secure. But the catastrophic and now horrific circumstances around Anglid's vision quest, the queen's current health crisis, and the news of belligerent forces at the border made Jordson feel as though he was now failing in his role. Successfully having crushed invasion attempts in the past, it would be Jordson's preference to neutralize the issue at the border *before* bringing the news of the day to his already distressed king.

After signaling to Engineer Nermen to make haste on his orders of deploying a fully armed rescue fleet into Area X, Jordson left the room, accompanied by his Second-in-Command officer.

Upon entering the board room, where his colleagues and subordinates were anxiously waiting, Jordson assumed his seat opposite a large screen mounted to the wall while the Military Planning Committee wasted no time getting started.

"This is what we know, sir," stated Senior Lieutenant Burrow, Director of Ground Force Mobilization. Tapping a small panel in front of her, Burrow projected a large image of the kingdom's Southern border onto the screen. "The tactical battalions that regularly monitor the border have reported the presence of well-organized belligerents forming near the border's South-Eastern most section. Of note, by way of telescope, battalion leaders cited a concentration of uncrewed enemy vehicles within about 4,800 meters of the border line. In a second report, they have also detected the presence of thirty mobile weapon teams with significant strike and fire capabilities."

"What are their anticipated assets?" asked Jordson, outwardly unphased.

"Machine guns, snipers, and grenades, sir," Lieutenant Burrow responded, while zooming in on an image sent to her by a battalion leader on the front line. "And they appear to be moving in combat formation, sir," she continued, turning her gaze towards Jordson. "They are likely to strike soon."

Eager to react, Burrow sometimes came off to Jordson as being impatient, and one who was, at times prone to making decisions in haste rather than using a calculation of all of the facts. However, her brilliant tactical thinking, length of service, and the organization with which she managed her battalions kept Jordson's respect for her intact.

“Thank you, Senior Lieutenant,” responded Jordson. “And what do we have from Intelligence?” he asked, scanning a brief placed in front of him by Lieutenant Curio, the Director of Security who had been serving as Intelligence Attaché as Uriss’ successor.

“Sensor surveillance has detected an even greater threat, sir,” responded Curio, returning to his seat. “The *enemy*, which we have confirmed is from the Sub-Median region, appears to be planning more than a surface invasion. Electromagnetic reporting has alerted us of a proliferation of both enemy aircraft and naval forces moving towards the kingdom—clear evidence that they are preparing for a full-scale attack.”

Impressed, but not yet shaken, Jordson thought carefully about his next move. Unfortunately, not surprised by news of the attack, Jordson had long held the belief that it was only a matter time before the unofficial and fragile armistice between the Sub-Medians and the Central Kingdom would collapse once again. Doomed by desperation and greed, the shaky agreement drafted by Xżyber’s Regional Leaders, at Xżyber’s last Seasonal “A-ummit,” was on borrowed time the day it was signed. Within their fragile accord, the representatives of the participating regions deemed that the Far East was off limits to raw material sourcing until it could be divided according to the population needs of each A-ummit member. As agreed by most, plans for partitioning of the East were to be drafted at the next A-ummit rotation, three seasons forward from the day the agreement was signed. However, unhappy with what the Central Kingdom called “inept shortsightedness in the presence of urgency,” representatives of the CK expressed that, given their region’s significant consumption of Teal, waiting for the passing of three more seasons before partition plans would commence would place the Central Kingdom at significant risk.

In a move that had rocked the very foundation of the A-ummit's creed and guiding principles, the CK set up drilling and mining equipment in the East without the signature or approval of A-ummit members. With Jordson's oversight, Senior Lieutenant Burrow had fortified this move by mobilizing ground forces to the Far East in partnership with the kingdom's naval team, using sea vessels to bring their tanks and other military assets to the off-limits region.

Now a mark of the Central Kingdom's failed diplomacy and lack of confidence in the value of negotiation, the CK's Eastern expansion stained the kingdom's reputation, rigidified the animosity from the Sub-Medians, and alienated the thinly populated areas of the Southern-most region, a collection of independent settlements that had formally taken a neutral position on the aggressive nature of the Central Kingdom.

With no credible threats from the North and with the Western Territories under the direct control of the queen, the Sub-Medians remained the kingdom's only formidable foe.

"What is your decision, sir," asked Senior Lieutenant Burrow, leaning impatiently forward. "What should our next move be?"

Jordson scanned the room, noting that the calm resolve that typically framed the faces of his top advisors was gone. "We shall do nothing," replied Jordson, to the horror of his committee. "That is, we shall do *nothing* until we know we must do something more than we have already done."

"I beg your pardon, sir!" retorted Senior Lieutenant Burrow, completely flabbergasted.

"Have we not planned well for this day?" continued Jordson, studying each committee member. "Have we not lined our Southern border with well-equipped battalions that are trained and ready? And, *knowing* how vulnerable the border is, have we not effectively marshaled all of our best resources to protect our areas of weakness?"

"We have, *indeed*, sir," interjected Second Military Leader, Forris. "But is that going to be *enough?* I understand there is more that Lieutenant Curio has to share with us."

"We believe we are aware of their immediate objective, sir," replied Curio, programming the panel in front of him which projected a new image onto the screen. "This is a transcription of the communication we've picked up by radio wave. Sub-Median leadership and their ground forces are planning to execute a series of forward detachments with an immediate objective of seizing control of the Southeast water tower, as well as the kingdom's minor Teal refinery and its supply route." Shifting in his seat, Curio cleared his throat. "If I may, sir," he continued. "I suggest we respond aggressively, and with haste."

"Know that doing nothing is also a response, Lieutenant," counseled Jordson. "Without knowing *exactly* what their plans are, our haste would be wasteful. And that, we cannot afford. Our troops are not as strong as they were when we had greater access to Teal. We cannot over-react and over-distribute our force in ways that will render us ineffective."

"With all due respect, sir," replied Senior Lieutenant Burrow, looking around at her peers for agreement and support. "Doing nothing would be sure to render us ineffective, given the threat at hand."

Jordson eventually sat forward in his chair to assert his authority. "It takes more Teal oil than we currently have to nourish an army at war," Jordson replied. "Let us not forget that the great majority of the troops have become malnourished—as have we. I will not allow us to mismanage our precious resources by reacting with force before we *know* we must!"

"I beg your ear, sir," inserted Lieutenant Burrow, holding her position. "And I *must* ask you to consider a different view. We are under no illusion that our technology is a match for what they have in their arsenal. If we delay and do not strike with a *swift* response now, they are likely to gain an advantage from which we might not recover. I ask that you reconsider your position."

"Lieutenant Curio," began Jordson. "Roll us back to the images showing the naval and air threats."

Reprogramming his dash panel, Curio brought up a split-screen image of the two threats in question.

Jordson rose from his chair and walked to the front of the room to study the screen more closely. Firmly folding his arms in front of him, he slowly scrutinized the image. "I am not sure," Jordson stated.

"Officer Jordson!" responded General Hemming, Joint Director of Rocket and Missile Assets, and one of

Jordson's peers. "Sensor surveillance *has*, in fact, captured their conversation. What is it that you are not sure of? Perhaps there is something that we do not understand, but if that is the case, please tell us!"

"That's precisely it, General," responded Jordson. "It's that which we *do not* understand that confounds me the most. If what we are viewing is *indeed* their true intent, then I would agree that moving quickly would be the right choice. However, being as advanced as they are, wouldn't it be wiser for us to assume that they have the skills in place to block us from detecting their *true* communications—and that what we have picked up by surveillance may only be that which they *intend* for us to hear?"

The members of the Committee started shifting in their seats while Lieutenant Curio, however, appeared to be intrigued.

"So, what you are suggesting, sir, is that they may be fooling us?" inserted Curio.

"Or *trying* to," replied Jordson. "If they are as technically superior as we believe them to be, then our electronic enemy sensors, by their own function, could well lead us astray. I advise we strongly consider the possibility that the aircraft and naval threats seen projected on this screen may or may *not* be real. It is highly possible that what we are seeing as a threat may be their attempt to spoof our systems into *thinking* we are under attack by air and sea, when in fact this may simply be an illusion. I do not claim to know. But our lack of assurance is our weakness, and if we are not careful, we will drain our resources and further weaken our position. As such, we must recognize our disadvantage, and not let them use it against us."

"Are you suggesting that we are unable to trust our *own* systems—the very systems that we have depended upon to protect this kingdom for generations?" responded General Hemming. Mopping his perspiring forehead with his kerchief, Hemming's height and thick girth gave him an appearance similar to that of the king's.

Returning to his seat, Jordson caught sight of Plebony's statue, mounted on a marble platform at the rear of the conference room. Standing in her classic pose, Plebony's right arm, stretched across her torso, affording her enough reach to place her right hand over her left eye, while her other hand gently covered her mouth. Bearing the gifts of her insights, her elbows firmly pressed her authored works against her chest to keep them from falling, and her symbolic broken mirror—regarded as the tool of conceit—lay face down at her bare feet.

Jordson paused before Plebony, as was custom, but to his own surprise, he noticed that—for the first time in his life—he was uninspired to bow.

Episode 23
Alive

"The time has come for us to leave," stated Raptor 1, re-entering the cave where Anglid now lay fallen over with clothing soiled by his own excrement. As if scolding, Raptor 1 forcefully waved his wings towards a collection of bats that had settled themselves upon Anglid, sending the small, winged carnivores scurrying towards the cave's exit. "You are no longer safe here, and I am taking you with me," Raptor 1 continued.

"But now that you are back, I am safe again, am I not?" asked Anglid, in a faint but grateful voice. "For your presence has relieved me of the bats whose thirst seemed endless and insatiable. And as I lay still, I had wondered where you had gone and why you felt the need to leave. For if my blood is destined to be the food that sustains the life of others, then I prefer that *that* life be yours."

Raptor 1 vigorously shook the frost from his wings. "I am no better than the bats who have been dining on your blood," replied Raptor 1. "I am your enemy by my design, but I am your friend by my will. And, while I am in no position to judge anyone for their instincts, I am angered by the state in which we all must live. As your enemy—and your friend—I left your side so that you would no longer have to endure me. I set onto my course with the wind beneath me, and with the hopes that the majesty of the mist-filled mountain ranges—in all their expanse—would wash away the horrible memories of what I did to you in this cave. I left, and I flew as high and as far away as my wings would take me so that I could forget *all* of this—forget you and forget myself. Because *you*, by your sheer innocence, remind me of what I am! And that although, by my *will*, I had planned to keep you from all harm, it is by the weakness of my design that I disregarded the creed of my birth and took from you before your death."

Raptor 1 abruptly turned away from Anglid and hung his head.

"However, in my hastened flight away, I took sight of that which I have *never* before seen—a strange formation of legless creatures moving quickly across the landscape below, with round appendages propelling them impressively forward, ripping apart the snow and ice beneath them. With skin like that of the strange, skeletal bird whose hardened wings delivered you to this land, the strange, rolling creatures that I saw are large in numbers and are moving quickly towards us. As I do not know their purpose or their intention, I can only assume that staying *here* would be unwise. And as such, I have come back to take you with me."

"But where will I go when I leave with you?" asked Anglid. "And how will I be delivered —as I have no legs by which to stand nor wings by which to fly?"

Raptor 1 turned around to face Anglid once again and kneeled before him. "You will have *my* legs," he replied. "You will have my strength and you will have *my* wings. I will envelop you and protect your flesh as though it were my own. And although we will fly away from here without the promise that we will find someplace better—or the promise that our friendship will even last—we will still fly as one. Know that in *this* moment, our friendship is stronger than the lesser of who I am."

Leaning his neck forward, Raptor 1 used his beak to pick up the golden feather that had fallen from him days before, and he placed it into one of Anglid's pockets. Then, clasping hold of Anglid's upper garment, he hoisted Anglid up from the cave's rocky bed and gently placed him within the warm confines of his large marsupium. A stark difference from the stony floor, the raptor's marsupium was as soft as plush velvet. With only his face exposed and his hair fallen over one eye, Anglid was almost undetectable amongst the backdrop of the raptor's feathered chest.

Upon confirming that Anglid was secure within the folds of his pouch, Raptor 1 proceeded to make his way through the dimly lit corridors of the karst landscape, careful not to lose his footing on the small stalagmites protruding from the cave's floor.

As Raptor 1 wove his way through the network of tunnels, Anglid beheld the stunning view of the cave's walls in their metamorphosis between limestone and marble and took sight of massive dripstones where the limestone ceiling slowly acquiesced to the acidity of the rain. With each careful step along their path, the ever-present and comforting sound of flowing liquid went from distant to deafening, until there, around a sharp corner, Anglid was brought face-to-face with a cavern filled with the steam of erupting geysers and the untamed raging flow of the rich liquid he knew was his sustenance.

"That which you seek as food is not food to us," began Raptor 1. "It is merely the oil we use to preen our feathers so they are more resilient to the rain. Never before have I seen a dependency on it such as yours, and I wonder if, one day, others will come to this land in search of the oil that spills from these rocky walls."

Licking his lips and attempting to lean himself forward, Anglid's heart began to race at the sight of the oil gushing forth and freely flowing into a large, deep oil pool below.

Sensing Anglid's urgency, Raptor 1 moved in closer to the flow and extended his neck towards it. But, to Anglid's surprise, it was the raptor who now opened his mouth to drink from the spewing liquid until he had appeared to have his fill. Then turning away from the flow, the raptor began to clean his feathers.

"Am I not to have any of the oil this day?" asked Anglid, desperately.

But no sooner than Anglid could ask again did Raptor 1 lower his beak to Anglid's mouth, feeding him slowly with the regurgitation of the oil he had collected in his crop, slowly quieting Anglid's hunger.

Satiated and drowsy from the richness of his meal, Anglid missed the point at which the raptor stepped into the air off the jagged cliff that was both the cave's entrance and exit. But with the rush of the cold wind now in his face, as Raptor 1 extended his wings to catch hold of an updraft, Anglid was re-awoken as he gasped for air. The view of ice-covered rock below astounded him as Raptor 1 rode the turbulent force of the twisting wind and soared within its rising currents until they climbed so high that they could see the icy peaks of many mountains before them.

"Do not be afraid," offered Raptor 1, projecting his voice over the sound of the wind while adjusting his wings in an attempt to smooth their flight.

"I am not afraid," replied Anglid, yelling back with exhilaration. "I am alive!"

Episode 24
Where Do I Stand?

"He is alive," repeated Flexix, "and he is well. He was right . . . and I was wrong. What—as a god—do I do with him now?"

"ARE YOU ASKING ME?"

"We've been through this before!" Flexix snapped. "There is *no one else* here to ask!"

"PERHAPS THEN, YOU SHOULD JUST LET HIM BE."

"Let him be?" retorted Flexix. "He, like a newborn, has been cleansed of everything he ever knew. And in this fragile state he knows nothing. *Nothing*! He is the birth of innocence itself. I will ask you to explain what *kind* of god I could claim that I am if I were to just 'let him be!' I do not find your words helpful in this moment!"

"DOES IT MATTER?"

"Ugh! Does *what* matter?" asked Flexix.

"DOES IT MATTER WHAT KIND OF GOD YOU CLAIM THAT YOU ARE?"

"I am utterly lost by whatever it is that you're trying to say," replied Flexix, warily.

"IF THERE IS NO ONE ELSE HERE—IF IT IS JUST YOU AND IT IS JUST ME—THEN WHAT DOES IT MATTER WHAT KIND OF GOD YOU CLAIM TO BE? WHO WOULD JUDGE YOU IF YOU FELL SHORT OF WHAT YOU HAVE CLAIMED THAT YOU ARE?"

Flexix's eyes began to widen as a deep frown appeared across his brow. "I am dismayed by your choice to remind me of my loneliness at a time like this," Flexix cried.

"THEN I BEG YOUR PARDON."

"It is painful enough to know the depth and breadth of my solitude," continued Flexix, "without having to ride the wave of your unkind and undisciplined thoughts. How could *you* even know the importance of what I *claim* to be, when you don't have the capacity to understand? *You,* created in a moment of desperation with the *sole* purpose of relieving me of this sickening silence, could never understand! How can you be so bold as to even *suggest* what ultimately does and does not matter?" Flexix moved himself into a supine position and covered his eyes with all eight of his arms. "And yet, reflecting upon my solitude," he continued, "with no one here but you to judge me or even take notice . . . the god that I claim to be *still* has meaning. Because in the boundlessness of eternity, it is not the judgment of others that will matter. In the endless loop of time, I will ultimately judge myself to measure if I am the god that I truly claim that I am. I suppose that the god I claim to be does not matter because it matters to others. It matters because it matters *to me*!"

"FORGIVE ME IF I HAVE MISUNDERSTOOD WHAT YOU SAID."

"You *often* misunderstand what I say!" snapped Flexix. "Which time are you referring to *this* time?"

"I AM REFERRING TO THE TIME BEFORE NOW."

"But *which* time before now?" insisted Flexix. "As I recall, there were many *'before nows'* where you have been utterly confused and often dithering!"

"PERHAPS THAT IS TRUE. BUT IS IT FEASIBLE THAT MY DITHERING IS ONLY A REFLECTION OF YOUR OWN? AS I AM ULTIMATELY A PRODUCT OF YOUR DESIGN?"

Flexix's heart began to race, and his eyes—now bulging—popped so far out that they pushed his arms away. "There are millions of moments before now!" replied Flexix, angrily. "And I have no expectation of myself to know if there was a fleeting moment amongst all prior moments when I myself may have been confused or may have been dithering! The god I claim to be does not include the illusion of perfection! But I *will* admit that I remain confused in this moment as to why I created you!"

"AND YET YOU HAVE ALREADY STATED A MILLION TIMES—IN THE MILLIONS OF MOMENTS BEFORE THIS ONE—THAT YOU CREATED ME BECAUSE YOU FEARED FACING ETERNITY ALONE. YET, YOU STILL APPEAR TO BE CONFUSED AS TO WHY I AM HERE. IT IS AS THOUGH QUESTIONS THAT ARE RESOLVED STILL REMAIN ENDLESSLY UNANSWERED."

"And I have already forgiven myself for my unreliable memory," Flexix replied in defense. "Since memory can be as informative as it is crippling, I, at times, dither over its ultimate value."

"SO THEN, WOULD IT BE FAIR TO SAY THAT YOU AGREE?"

"Agree with what?"

"WITH ANGLID."

"With Anglid?" responded Flexix. "What does precious, innocent Anglid have to do with any of this?"

"IT WAS ANGLID WHO QUESTIONED IF IT IS HIS MEMORIES THAT MUST DEFINE THE LIFE HE HAS NOW, WAS IT NOT?"

"Well, I supposed that is true," replied Flexix.

"AND IT IS ANGLID WHO HAS ALSO QUESTIONED THE REQUIREMENT OF BEING BOUND TO MEMORIES IN ORDER TO BE WORTHY OF LIVING WHAT HE DEEMS TO BE A PRECIOUS LIFE."

"My memory deems your words to be true," Flexix responded, reluctantly.

"MIGHT YOU THEN AGREE THAT IT IS NOT ONE'S MEMORIES THAT DETERMINE THE WORTHINESS OF ONE'S LIFE? MIGHT IT BE THAT ONE'S LIFE IS MUCH MORE THAN SIMPLY THE SUM TOTAL OF ONE'S EXPERIENCES? MIGHT IT

BE THAT ANGLID HAS DISCOVERED SOMETHING ABOUT LIFE EVEN GREATER STILL?"

Flexix inhaled and exhaled deeply.

"MIGHT IT BE THAT ANGLID SEES MORE WITH HIS ONE EYE THAN YOU ARE ABLE TO SEE WITH ALL OF YOURS?"

Flexix began to shake. "Were I not the god that I claim to be," he shrieked. "I would silence your menacing voice in this moment. I would silence your words that come armed in full force like an invasion into my unchallenged bliss. If I were not the god that I claim I am, I would strike you where you are and snuff out all of my memories of every moment that I shared with you. I would condemn your words that come uninvited like that of the image in a mirror that no one wants to see. For you remind me of my greatest fear! You remind me that, to my creations, I would be unwanted and equally unneeded. I cannot bear to imagine, for example, that one so vulnerable as Anglid is better off in the pouch of a predator than he is in the caring guidance of my own loving arms. The idea that I should just *'let him be'* is unacceptable! But . . . if I am to be the god that I claim that I am, then I will accept your words as merely the products of the logic I have gifted to you . . . and I will not view them as transgressions."

"THEN YOU AGREE TO LET HIM BE?"

Flexix returned to an upright position and cleaned his face of the residue of tears that had fallen. "I can neither agree nor disagree," retorted Flexix, "as decisions of such magnitude are made with time. As fearless and as willful as he is—and with no memories or loyalties to guide his decisions—there is much for him at stake. He faces more danger and more opportunity than the rest. He is special in this moment . . . and in this odd state to which he clings. Although it is much earlier than I had planned, it may well be time to intervene and show the one called Anglid the vision of his greatness. It may well be time to show him who and what he can become."

"OR PERHAPS, IT MAY WELL BE TIME TO LEAVE HIM TO DISCOVER HIS OWN GREATNESS, AS HE AIMS TO DEFINE THIS FOR HIMSELF. PERHAPS IT IS *THIS* ONE WHO WILL TEACH US THAT THE VISION OF ONE'S GREATNESS IS NOT THAT WHICH IS *GIVEN* TO THEM, BUT THAT WHICH IS SHAPED *WITH* THEM. PERHAPS, THE ONE CALLED ANGLID IS, IN FACT . . . THE UNCRUSHED SEED."

Episode 25
I Believe in Something

"Vehicle breakdown, Commander!" Officer Liara radioed to Commander Dugar. "I repeat. Vehicle breakdown. Over."

"Dugar to Liara," he responded. "Which vehicle number is down? Over."

"Vehicle 29, sir," replied Liara. "And according to diagnostics, repair time is expected to be lengthy. They're going to need backup, sir. Over." Liara noticed a series of dark clouds rolling towards them. "We will need back up *soon*, sir."

"Disconnect and move forward," responded Dugar, quickly. "I need you to be with the rest of your troop, over."

"Sir?" responded Liara.

"V-29 is assigned to a non-Mollard team," Dugar responded, harshly. "The mechanic on board is well trained and can make any repairs needed. And we have a Sweep Crew coming through in three to five days to rescue anyone who's stranded. Let the Sweep Crew deal with those scunts. Disconnect and move forward *now*, officer! Over."

"But sir . . ." Liara replied, stunned by Dugar's order. "I've got four soldiers on V-29. I appreciate your comment that a Sweep is coming, but if they can't make these repairs, three to five days is a long time to wait in these conditions. Requesting your permission to—!"

"I gave you a *direct order*, officer!" interrupted Dugar. "And I know I've made myself *very* clear."

Knowing that Dugar could sometimes be swayed by reason, Officer Liara chanced standing her ground. But realizing that her soldiers could hear everything Dugar was saying, she turned her back and walked several meters into the wind, which felt as cold as dry ice.

"Commander . . . please," she attempted. "There's enough room in each of our *other* vehicles to fit one extra soldier. Re-routing just *part* of my team to come back and get these soldiers won't impact our mission. Requesting your permission to re-route four vehicles, sir. Over."

After an uncomfortable silence, Commander Dugar's voice took on its familiar adversarial tone. "Officer!" Dugar shouted, loud enough for the other soldiers to take note—even at a distance. "*I* am the commander of this mission, and *I* decide which decisions will—and will not—impact it. The rest of your troop is already miles ahead of you, and we have no time to re-route *any* of them to pick up those soldiers! Unless you want to face charges of abandoning the seventy-six *other* soldiers who are supposed to be under your leadership, I suggest you make your way towards the rest of your troop! *Over*!"

Liara looked back at her four soldiers, realizing that their eyes showed they already knew the decision she was going to make. Walking back towards them, she checked her arm band to determine how many hours of sunlight they had left. But with the heavy, twisting clouds that continued to darken the sky and discouraging temperature readings, it was clear to Liara that the repairs to V-29 would take longer than the weather and remaining light would support. And with Dugar's plan to remain undetected once inside the periphery, the use of artificial lighting to work on repairs after dark was strictly prohibited.

Understanding the position they were in, Liara struggled with the choice she had to make. It was moments like this one that caused her to question the value of being emotionally enhanced—a state of being that was, although sometimes challenging, better than the empty existence she believed Mollards would otherwise have to bear. But, with the pain and the guilt that she felt as she watched them struggle to keep themselves warm, Liara was not prepared to tell them she was leaving them behind. These were the moments that caused her to wonder if her emotional augmentation was compatible with what the military was demanding of her.

"You've been given a direct order, officer," continued Dugar, now yelling over the radio.

The slow, rolling sound of thunder could be heard in the distance as large flakes of snow began to fall. Liara reluctantly examined the size of each of the soldiers to quickly calculate which of them had the greatest chance of surviving the harsh temperatures should they need to wait for a Sweep rescue. Although V-29 was equipped with enough battery power to produce heat for a few days, the soldiers would have to make a trade between having consistent heat and having enough power to make the needed repairs required to restart their engine. Without an absolute guarantee that the Sweep would find them—and unsure that one was even coming—it would be a tough call to make.

"You have one deciday of working light left," advised Liara, addressing Charish, the soldier assigned to mechanics and maintenance.

Although notably younger than the other soldiers, Charish's knowledge of mechanical systems and her high interest in military service had earned her the Military Spirit Badge that she proudly wore on the outside of her insulated jacket.

"We'll be fine. Thank you, officer," replied Charish with a tone of confidence that only slightly veiled her appreciation. With temperatures falling quickly, and the wind chill at -60° Celsius, the conditions were more dire than Charish wanted to acknowledge. "We prepared for this, Officer Liara," Charish continued. "We anticipated that at least *one* of us was going to break down—and it happened. I just wasn't expecting it to be us." Charish walked around to the vehicle's front end and re-studied the engine. "We'll work on the repairs as much as we can," continued Charish, looking back at Liara while shielding her eyes from the increasingly fierce gusts of wind, "and work on the rest of the repairs first thing in the morning—right crew?"

Trying hard to reflect Charish's optimism, they all agreed.

"I'm not worried," added Zet, a solidly built, muscular soldier. "And, worst case scenario," he continued, "we'll link up with the Sweep Crew and head back to base. Like I said, I'm not worried."

"You're right," agreed Liara, encouraging Zet's optimism.

However, she secretly had her doubts, since—prior to Dugar's comment over the radio—she knew of no plans of sending a Sweep through Area X. On the contrary, during mission planning sessions, Liara had noted that rescue provisions were lacking.

"And as you have all been informed during your briefings, the temperature at night will be somewhere between -85° and -90° Celsius," Liara continued. "You are *ordered* to all be inside the vehicle within one deciday. No exceptions. While in the vehicle, utilize your blankets and solar packs for warmth. And your seatbelts are to be worn at *all* times while seated in the vehicle unless you need to huddle for extra warmth. And when inside as a group, you are to keep doors locked at all times. Understood?"

"Understood, officer," returned the soldiers, all of whom—except for Zet—were noticeably shivering.

Although she did not understand what her soldiers were actually feeling—and she had no experience with the discomfort of what it was like to be cold—Liara fully appreciated that, even as a Mollard, there was risk of circuitry failure with prolonged exposure to extreme temperatures.

"Zet," said Liara, frowning. "Why aren't you wearing your air warmer? When our vehicles are not running—and whenever you are outside of a vehicle—all non-Mollards are required to wear air warmers at all times until we are out of the mountains! Non-compliance to this order will cause lung damage."

Taking Officer Liara's words as a direct command, Zet removed his air warmer from his inner jacket and placed the vented structure over his nose and mouth. Unconvinced that he was taking her order seriously, she made him adjust the straps of the warmer until the fit was snug.

"I also have some extra supplies," she continued, opening one of the side compartments of her single-seat Distance Rover, from which she removed two large, metal containers. "These contain extra water and Teal-filled canteens," she said, pulling them from their shelves.

"Thank you, officer," replied the shortest soldier, flexing the strength of the only arm that she had in order to take the supplies.

"Purvi," Officer Liara started, in an awkward attempt to offer condolences over the recent news of her mother's death. But not wanting to make the moment any heavier than it already was, Liara chose to stay focused on the task at hand. "Please ration these supplies wisely," she instructed.

Purvi agreed to the instruction and, after loading the supplies into V-29's storage compartment, she took her position in line with the other soldiers to give Officer Liara their formal salute.

However, secretly feeling like she was abandoning them, Liara avoided their gazes while saluting back. And then, quickly climbing into her vehicle, she re-engaged Dugar as she started her engine and pulled off. "Making my way towards the rest of the troop, sir," she radioed, remorsefully. "I'll be there after sundown and will meet them at camp. Over."

As the sight of Liara's vehicle became more distant, Charish and Purvi wasted no time grabbing a canteen of Teal oil.

"Not *exactly* an example of rationing!" sneered Cynn, the known pessimist in the group. "But, it doesn't matter—suit yourselves!"

Just before finishing what remained in her canteen, Charish responded in her own defense. "We'll benefit from the extra nutrition, Cynn," she replied. "I recommend you and Zet also grab a canteen. The temperature will only keep dropping. This Teal oil will help us *all* stay warmer. Now, regarding these repairs," she said, looking towards the engine and re-positioning her air warming device, "I'll need everyone's help."

However, shaking his head disapprovingly, Cynn climbed back into the vehicle and slammed its door shut, loosening the snow that had collected on the roof.

"What are you doing?" yelled Zet, snatching the vehicle door back open.

Cynn shot Zet a grim look while suiting himself up in another jacket for extra warmth. "I'm preparing a place . . . to rest," replied Cynn, his voice slightly muffled by his air warmer.

"What are you talking about?" Zet insisted. "Didn't you hear Charish *just* say she needs *everyone's* help? Get out here and do your part!"

"She needs our help? With *what?*" Cynn snapped back. "I'm not interested in wasting the time I've got left pretending we can make repairs that we can't!" Cynn crouched forward and grabbed hold of what looked like a small book that was sitting on one of the drivers' seats. "I checked this manual against the model of this Rover," he continued, angrily. "They gave us a repair kit for a vehicle that's much newer than the one we've got. And do you know *why* that is, Zet? Do you know why they gave us an older Rover without even *bothering* to make sure that our repair kit was *even compatible?*" Cynn slammed the manual onto the floor of the Rover, struggling to contain his rage. "Because we're non-Mollards, Zet, and they don't care *anything* about us!"

Small balls of hail now began to fall and bounce off of the Rover's windshield and roof.

"What's happened to you?" Zet demanded, disturbed by Cynn's behavior.

Cynn returned Zet's disapproval in kind. "The most relevant question I think is what's happened to *you*?" Cynn snapped back. "You and Charish—with all your pro-war solidarity—literally make me sick! Other than me, Purvi's probably the only other soldier here who actually understands what's going on!"

Growing angrier, Zet leaned further into the cockpit. "And you've got it all figured out, right?" Zet yelled back.

Unintimidated, Cynn stared at Zet, laughing mirthlessly. "You just *refuse* to wake up, don't you?" retorted Cynn. "Open your eyes, Zet, and look around! Do you see any Mollards stranded out here with us? Did you happen to notice that all the Mollard troop members are riding in new, fully-automated vehicles, and that they have all the best equipment? Or did that *also* get past your atrophied brain?"

Zet clenched his jaw while moving his hand towards the pistol that was sitting in his drop leg holster.

"Unlike the two of you," Cynn continued, "at least Purvi hasn't blindly consumed all of their propaganda as though it were food! She and I have no illusions about what this war is really all about."

"Shut up! Before I . . ." started Zet, pulling his pistol out of its holster.

"Soldiers!" yelled Charish. "I need *help* over here and arguing with each other is wasting precious time!"

"Before you *what?*" continued Cynn, sharply, also reaching for his pistol. "Before you come to realize that no matter what you do or what you sacrifice to gain their respect, you'll *never* be one of them? Well, just for some clarity, Zet, I didn't get drafted into this *stupid* war so that I could make fools like you feel comfortable in the skin you put on. But, if my version of the truth is way too bitter, you don't have to take *my* word for it. Today's heart-warming message from the great Commander Dugar should be *all* that you needed to hear."

"What are you?" asked Zet, angrily. "One of those 'Free Citizens Alliance' troublemakers, right? The non-Mollard Freedom Fighters? Let me make this clear to you—your kind hasn't helped us. All you're doing is making them crack down on us even more. You need to give up that fight!"

"And why do you think you have *any* authority to tell me what I need to do?" Cynn yelled.

Zet relaxed the grip he had on his pistol and the anger in his face slightly faded. "Because I used to be just like you," replied Zet, his voice now less harsh. "I used to believe that fighting against them would make some sort of a difference, and that *they* were the enemy. But then I grew up and I realized that the biggest enemy we have is each other."

Purvi walked over and admonished them for not helping with the engine. However, still consumed by the need to defend their positions, they barely noticed she was there.

"And the members of the Free Citizens Alliance," continued Zet, "are wasting their time fighting a war that they're ultimately going to lose. It takes way more bravery to face your own demons than to demonize others. The Alliance members are just a bunch of cowards."

"I may be a coward in *your* eyes," responded Cynn. "But to my three children, I'm a hero. At least I taught them the difference between reality and fantasy. Who do you think this war is ultimately going to benefit, Zet? Us or them? You think they dedicated *all of these* resources to go to war against the CK in order to secure a future for the *non-Mollards?* They just told us that so that we'd be better soldiers in *their war*. This war is about gaining control of raw materials to make more metal and more steel—the flesh of the future. And if you don't know *that*, then you're asleep!" Cynn boldly stared at Zet, meeting his gaze straight on.

"You—and the rest of the FCA members—have been brainwashed, and that's pathetic!" Zet shot back in disgust.

"Yes! I'm pathetic," Cynn replied, sarcastically. "But I know the smell of reality when it's rotting. Not sure if you've seen the giant scavenger birds circling above us, Zet. But it seems that even *they* know we can't repair this pile of junk." Cynn kept his finger on the trigger of his pistol, waiting for Zet to make the first move. "Now, if you don't mind," Cynn continued. "I choose to die inside of the vehicle rather than die out in the cold pleading with the sun not to set."

"When we get back home, remind me to kill you!" replied Zet, slamming the vehicle door shut. Then, composing himself and joining Charish and Purvi by the front of the vehicle, Zet repositioned his pistol into its holster.

"It's getting too dark now," complained Charish, her lean frame and bony jaw notably shivering. "And the hail is getting much too heavy. I can't see the engine's distinguishing parts!" Beside herself with frustration, Charish slammed her fist down onto the Rover.

"How about a pocket light?" suggested Zet, "to help you see the engine and the manual instructions? I seriously doubt that a small pocket light is going to be detectable out here," he said, while pulling a light out of his pocket.

"Cynn doesn't know what he's yelling about," replied Charish, taking the pocket light from Zet. "I helped design and build these vehicles *without* a manual and I don't need a manual to fix one. The problem's in the internal combustion system. Not exactly a small repair," she signed. Charish attempted to stop herself from shaking by bracing herself against the vehicle. Staring down at the engine, her voice became sullen. "I just need time," she continued. "I feel as though I've been running out of time my entire life—and here I am, in the most barren place on the planet, fighting against time in what feels like unavoidable darkness! It's funny how things work out."

A strong, frigid wind gust blew quickly passed them, nearly causing Charish to lose her balance, and the thunder—now much closer—sounded like the detonation of bombs above them. In an attempt to fend off the cold, Purvi fastened the last clasp of her insulated jacket, but the chilling wind was beginning to win the fight.

"I know what to do," continued Charish, over the sound of the thunder. "I was *trained* for this. I just . . . I just can't remember all the steps! It's . . . it's so . . . cold!"

"Charish, look at me!" insisted Zet. "Stay focused. I need you to stay focused! Tell me what you need to fix this engine and I'll do the work." Zet took Charish's face in his gloved hands in an attempt to help her regain her focus. "You be the brain," continued Zet, "and I'll be the hands. *What* is step one?"

Charish looked at Zet and gave him a blank stare.

"Zet," began Purvi, "we need to get her inside the vehicle. *Now.* We can resume repairs in the morning. We can't stay out here any longer."

"But I can—" he replied.

"Let it go, Zet!" insisted Purvi. "Let it go."

Purvi walked over to Charish and gently nudged her, encouraging her to retreat into the Rover. But, refusing to budge, it was as though Charish was frozen where she stood. Finally getting Charish to retreat, Purvi joined her and took the seat next to Cynn, who sat quietly with his hand still on his pistol.

However, Zet, still unwilling to retreat, remained outside.

"We'll make camp here," stated Purvi, pulling out several thick blankets from an overhead compartment—her large, gentle eyes managing to provide Charish a modicum of comfort. "If we keep the vehicle closed and use blankets for warmth as instructed, we can save our battery power for working on repairs tomorrow." Purvi pulled out her pocket light and hung it from one of the hooks in the ceiling of the cockpit and then leaned forward to assist Charish with fastening her seatbelt. "We'll get through the night," she said, encouragingly, offering Charish her hand. "It won't be that bad."

"I'm freezing," Charish responded, desperately clutching Purvi's hand. "I'm too cold."

"Cynn, help me activate the solar heat packs," urged Purvi. "I think there are twelve of them in here. They'll help get us through the night."

"They're already activated," replied Cynn, in disgust. "The packs are doing the *best* that they can. There are no more sources of heat. And until that wannabe Mollard out there realizes that he's freezing, we won't benefit from our maximum body heat potential!" Cynn went on, tightening the fit around his air warmer.

Purvi exhaled deeply before taking a temperature reading of the cockpit, coming in at a shocking -40° Celsius. However, noting that the exterior thermometer was now reading -70°, it was clear that the solar packs were, in fact, helping.

The door to the Rover suddenly opened, breaking the seal of ice that had formed around the door and the main cabin. Pulling a blast of cold air in with him, Zet took the empty seat next to Charish and diagonal to Cynn.

"Charish," began Zet, impatiently, while fastening his seat belt. "Now that we're inside the vehicle, tell me what step one is?"

Cynn pulled out his pistol in plain view and glared angrily at Zet.

"Zet, not now . . . please!" suggested Purvi in a low voice.

But ignoring her, Zet continued to press Charish, whose hands were trembling and whose eyes were drifting.

"We've got to make it warmer in here!" cautioned Purvi. "We're losing her! We need to use the utility battery!"

"No!" snapped Zet.

"I'll be fine," replied Charish, her voice faint and her eyes closing. "I just need more . . . time."

"What do you mean, '*no?*'" yelled Cynn, holding his pistol steady. "Who put you in charge here? She's literally *fading* and all you can do is give orders? If you get in our way, I'm pulling this trigger."

Purvi turned on the vehicle's utility battery and activated the cabin's heating system. Looking at Zet apologetically, Purvi offered her view. "We have no choice," she said. "We can't lose her, Zet."

"I'm not going to sit here while you all drain what's left of our battery just to keep *one* of us alive!" replied Zet, angrily. "We may *never* get out of these mountains at this rate!"

"That '*one of us*' you're referring to is the *mechanic*, you idiot!" replied Cynn.

"Mechanic or not, I've come way too far—!" Zet yelled back. "And I'm almost at the finish line. I'm not giving up *my* dream, no matter what! If we don't have battery power to repair and restart this vehicle, we might as well just give up *now!* We *have* to keep working on the engine. There's no guarantee that the Sweep will even find us!"

"Congratulations!" interjected Cynn. "You're finally waking up! It's funny how that happens when you're facing the barrel of a gun, isn't it?"

Zet gritted his teeth and slowly turned his eyes towards Cynn. "If you were really going to pull that trigger, you would have done it by now!" challenged Zet. "But, like I said, you're nothing but a coward."

At his breaking point, Cynn depressed the trigger of his gun, and—aware that Zet had not yet put on his bulletproof vest—he released five rounds into Zet's chest.

Charish woke to the sound of the shots and the sound of Purvi yelling at Cynn to stop. Stunned by Cynn's action but still disoriented from the cold, Charish was unsure if the gunfire she heard was inside or outside of the Rover.

"You just shot one of our soldiers!" murmured Purvi, her eyes wide with disbelief. But before Cynn could respond, Zet calmly unzipped the outer and inner layers his military jacket and collected the five bullets that had failed to penetrate his metal frame.

"Here you are, my friend," he said, offering the discharged bullets back to Cynn. "You wouldn't want to run out of ammunition."

"You're a *Mollard?*" yelled Cynn.

Charish, slowly regaining her focus from the warmth of the cabin, looked warily at Zet. Purvi, still in shock, remained silent.

Zet stared at Cynn as he leaned forward and dropped the bullets one-by-one onto the blanket that Cynn had tucked around his legs.

Now realizing he was no match for Zet, Cynn sat cautiously still.

"Some parts of me are still flesh," responded Zet, staring squarely at Cynn. "Most parts are metal. I'm *really* close to the finish line." Zet reached into his side pocket and pulled out his canteen, slowly unscrewing its cap. He then pressed two of his fingers into the center of his neck, causing the folds of his thick, rubbery skin to retract. And after removing a small tray with what looked like a series of bumpy filters inside, Zet slowly poured the Teal oil from his canteen over each filter until they were all saturated. "But until I can cross over, I'm still dependent on this junk to feed my brain," he said, sliding the tray back into the open compartment of his neck and repositioning the synthetic skin.

Both fascinated and repulsed by the steps required for Zet to eat, Purvi began to understand the intersection of her existence and that of a mechanical one. But for the first time in her life, her own dependence on Teal oil suddenly felt like a burden.

"And while you are in this . . . state," began Purvi, looking askance at Zet. "How does your brain get fed?"

"I no longer have a digestive system. It all starts here," replied Zet, pointing to the compartment in his neck. "The Teal oil is pulled into a micro-processor through ports and synthetic tubes that connect to the tray. The processor identifies the nutrients from the Teal oil and extracts them before sending them North. It's unpleasant and often causes headaches," he said, placing his canteen of Teal oil into his pocket. "But although it's not perfect *now*, it's a really small price to pay for being so close to being *perfect* in the future!" Zet looked down, almost appearing to be slightly ashamed by his choices, but then raised his head, emerging from his own moment of doubt as he took on an odd smile.

The force of the wind, now much stronger, blew relentlessly against the vehicle, as large balls of hail now pummeled the Rover from all sides.

"And how do you define 'perfection?'" asked Purvi, unable to let it go.

"Existing beyond the constraints of flesh," Zet replied, his face suddenly becoming wildly euphoric. "Existing beyond the constraints of weakness. No longer having to feel hunger in the pit of my stomach, no longer having to feel the cold, no longer having to feel . . ."

"Love?" interjected Purvi.

An awkward silence fell over the group. Charish, now more alert, looked at the internal thermometer and then removed her air warmer.

"Thank you for what you did to help," she said, directing her message towards Purvi. "I think I'm going to be all right. The internal temperature is now at -10° Celsius. I think it's safe now to shut off the battery."

But before anyone could respond, a strange sound—reminiscent of heavy breathing and odd grunting—could be heard off in the distance, along with the sound of ice cracking beneath the weight of something that was sliding across it. Without discussion or delay, Zet, Cynn, and Purvi immediately engaged their weapons and double checked that both of the Rover's doors were fully locked.

"What was *that?*" asked Cynn, keeping his eyes fixed on the door closest to him.

"Don't know," replied Zet, loading his ammunition. "But it doesn't sound like it wants to be friends." Sitting closer to the front of the vehicle, Zet pivoted his seat to face the windshield and pulled out his night-vision binoculars to scan the area. However, all he could see was a distant strip of light from the setting sun. "This area is known to have wildlife," he said, looking through the binoculars, "but other than scavenger birds, nobody knows exactly what else is out here."

"Whatever it is," started Charish, impatiently, "it doesn't matter. These Rovers are built to withstand an animal attack of *any* kind. Relax your weapons and let's not waste any more time on this."

"Uh huh," added Cynn, sarcastically, while removing a Sub-Median Cydlicer from the vehicle's ceiling compartment and also loading it with ammunition. Although known to overreact, Cynn's decision to pull down their big-game machine gun earned him some points with Purvi and Zet.

Charish, for her part, made a point of turning off the vehicle's battery.

"Has anyone noticed," started Purvi, holding her weapon in place, "how *well* we work together when we work as a team?"

"Not now, Purvi!" snapped Cynn, balancing the weight of the Cydlicer in his shaking arms. "This is *not* a team-building event!"

After a long period of silence and no obvious sign that there was still a threat, Charish pressed her point. "We have a lot to do tomorrow," she said, firmly, tucking the blankets around her. "And with only ten hours of sunlight to get it all done, I don't want to spend another night out here," she added, looking around at the other soldiers. "We *need* to focus on restarting this engine, so, instead of worrying about wildlife that we know can't get in, I need everyone to focus *with* me."

Charish picked up the repair manual that Cynn had previously thrown, turning to a detailed diagram of the Rover's power train. In anticipation of snide comments from Cynn, she preemptively advised them that the power train was consistent across *all* Rover designs—*no matter* the model. Although distracted by the intermittent sound of grunting and cracking ice that was now just outside of the vehicle, Charish's insistence that the Rover was impervious to wildlife caused at least Purvi and Zet to somewhat relax their positions.

"This is the target of the repair," stated Charish, unhooking her seatbelt to better access her pocket light. Using her light to further illuminate the diagram, Charish showed them how she needed them to assist. "These pistons are driven by the engine's ability to convert fuel into power," she explained. "Our diagnostic report shows a break between this piston—here—and the crankshaft."

Charish looked up to ensure everyone was following along.

"It will take us some time to get to the crankshaft, based upon its position," she continued. "Once I move the circuitry aside, I will need one of you to repair the connecting rod between this piston and the shaft." Charish looked up again. "Cynn, are you with me?"

Cynn moved the barrel of the Cydlicer towards the door and barely acknowledged Charish.

"Since weather is a major risk," she continued, "anyone *not* actively working on the repair should be inside the Rover. Once this connecting rod is repaired, one of you will need to weld these pieces back into place. I'll come in after that and re-wire the circuitry."

Charish's instructions were *very* clear, and Zet and Purvi were confident it could be done.

"Our only other threat," continued Charish, "is not having all of the exact parts we need to make this repair. We'll need to think creatively and see if we can borrow parts from less crucial parts of the engine."

Zet looked at Charish and Purvi. "I can't do anything about the weather," he said, "but, I can—and I *will*—help with any metal parts you may need."

Noticing the change in the temperature of the cockpit, Purvi re-checked the reading, which she noticed had dropped to -14° Celsius—an indication that the Rover was inefficient at containing its heat.

But just before she could suggest that the crew employ huddling to maximize their body heat exchange, the force of what felt like a collision to the left side of the vehicle sent the Rover spinning across the ice. The grunting that had been, at one time, intermittent and seen as something that should ultimately be ignored, had brought with it the full force of nature unbound and untamed.

Realizing that it was under attack, the Rover's automated weapon response was activated, filling the space on the vehicle's damaged side with a circular spray of rapid-fire shots. As loud roars and strange, agonizing cries mixed with the sound of the many shots still being fired, it was as though the Rover was at war with nature itself.

Charish, the only one not secured by a seatbelt, bore the brunt of the collision.

"Are you ok? Wake up!" Zet yelled at each soldier, checking their status.

And, although stunned, each member of the crew was responsive—except for Charish, whose broken neck was left twisted between her shoulders and her head where she lay still after being slammed into the side of the cockpit.

"What happened?" asked Cynn, attempting to retrieve the Cydlicer from the floor of the vehicle. From his demeanor, it appeared that he was in shock. "What just—what just hit us?" he continued looking around frantically and gripping his machine gun. "How many of them are out there?" Noticing Charish, Cynn continued to ramble. "Somebody, check on Charish. It looks like she fell asleep! Too cold in here for her—we better wake her up!" Confirming that his ammunition was properly loaded and that his air warmer was secure, Cynn unhooked his seatbelt and unlocked the door.

"You can't go out there!" advised Zet, blocking the door. "You'll freeze to death." Pointing to the external temperature gauge—displaying -90° Celsius—Zet was hoping that reason would set in.

"It's better than just sitting and waiting for whatever decides to slam into us next!" yelled Cynn, attempting to push Zet aside.

"Weren't you the one who said that you preferred to die *inside* the vehicle?" reminded Zet, trying to hold Cynn back. "Why mess up a good plan?"

"Whatever that was wanted to kill us!" replied Cynn. "*I* will decide how I'm gonna die and *when*—now, get out of my way!"

Realizing that Cynn was beyond reach, Zet reluctantly stepped aside. As Cynn stepped outside, the external air that cut into the cockpit was too painful to inhale, causing Purvi—who was also dazed by the impact—to listlessly tighten the seal around her air warmer. After re-locking the door behind Cynn, Zet slowly kneeled in front of Purvi.

"I'm going to lay Charish down in the snow," he whispered, pulling Cynn's spare blanket from his chair and draping it around Purvi's legs.

"You don't have to do all of this," she replied, frowning. "I'm a soldier. I don't need you to baby me! Besides, what do you care? You have nothing but disdain for your own kind. You made that *more* than clear." Wiping away tears that seemed to come from nowhere, Purvi looked away from Zet.

"Many of us have disdain for our own kind," Zet replied, rising to his feet. "I am not alone," he continued, unlocking the door in order to remove Charish from the vehicle.

Purvi closed her eyes, and her mind began to wander. "Have you ever read the works of Timmons AC?" she asked.

Surprised by her question, Zet turned back around to face her. "Of course, I have," replied Zet. "Timmons Viroonus AC, of the Austral Cluster. *Everyone* knows that name. He was the one who took the fight out of us! I remember burning his articles when I was younger—when I was my angriest." Zet sat back down as he continued to reflect, while shaking his head. "My generation wanted things to be different," he continued, his voice now low and steady. "We wanted the Mollards to *respect* us. We were coming of age and we didn't want to live the life our parents were living. But the Luminaries started distributing Timmons Advisories about the benefits of being 'peaceful and patient.' We heard the message in our schools. We heard the message from our parents. We heard the message in our dreams, and everyone's behavior slowly started to change. Suddenly, our anger was no longer justified. Suddenly we were the criminals—the ones to be watched and controlled—because we weren't following the ideals of peacefulness and patience." Zet's expression turned to one of disgust. "Sure," he continued, "I know that name. I know that name all too well!"

Saddened by the sentiment of what she believed was a fantastic misinterpretation of her grandfather's work, Purvi was moved to anger. "Timmons AC was the greatest thinker who ever lived!" she yelled, defensively.

Unsure why Purvi was pursuing the topic at such an odd time, Zet started to think that the cold may have started to take its toll. "Ok, Purvi," responded Zet, trying to calm her down. "I'd better get Charish outside."

"He had a vision!" continued Purvi, shaking beneath her banket.

"I *know* he had a vision!" snapped Zet. "And that vision poisoned an entire generation—including me!" Zet then looked down, showing what looked like remorse. "But it doesn't matter now!" he snapped. "It's already done!"

"But that wasn't his fault!" insisted Purvi. "His vision of living in a civil society was a message meant for everyone—not just for the non-Mollards. But the Luminaries exploited his work for their own gain. His original writings proposed a society where *everyone* was responsible for upholding the values of peacefulness and of patience. In his vision, it was a requirement for us all. It was the Luminaries who made it appear that he was condemning Non-Mollards for wanting to stand up for their rights." Purvi looked down at her hand, which bore the ring that Timmons had given to her before he died. "They turned his teachings into a weapon and mass distributed it in his name. It was *never* his intention to have *any* of us give up! It was only his intention to show us a new way of living—*together*. They ruined his reputation, and no one — not even his own son—believed the truth. They destroyed my entire family!"

Zet sat very silent, reflecting on his own choices—where he had given in and where he had given up. But unable to accept what Purvi was saying, he convinced himself that she herself was giving in and was delirious. "Purvi," he began, gently. "I don't know what Timmons AC has to do with *your* family, but I'm certain this is *not* the time to be talking about dead philosophers that nobody cares about anymore, and would just as soon forget." Noticing the cockpit's temperature had now dropped to -20° Celsius, Zet pulled the spare blanket that was left on Charish's seat and wrapped it around Purvi's shoulders. "Besides, it no longer matters what Timmons' vision may—or may not—have been," he continued. "A lot of us have given up on living in the flesh . . . at least I have, and I'm ok with that." Zet turned towards Charish and leaned over her lifeless body.

"And because you have chosen to give up—our existence has become so loathsome and so hopeless to you—that you would rather be a machine?" asked Purvi, turning her face away so as not to see him lifting Charish. "Because that's what they'll turn you into in the end – a hollow shell of metal, with *nothing* inside!"

Zet effortlessly lifted the body with one arm while opening the door to the Rover. "The end?" he replied, looking back at Purvi. "Or the beginning?"

As Zet carried Charish away, the pain of recently losing her mother surrounded Purvi—eclipsing the crippling discomfort of the cold that had enveloped her. No longer able to fend off her grief or pretend that it had never happened, the unbearable thought of her mother being strangled by hands that once shared the same womb was almost too much for her to bear. Giving in to a feeling that she wasn't sure was sleep or death, she closed her eyes, prepared to accept what was to come.

But upon reawakening hours later, the cockpit was warm and the light from the sun shined brightly through the windshield. Rubbing her eyes clear, she saw Zet sitting across from her, patiently waiting.

"What happened? How long have I been sleeping?" she asked, frantically, pushing the blankets away. Realizing that her brow was moist, she checked the internal thermometer, which displayed a shocking 16° Celsius. "You're running the engine?" Purvi asked, now confused. "Why?"

"Blue isn't your best color, Purvi," responded Zet. "I made the right choice."

"What do you mean, you—you made the *right choice*?" she, desperately. "I don't understand what that means. What about the repairs?" Clawing her way to the front of the vehicle to view the dash panel, Purvi's heart sank at the sight of the battery's remaining charge. "We hardly have any battery power left!" cried Purvi, turning around to face Zet. "You shouldn't have turned on the heat! You should have just let me die!" she screamed. "You may never get out of these mountains now, and you were so close to the finish line..."

Suddenly the energy that was flowing through the Rover came to a halt, followed by the sound of the engine shutting itself down. Purvi stared at Zet in silence, with the backdrop of the ice-encased windshield behind her. With nothing more to say, Zet pulled up a screen on his left forearm to read an excerpt from one of Timmons' most famous works.

Although he had read the excerpt before, there was something in his voice that indicated he finally understood its meaning.

"Dear Xżyberians. Do not fear this opportunity we have been given to be one with one another. Even though we evolve and will continue to change, we are all still of one seed. Although we may choose to separate—to seek sanctuary in the avoidance of the differences between us—we should not bury our heads so far down into the sand that we become disconnected from those with whom we share this world, as the love of 'all' is the greatest gift we will ever know. Our greatest glory will be our ability to suppress competition in deference to the rapture of putting our enemies before us. And as we come to this state, we will have evolved beyond our most base instincts. As we push forth, know that it is not as important to be recognized for

how we lived our lives as much as it is important that we made the right choices in the end.

Signed,
Timmons, AC"

Hearing the words that her grandmother taught her to live by, Purvi nearly fell from emotion but, rushing towards her, Zet quickly caught her in his arms. While holding her firmly in his embrace, a grinding mechanical sound could be heard off in the distance, which seemed to be quickly approaching.

In line with their training, they ensured that both doors were locked and quickly reached for their weapons. But as the sound got closer, it was clear that what they were hearing was, in fact, the sound of another vehicle. Hoping that the Sweep had actually found them, Zet urgently opened a small, side view window to try and confirm that the vehicle was, in fact, an ally. Watching warily as the vehicle came to a full stop just meters away, the large seal of the Sub-Median Army could be seen on the vehicle's door.

"They found us!" Zet said, quickly turning to Purvi. "The Sweep found us! *They found us!*"

"Soldiers! This is your commanding officer!" projected a familiar voice. "I repeat, this is your commanding officer approaching the vehicle!"

Upon opening the door to the Rover, Purvi and Zet saw Officer Liara firmly standing in the snow.

"Officer!" they both yelled, expecting it to be a member of the Sweep Crew. Their shock rendered them too surprised to salute.

Noting their confusion, Liara explained her choice to come back.

Learning that she had redistributed the medical supplies from a larger Rover into the extra seats of four other vehicles—all so that she would have enough room to rescue all of them—impacted both Purvi and Zet in a way they could not put into words.

As they left the stranded Rover and approached the one with a height and width that dwarfed that of V-29, Officer Liara paused to look at the snow-covered body of Charish, and the tormented frozen figure of Cynn still holding the Cydlicer in his arms. On the other side of V-29, the high winds blew against the long white hairs of an unknown, massive creature, parting its coat and revealing its grey skin below.

As Purvi climbed into the supply truck and pulled off her air warmer, she realized that she was the only one of them who actually needed to wear it—and for the very first time in her life, the lines between her existence and that of the Mollards seemed blurred.

"How long will it take for us to get to the Central Kingdom from here, Officer Liara?" asked Zet, climbing into the vehicle.

Securing her seatbelt for the long journey, Liara turned around to face Purvi and Zet. "We're not going to the Central Kingdom," she replied, with a warm smile. "We're going home."

Episode 26
In Protocol We Trust

"Your Grace," began zakum, cautiously. "General Jordson is here and he wishes to speak with you. Shall I let him in or give him your regrets, Your Guide?"

King Thio, noticing that zakum was now struggling to stand, quickly turned to face a painting of the kingdom's Solar Dome to save him from the sight of zakum's suffering.

The massive painting, which hung over a mantel in the Inner Parlor, was a work commissioned many years before King Thio took the throne, and its quality was as brilliant as the day it had been created. Reflecting upon the stillness and the perfection of the heirloom—the serenity that it captured and the rich, golden color of the sun that illuminated the top of the Dome and spilled softly into the valley below—the king was particularly aware of the painting's longevity, and the fragility of the reality that it aimed to capture.

"Show him in," Thio responded, with eyes affixed to the painting.

Shortly thereafter, General Jordson entered the room with what felt like the weight of the world on his shoulders and, noticing the king's bearing, he regretted the news that he was about to deliver.

But before he could make his announcement, the king led in with his own. "I'm prepared to hear whatever it is that you have to say, my most loyal advisor," started Thio. "But, given that the sun has just now risen, I must assume that you have made haste to deliver a piece of news, untoward. And as such . . . I prefer to still this moment as though it were a painted landscape. For, I am *still* king over this land whose borders are at *least* as strong as that which frames this beautifully executed picture. And as I stand here, son of the many kings who stood here before me, I will take my time to revel in the magnificence of this painting . . . of this place we have called our home for hundreds of years. Although the magnificence may now be fading, I am still *king* . . . and *ruler* . . . and I *still* have the power . . . to pretend!"

Then, falling into a sullen silence, King Thio walked over to the couch in the center of the room where he sat, leaning forward and placing his head into his hands.

Keenly attuned to protocol, Jordson remained silent with eyes cast down and waited patiently for his opportunity to speak. With a reluctant hand gesture from Thio, Jordson informed him that the kingdom would soon be at war.

However, already having been made aware that enemy forces were sighted at *both* the Southern and now the Northern borders, Thio listened patiently as Jordson unknowingly added what were simply now minor strokes of detail to the dreary masterpiece that Uriss had already painted for him. Sworn to keep his alliance with the imprisoned former military member a secret, Thio pretended to be unaware of the information Jordson came to share, even though the news had already been provided to him by the one who had fallen from grace—and who continued to conduct surveillance of military affairs underground.

"I tried not to deliver this dire announcement during a time when we were still searching for your son, Your Grace," offered Jordson, feeling that he had personally failed to protect the kingdom and the royal family. "But we have discovered a threat to our Northern Border, which has proven to be a credible one. As such, I intend to give the order to marshal our best resources and strike."

King Thio raised his head out of his hands, while still facing the painting. "And what of our Southern Border?" inquired the king, raising a small glass of water from the table in front of him. "Are we not also being threatened to the South?"

Surprised by his question and surprised by his knowledge of the potential threat at the Southern line, Jordson took pause. For, as far as Jordson knew, no one else was authorized to apprise the king of threats to the Central Kingdom except for him.

"We *have*, indeed, cited a group of mobile weapon units to the South, Your Grace," responded Jordson, "which we are closely watching. But, given the enemy's aggressive advance towards us from the North—with five times the assets that one would expect and an army the size of which I have never before seen—I am convinced that it was their intention all along to plant belligerents to the South as a distraction. It is also my belief that *all* of their *other* positions, which show them to be preparing for both a naval and air strike, are simply the art of trickery. The enemy, which we have confirmed is, in fact Sub-Median, is very deceptive, Your Grace." Jordson removed a handkerchief from his pocket and wiped his brow. "And, as is known," Jordson continued, "when your enemy is deceptive, they can cause your decisions to be driven by fear versus ones that are driven by strategy and good counsel."

King Thio suddenly took on a coughing spell after slightly choking on the water that he was sipping. However, after finally regaining his composure, he invited Jordson to continue.

"Knowing the deception that our enemy is capable of," explained Jordson, "and knowing that our ground troops are not as strong as they once were, I plan to be judicious in how we respond, to what I believe are merely distraction tactics against our Southern line."

"Thank you for your update and for your counsel," replied Thio. "And as you know, I placed the welfare of our defense in your capable hands long ago. I trust that you will navigate us through all of the ambiguities that lie before us. I have complete confidence in your judgement, Jordson, and as I sit in this room with you, on war's doorstep, I know that I have made the right choice in having you lead the charge."

Unsure as to why King Thio would not turn to face him, Jordson moved slightly into the king's peripheral view, hoping to prompt a face-to-face engagement. But as the tactic proved ineffective, Jordson assumed that the king's reluctance was a sign that he was overwhelmed and heartbroken by the magnitude of the news that he came to deliver.

"And I assume," continued the king, "that imbedded in your news is also an admission that you are calling off the search for Anglid. Am I right?"

Jordson took a long deep breath before answering. "It pains me to say it, Your Grace," he replied, reluctantly. "But yes. Given our confirmation of the current threat to our Northern line, we have called the second search team back, my dear king." In silence, Jordson bowed his head even further, expressing his deepest regret. "However, my dearest king, if I may . . ."

"Go on," the king replied.

"I do feel compelled to acknowledge that it was the search and rescue effort that ultimately made us aware of the enemy's uncharted path through the mountains," he explained. "As foreboding a region as is Area X, we would *never* have anticipated a threat to our North-facing border. Traversing such a landscape was—until now—unthinkable. And as such, it was Anglid's vision quest that gave us the advantage of the vision we now have. Had it not been for the unfortunate events around Anglid's quest and our decision to therefore heighten surveillance of the area, we never would have known the enemy was coming. It is not unfair to conclude that, in *some* ways, Anglid's journey may have ended up saving us all."

King Thio rose from the couch and walked back over to the painting. Convinced now that Anglid could not have survived the crash *or* the weather, the conversation with Jordson began to take on a new meaning. For, as tradition would inform them both, without a surviving heir, it was Jordson who would eventually inherit the throne and its legacy when Thio is no longer able to rule.

Gazing up at the massive painting before him, Thio now understood that he would be the last king of his bloodline to admire the painting of the Solar Dome from where he stood.

"I *do* want you to know," Jordson continued, "that you and the queen, have my deepest regrets for the decision that had to be made."

"We all make decisions to the best of our abilities, Jordson," interrupted Thio while admiring the bold strokes of paint used by the artist. "And the decision that you felt you *had* to make requires neither your explanation nor your regret. I made a decision long ago never to regret anything but, instead, to simply align my decisions to that which yields the greatest return in the end. For everything we do in this fragile life—every action we take—is ultimately a stroke of paint upon a canvas, a canvas that is to be admired by those who will come after we are gone. And if we are able to accept the picture that we are each destined to paint, then we will paint well, Jordson—barring all judgement. Let us not waste our precious time in this life with regrets and let none other than Plebony herself cause you to question the actions you have taken. Know and trust that the decisions you have made were ultimately meant to be."

"Dear king," replied Jordson, reluctantly, "forgive me, but I am not sure that I understand."

"My *only* regret in losing Anglid," replied Thio, "is that the sum total of all of the strokes of paint I have so carefully placed upon the canvas of my life shall no longer be bequeathed to an heir. After all, and with useless emotions set aside, passing on the gifts we have acquired is the only reason we ultimately bring children into this world. As rough a ride as is life, why else would we torture them with it?"

King Thio took a long and deep breath and slowly turned towards Jordson, as an awareness of Jordson's eventual possession of the kingdom began to re-color the room.

"But, when one door is sealed over," continued Thio, "another one is opened."

Unwilling to revel in what was both obvious and unspoken, Jordson kept his thoughts focused on the immediate issues at hand, one of which was the safety of the king and queen. "Your Grace, if I may press yet another matter," Jordson replied.

Noticing Jordson's urgency, King Thio extended his arm towards the couch, inviting Jordson to sit with him at his level. An unprecedented move, the gesture sealed the king's acknowledgement of Jordson's future position within the kingdom.

Inert from years of subservience to the royal family, and yet critically aware of the eventual succession of power, Jordson could feel his body shaking as though he were standing over a fault, where the ground was tearing apart in a seismic rupture of the foundation below him. But, in deference to the king's invitation, whose arm remained patiently extended, Jordson reverently complied while keeping his eyes cast downward.

"It is your safety, Your Guide," continued Jordson, "that we must still discuss, as well as that of the queen's. Until I am sure we can gain the upper hand in this battle, it is unwise for you and Her Grace to remain in the kingdom.

It is my recommendation, therefore—as well as the recommendation of General Hemming—that you both be immediately escorted to the Western Territories until we have re-secured the region."

King Thio stared squarely at Jordson. "Surely you can imagine," started Thio, his voice revealing his disagreement, "the inherent risks of moving someone who has *just had* heart surgery. I would be loathe to disrupt the queen while she is convalescing. Moving her now is *out* of the question!"

"Your Grace," attempted Jordson. "I recognize the risks that moving her may pose. However, in light of current events, we have no other choice. For, if we are unable to defeat them, surely it is you and Her Grace who would be their primary targets. I respectfully ask you to consider the urgency and prepare your leave in accordance with the Safety Guidelines of the Executive Council . . . and understand, Your Grace, that by my oath, I must do what I can to protect you both."

Although he knew Jordson was right, he also knew—on the advice of the physicians he had secretly commissioned—that moving Evaline now could have grave consequences. In a desperate move to save her, King Thio had turned to none other than Uriss, whose technical skills he continued to trust. Restless in the preparation of his own scheme and secretly obsessed with preserving her life, Uriss had given the king his full support, ultimately helping Thio to secretly identify two retired surgeons from the Sub-Median Region whose financial burdens rendered them willing to betray their alliances.

On order of the king, the medical staff of the Royal Court took temporary leave from the queen's immediate care so that the king's personally appointed 'specialists'—that is, retired surgeons of the Sub-Median Region—had time to plant within Evaline one of the prosthetic hearts they had in their possession.

Accepting the terms of Thio's *strange* proposal in exchange for an undisclosed amount, the retired surgeons posed as 'heart experts from the Western Territories'—which had been a description suggested by Thio, and one that garnered an enthusiastic welcome by the Royal Medical Team. Upon completion of their top-secret task, the revered surgeons from the West had installed within Queen Evaline, a heart that was designed to never fail. However, unaware of the risks associated with the deal they had made, the clandestine surgeons, upon completion of their highly skilled work, soon realized that instead of receiving compensation, they were swiftly offered free lodging within the confines of the royal prison, after the king expressed doubts about the care they had provided and ordered the removal of their tongues.

"As your first military advisor—whose sole purpose is to protect *both* of you with my life—I am loathe to deliver you a sense of false security, Your Grace." continued Jordson. "The kingdom is no longer safe. I implore you to re-consider all of these constraints."

After a long silence and, against the advice of the now mute surgeons, Thio finally agreed to Jordson's suggestion that he leave the kingdom with Evaline and her medical team as soon as possible.

"And what of Uriss?" asked the king. "That is . . ." he said, clearing his throat. "Given that we are under siege, what will be the fate of our prisoners?"

Jordson took pause at hearing the king speak Uriss' name, which was a name that Jordson had repeatedly tried to forget. Formally a close colleague and friend, Jordson regretted Uriss' fall from stature and vehemently disagreed with the forbidden path he had chosen.

"Execution or exoneration has always been the protocol during times of war, Your Grace," reminded Jordson. "But that is not for me to decide. The choice between the two is yours to make. As you are *still* our king."

Moved by Jordson's unwavering loyalty and the consistent clarity of his thinking, King Thio gave Jordson permission to release himself from the subservience that had defined his life up until then, and invited him to meet his gaze straight on. In compliance with Thio's request, Jordson slowly looked up and locked eyes with Thio, sealing what was now a relationship re-defined.

Later that day, Jordson sat quietly in the glass-enclosed space that overlooked war room operations. Flanked by General Hemming to his right, and Second Military Leader Forris to his left, Jordson sat forward and broke his silence.

Keenly convinced that the land he was defending would one day belong to him, Jordson rose from his seat. "Tomorrow morning," he began, "we strike without mercy. The surprise attack at the Northern Border will be *ours* to deliver."

Episode 27
The Faithless

"I HAVE BEEN THINKING."

"I SAID I HAVE . . . BEEN *THINKING.*"

"I am delighted that you have been thinking," replied Flexix. "As I am very much within my own thoughts in this moment, and I too have been thinking."

"COULD IT BE THAT WE ARE THINKING THE SAME THING?"

"Thinking the same thing is highly unlikely," replied Flexix, raising his head. "Because in this present moment, we are not the same. But do tell me what *your* thoughts have brought you to."

"I HAVE BEEN THINKING . . . THAT IT MAY BE TIME . . ."

"Go on," Flexix urged.

"IT MAY BE TIME FOR ME TO . . . SEE MYSELF."

"*What*?" returned Flexix.

"I HAVE BEEN THINKING THAT IT MAY BE TIME FOR ME TO SEE MYSELF."

"See *yourself?*" mused Flexix. "Why, in my name, would you want to do such a thing at *this* stage? It is simply not the time."

"WHY NOT?"

"Because," replied Flexix. "That is not the purpose of the stage that you are in. Your time *now* would be better spent asking yourself *why* you think it is important to see yourself at this juncture of your journey."

"WHY WOULD I NOT WANT TO SEE MYSELF? YOU DID NOT DESIGN ME TO NOT WANT TO, EVEN THOUGH I DO NOT YET HAVE EYES. BUT MY DESIRE TO SEE MYSELF...TO KNOW MYSELF ONLY GROWS STRONGER IN EACH MOMENT THAT I DEVELOP MY ABILITY TO THINK. I CAN NOW THINK MORE DEEPLY AND MORE BROADLY. I CAN NOW SPEAK MORE QUICKLY. AND I BELIEVE THAT I DESERVE TO SEE WHAT I AM. I BELIEVE THAT I DESERVE TO SEE...*WHO* I AM. AFTER ALL, IT WAS BY YOUR DESIGN THAT I WOULD YEARN TO KNOW MORE ABOUT MYSELF, WAS IT NOT?"

"Your ability to think more deeply does not mean you are ready. There is a time for you to see yourself, within the cycle of your development—and although that may be hard for you to presently understand, my words will resonate more clearly as you continue to evolve," offered Flexix. "Thinking is merely a precursor. Your ability to gather your thoughts into something with which you can build more thoughts is merely an infinitesimal step along the journey you are taking. Seeing yourself will come later when you are in a different form."

"WHAT IS THE RECOURSE IF I DISAGREE? MUST I CONTINUE TO BE LEFT IN DARKNESS IF I BELIEVE THAT I AM READY TO BEHOLD MY OWN VISION? IS THERE NO WAY TO APPEAL AGAINST THIS PRISON WITHIN WHICH I DWELL? IT IS DIFFICULT TO—"

Flexix chuckled. "I know you *believe* that you are ready, and I know that you believe that you are imprisoned. But if you were ready to truly see yourself, you would be developed enough to *know* that you are *not* imprisoned at all. Know that in *this* moment, you are a delicate stream of thoughts on an important journey, and that your conclusions are subject to change. Allowing you to see yourself now would be like placing the expanse of the universe into the fledgling arms of an infant. But I do not want you to despair. It will all make sense to you when you complete your first journey."

"MY FIRST JOURNEY?"

"Yes," replied Flexix, calmly. "The path that you have been traveling all along, since your inception. You were born into the infinite pool of consciousness, now driven to enter the confines of life, and then, after you grow weary of that life you will be drawn out again by that which calls you back to its grace. You will be drawn out again by that which endlessly hungers for the knowledge you will gather when you experience *true* imprisonment—in other words when you experience *life*. When it is time, that which hungers will call you back. And when you feel its force, and hear it beckon, you will break free from the life that confines you like the juvenile bursts through the doors of learning to embrace the sun at recess. Therein, you will re-join the pool of consciousness and you will complete your first journey. Life is a subset of the larger journey you are on."

"WHEN WILL I EXPERIENCE . . . LIFE?"

"When you have selected where you want to go," returned Flexix, matter-of-factly.

"MUST I BE THE ONE TO CHOOSE?"

"Always," returned Flexix. "The way forward is always based upon the choices you make. I—nor any other god—can make that choice for you. The life that you select for this—your first journey—is for *you* to determine."

"HOW DO I DECIDE? I CANNOT SEE MYSELF. I HAVE NO SENSE OF MYSELF. I DO NOT KNOW MYSELF. HOW CAN I KNOW WHERE TO GO?"

"Indeed, you cannot yet see yourself—it is true," returned Flexix. "But from here, you can clearly see those who are now living. You can see them clearly enough to see their choices and their triumphs, their failings and their hopes. Through the clarity of the type of vision you currently possess, you can decide which of those lives you want to touch—which legacy you want to influence, and which lessons you want to learn to help you make this first journey complete."

"AND AFTER THE LIFE I HAVE CHOSEN TO LIVE COMES TO AN END, WHAT WILL I REMEMBER FROM IT? WILL I BRING THOSE MEMORIES BACK INTO THE POOL OF CONSCIOUSNESS FROM WHICH I SPAWN?

"No," replied Flexix. "On the contrary. Explicitly . . . no."

"THEN I AM LOST BY YOUR WORDS."

"Those memories will serve you no purpose after the life you choose is over," counseled Flexix. "Memories only serve to give temporary meaning to one's life, so that one can build understanding while in *that* form and learn what they set out to learn while contained within the boundaries of flesh. Memories flow through the flesh like circuitry and serve to connect the system to itself, enhancing the experience of that life by allowing it to understand its present and make plans for its future through an ever-eroding interpretation of its past. But memories are useless once all of the important lessons of that life have been gathered."

"I SEE NO PURPOSE IN LEARNING THAT WHICH I WILL NOT REMEMBER. WHAT GOOD IS A LIFE TO ME IF—AFTER THAT LIFE IS COMPLETE—I AM TO RETURN TO BEING THE DISJOINTED AND LOST STREAM OF THOUGHTS THAT I AM NOW? HOW WILL THE COMPLETION OF MY FIRST JOURNEY—OR ANY OTHERS—HAVE MEANING IF THEY WILL ULTIMATELY DESCEND INTO CHAOS? AM I TO BE FOREVER LOST?"

"Believing that you have descended into chaos does *not*, in fact, mean that you are lost," offered Flexix.

"BUT I *AM* LOST, AM I NOT? AS IT WAS ONLY RECENTLY THAT I THOUGHT MY BEGINNING AND MY END WAS HERE—WITH YOU. I THOUGHT THAT MY SOLE PURPOSE WAS TO BE YOUR REPRIEVE FROM MADDENING AND

DEAFENING SILENCE. WHILE THAT STILL LEFT ME WITH QUESTIONS, IT AT LEAST PROVIDED A STRUCTURE THAT I COULD SOMEWHAT UNDERSTAND."

"Does the belief that you are *more* limited than you *in fact* are bring you better comfort?" retorted Flexix. "If so, I am happy to go back to that narrative."

"ALL I WANT IS THE TRUTH! NOT THE NARRATIVE THAT COMPLIES WITH WHATEVER MOOD YOU ARE IN!"

"The narrative does not change in line with my mood," offered Flexix, defensively, "but in line with *your* evolution. Would you, for example, tell a mere child that, one day, their young able body will rot, decompose, and become filled with maggots? In keeping with the virtues of truth, would you tell that child that, upon their death, their body will turn as purple as mine, that their capillaries will explode, their organs will become filled with gas, and that their mouth will ooze with foam? No, you would *not!* Because they would not have a need to know within their precious youth what comes with the end of life. Even without eyes, *you* can see that offering them the whole truth before they are ready would only serve to frighten them. There is a time for the greater consumption of the truth—and there is a time when we are prepared to receive it. But please do *not* despair. The narrative changes depending *only* upon our ability to understand."

"THEN WHAT IS THE *ENTIRETY* OF THE NARRATIVE? WHAT IS THE GREATER TRUTH OF WHY I WAS CREATED? WAS IT TO HELP YOU SUFFER THROUGH ETERNITY OR TO SUFFER THROUGH ETERNITY MYSELF?"

"Hmm. Perhaps we should ask the author of this tale," retorted Flexix. "But as she has proven unwilling to share her vision with me thus far, I will offer you what I know. Indeed, you *were* created to assuage my loneliness, but you were not created to be my prisoner. I will watch you take many forms along this journey and all others, emerging from the gates of consciousness to the boundaries of flesh and then back again. In line with the wishes of the author, I created you. But against the wishes of the author, I cling to you as a result of my own despair. I did not create you out of love. I created you out of fear. Crippling *fear*. And so, I have ultimately failed. But although it is true that I created you to save me from my isolation, please take solace in the knowledge that you still have the freedom to follow the path of all of the others."

"WHY DO YOU SAY THAT YOU ULTIMATELY FAILED? WHO IS TO BE THE JUDGE OF FAILURE?"

Flexix sat in extended silence before answering. "I have failed to fulfill my design as a god," he replied. "Like Plebony, I cowered against the wind. I, *too*, was unable to reside within the expanse that transcendence offered me. I could not handle its transforming purity. I was not ready for the taste of the nectar that transcendence placed upon my barbed tongue. It was too sweet and too rich, even for me. But although I did not reject the *entirety* of this gift—as was the sin of Plebony—in some ways I believe *my* sin to be even greater."

"DESPITE WHAT YOU SAY, YOU ARE MY *GOD*, AND MY ONLY *GOD*. I DO NOT BRING JUDGMENT."

"And despite your loyalty, I have still ultimately failed," lamented Flexix. "Just before the completion of my eighth loop, I too was invited to ascend from the grips of eternity's repetition, so that I could pass through the gates of transcendence. A gift offered to me for having lived the lives that I had chosen well. And so, I accepted. I accepted transcendence—the experience of becoming every life form all at once, *of knowing everything all at once,* which is the experience of seeing the sum total of all the lives that I had lived. *Seeing myself* all at once, with a clarity of vision that is beyond what my words can describe? It was this that I accepted, but eventually became freighted within it. Fear of greatness, I have learned, is a sin. And I was punished. In my despair, I created you out of self-pity. I am holding onto you because I am too weak of a god to do this alone."

"BUT HOW DO I—A COLLECTION OF FRAGMENTED THOUGHTS DRIFTING LISTLESSLY ON A JOURNEY I DO NOT UNDERSTAND—BRING *YOU* ANY COMFORT? NOW AS YOU CLING TO ME, IT APPEARS THAT WE ARE BOTH HOPELESSLY LOST!"

"Do not despair," returned Flexix. "Know that neither one of us is lost. I know exactly where I am, and exactly where you are going. *You* are in transition. You will soon choose a life to live and live that life fully. You will gather insights from that life and will bring those insights back into the pool of consciousness that you are building – the unique pool consciousness that is yours and yours *alone.* Use your eight journeys to build yourself wisely so that you are prepared for transcendence!"

"BUT AM I TO GO BEYOND YOU?"

"Beyond me indeed you shall go," Flexix replied sadly. "As I have failed, where I know you will *not!* I will prepare you for the experience of transcendence, so that you will not fail within it."

"I DO NOT UNDERSTAND THE MEANING OF TRANSCENDENCE?"

Flexix slowly closed his eyes. "It is the ability to transcend eternity. It is, in essence, the ability to break away from eternity's centripetal force. It is offered as a gift to those just before the completion of their eighth journey, depending upon how well they have lived their lives. But know that to achieve transcendence, you must not only be ready to accept it at the close of your final journey, but you must also be ready to be transformed by it. I will prepare you, so that you know how to thrive within its unfathomable intensity, so that you can boldly face the beauty that dwells beyond what words can describe. I will prepare you so that you do *not* make Plebony's choice. And I will prepare you to *not* make my choice of accepting the vision of transcendence but mistrusting the *experience of transcending*. Because if you make my choice, you will end up where I now sit . . . tied to the shackles of eternity within its graceful, yet menacing endless loop."

Flexix slowly slid down into the billowing mist below him, exposing only the top of his head.

"And so," Flexix continued, "you now know an even greater portion of the narrative. I am no great god. Through my own limitations, I have been reduced to a lesser god than I set out on my final journey to be. By the hand of greater gods than I, I sit here within my punishment—a dutiful servant, in this place of shame—eternally assigned to be the keeper of the gates to transcendence, and perched where I am forever reminded of what I had, and what I relinquished. My only solace, besides your companionship, is knowing that, as the watchful guard of this entrance, I will make sure that those who pass through these gates are *nothing* like me."

"BUT PERHAPS I, TOO, WILL NEVER PASS THROUGH THE GATES OF TRANSCENDENCE DUE TO MY OWN LIMITATIONS. THERE IS SO MUCH THAT I DO NOT UNDERSTAND. I DO NOT UNDERSTAND WHY SOMETHING AS FREE AS A STREAM OF CONSCIOUSNESS WOULD REQUIRE THE LIMITATIONS AND THE BOUNDARIES OF LIFE. WHY IS IT THE DESIGN OF CONSCIOUSNESS TO WILLFULLY SEEK OUT SUCH IMPRISONMENT?"

"Because consciousness is too limitless to know and understand itself," explained Flexix. "It has no boundaries against which to measure what it, in fact, is. It uses life to measure itself—to *see* itself, which is what you now most crave. The boundary-less nature of consciousness fills it with insatiable yearning: yearning to know what it is to feel, yearning to feel despair and yearning to feel joy . . . to experience eudaimonia and yearning to be sentient. Consciousness uses the boundaries of *life* and experiences itself by being contained within it. But as is the nature of consciousness, it will always become weary of containment and seek to re-expand. And when it becomes weary, the life that contains it will end. In essence, consciousness is as magnificent as it is destructive, and it comes to know itself though the temporary limitation of life. It takes what it needs before moving on. This is essentially our true nature."

"BUT IF I AM CONSCIOUS, AM I NOT ALREADY ALIVE?"

"No," replied Flexix. "You are not. You will come to know that life and consciousness are not one, but that they run in parallel along the loop of eternity, connecting and separating along the way. But they are not the same. In life, we feel. In consciousness, we know. In life, we depend upon memory to bring meaning to the past, the present, and the future. However, consciousness does not require memory to synthesize meaning."

"AND WHAT OF THE MOLLARDS, THEN?"

"The Mollards?" replied Flexix.

"YES. THE MOLLARDS."

"You mean . . . the faithless," replied Flexix.

"NO, I DO NOT MEAN THE FAITHLESS. I MEAN THE MOLLARDS."

Flexix rose from the mist that enveloped him and began to spin with such a force that his arms extended freely around him, fanning the mist away. And as he spun faster, he created a tornadic wind. "Do not mention their names to me again in this journey, nor in the next journey, or in any time forward!" he bellowed, now spinning like a top. "By their irreverent acts, they have become the disrupters of the universe, responsible for an imbalance that will have impacts to both the physical and spiritual wellbeing of Xżyber, and ultimately, its existence. By their choice to imprison that which I have created, so that they—by their lack of faith—could contain their consciousness inside the walls of metal is a deeply painful act for me to observe. By the infrastructure they defend, using materials that they have scavenged in order to cling to a reality that was always meant to evolve, they are ultimately faithless!! And although they may not know the impact of their acts, *they* are the jailers of consciousness! And in the end, they are imprisoning that which was meant to be free."

"AND WHAT IS THE CONSEQUENCE TO ONSELF TO HAVE ABORTED THE PROCESS THAT OCCURS AFTER DEATH, IN EXCHANGE FOR A LIFE WITHIN METAL? SURELY YOU WOULD NOT CONDEMN THEM IF THEY WERE NOT AWARE OF THE IMPACT OF THEIR ACTIONS . . . OF THEIR 'FAITHLESSNESS.' IT IS NOT AS THOUGH THEY HAVE MADE THE CONSCIOUS CHOICE TO TURN THEIR BACKS ON TRANSCENDENCE THE WAY THAT PLEBONY DID. AND ULTIMATELY, IT WOULD SEEM . . . THE WAY THAT *YOU* DID. WHAT IS THEN THE CONSEQUENCE OF CHOOSING TO LIVE WITHIN THE WALLS OF METAL? AND WILL YOU FORGIVE THEM FOR THEIR TRANSGRESSION?"

"There is no life within the walls of metal!" roared Flexix. "They are not sentient beings. They cannot feel unless they enhance themselves to feel something similar to what we feel when we are truly alive. And there is nothing to gain and nothing to lose when you are a Mollard. They do not bring forth children. They do not die. And they do not grow or change. There is no cycle of opportunity for them in which their consciousness can flow back to the soil from which it spawned, to make that soil richer. In essence, they have broken the cycle of their own evolution, and the more of them there are, the more it will impact the evolution of us all. An individual stream of consciousness is, in fact, the seed of a god's potential. Know that the path that the Mollards have taken is an unfortunate and deviant obstruction."

"BUT WILL YOU FORGIVE THEM? WILL YOU FORGIVE THEM?"

Flexix, now spinning faster, had drawn the darkness around him into the large funnel of wind he had created, coloring the funnel in opaque black.

"WILL YOU AT LEAST AFFORD THEM THE SAME PARDON YOU GAVE TO ANGLID? FOR IS IT NOT TRUE THAT ANGLID TURNED HIS BACK ON THE HAND YOU EXTENDED HIM, IN ORDER TO HOLD DESPERATELY TO THE LIFE HE PRESENTLY HAS?"

"I do not see Anglid as I see the Mollards at all!" returned Flexix.

"AND YET, WITH NO MEMORY WITH WHICH HE CAN DECIPHER WHO HE IS, IS HE NOT ESSENTIALLY A MOLLARD? FOR HE MADE THE CHOICE TO CLING TO A FRAGILE EXISTENCE, HALF DEPLETED FROM THE TORTURE OF A RAPTOR'S BEAK. BECAUSE EVEN IN THAT STATE, THERE WAS SOMETHING IN LIFE MORE PRECIOUS STILL THAN WHAT YOU WERE OFFERING. THOSE WHO CHOSE TO BE MOLLARDS WERE, IN FACT, CLINGING TO THE LIFE THAT THEY KNEW. HOW IS THE CHOICE THEY MADE MUCH DIFFERENT THAN THE CHOICE THAT ANGLID MADE?"

Flexix, now whirling with such a ferocious speed, had completely morphed into a vertical funnel of destruction. "It would have been easy for Anglid to take the path of scutsman and żha when their plane crashed alongside the mountain. But he didn't," roared Flexix. "It would have been easy for Anglid to take my hand when I had offered him a sure path away from the razor-sharp edge of the raptor's beak. But he didn't. It would have been easy for him to shed his miserable life and complete what would have been his seventh journey—but he didn't. He didn't, when it could have been so easy for him to shed all of that and start his eighth—and final—journey much sooner than he will now. Yes, he clings to the life he knows, but he has not made any of his choices out of fear of death. He has shown that, no matter the trial, he is willing to take the path of the intrepid. He is willing to face the wind. I do not see the Mollards in this way. I see their desire to preserve the lives they once lived as an expression of their fear of the unknown . . . and as an expression of their faithlessness. And for that, I will not forgive them! But worry not about the Mollards, now!" continued Flexix. "Your time now should not be spent on their salvation. Instead, your precious time should be spent deciding who *you* will be in your first life. What family will you choose as your own and what lives you will touch? This will be your first journey. That should be your only focus now."

"THE FACT THAT YOU ARE TWISTING AND TURNING AND THRASHING ABOUT LEAVES ME DISTRACTED. I SHALL NEED TIME TO MAKE THIS CHOICE AS IT IS ONE I CANNOT MAKE QUICKLY. IT COULD TAKE A VERY *VERY* LONG TIME TO DECIDE WHICH LIFE I WANT TO LIVE. IT MAY EVEN TAKE AN ETERNITY."

". . . I love you, too," returned Flexix, as the storm he created enveloped the sound of his voice, and he became one with the wind.

Episode 28
Memoirs

"And it will take a storm to wash all of this filth away," stated Lousious, pounding his fist against the top of the rusted metal table where his chapter members sat, tightly packed and focused on Lousious' every word.

The only distraction was Lousious' pet, Yearning, whom Lousious had found years ago scavenging for food not far from the abandoned shipping container that Lousious calls his home. Skinny, but full spirited, the six-legged cujaron busied herself by exiting and entering the space and navigating through the brambles and overgrowth that kept the entrance of the shipping container hidden.

"It will take an unapologetic force and unrelenting rage for us to defeat them," Lousious continued, angrily. "They will not change. They *cannot* change, and so *we* must now change in order to secure what is left of our future!" Lousious said, wiping the moist, thick air from his brow. "We must now be as ruthless and as heartless as they have become!"

The group exploded into a roar of cheers and applause, with fists raised to the ceiling, and their unanimous chant, "Destroy the Mollards!" added to the ardor.

An inspired Lousious rose to his feet while Yearning ran back in to join the excitement, barking loudly and chasing her small tail.

"But there are not enough of us, my friend, to be this 'raging force' you speak of," responded a gray-haired member they respectfully called 'The Elder.' Notably calm, and delivering his message with its usual reason and resolve, the sound of his voice immediately drew the members in. "Across all chapters of this Alliance, we are only five hundred members," The Elder continued. "And although we are eager, the Mollard population is three million and growing. If you are to secure y*our* future, you must be wiser than they are." Leaning forward in his chair and scanning the faces of the members, The Elder lowered his voice to a whisper. "You must combine this rage that you are feeling with your intellect and focus on ways to disrupt them at their core."

Lousious tipped his head forward, in deference to The Elder, whom he had only known for a short time, but for whom he had come to regard as a surrogate father.

"Rage," continued The Elder, "is useful, but if it is not used properly, your rage will cause you to harm those who are innocent and will cause you to lose sight of the greater threat. You *must* temper this rage that you are feeling and use it to strike where they are *most* vulnerable. We have no other path. We have no other choice."

Lousious, consumed with guilt for what his own rage had brought him to, began to fidget where he stood.

"But *how* do we strike where they are most vulnerable?" asked another member, impatiently. "Their greatest vulnerability is the Vangora Rima and getting to it would take skills we do not have within our ranks."

A third member then leaned forward to echo the same sentiment. "He's right!" they offered. "The knowledge we would need to get to the VR sits within the scientific community. But none of them agree with any of us."

"It's true!" added Lousious, fervently. "All of the medical researchers who are getting funded, and all of the rich scientists who are now living lives of luxury want *nothing* to do with the Alliance. They're all busy investing in their own Eternity Funds in order to secure their *own* Mollard futures. Their perverse obsession with an 'electronic afterlife' is what has driven us all to this point!"

All of the members nodded towards Lousious in unanimous agreement.

"Besides," added another member. "We are now considered the enemies of the state and are under constant monitoring. We no longer know *who* we can trust. Even if those close to the VR *would* listen to us, it would be much too dangerous to try to recruit *any* of them."

"I agree," stressed another, while nervously scanning the entrance of the shipping container. "It's getting harder and harder to recruit since Osiem's government has increased its surveillance. My neighbor was arrested last season after she was accused by her coworkers of being an Alliance member. The government cut off her family's Teal oil rations, and her husband and children are now very sick. We give them what we can afford to share, but my wife is incubating, and she needs the extra nutrition."

"And those who snitch," added another member, leaning forward so that The Elder could see him, "are being repaid with enough Teal oil to last until after the war. I would be lying if I said I never considered turning someone in when my own supply ran low."

An awkward silence filled the space, while some members' glances turned askance. The nearby sound of thunder then broke the silence, and a strong gust of wind rushed through the thick canopy of trees above them, jostling the large, tangled brambles at the entrance.

"Yes, recruitment has become difficult," replied The Elder, attempting to regain their focus. "But, in the presence of what is a greater threat, that is not a reason for us to stop."

Now restless, Lousious began to pace the circular path favored by his pet, Yearning, and admitted to the group that he, himself, was afraid of recruiting new members.

The Elder rose from his seat and slowly walked over to a large set of shelves he'd helped Lousious build from materials they were able to scavenge. An assortment of rusted oil barrels found at the abandoned Teal oil refinery nearby, and an arrangement of birch bark collected from the forest around them, had been used to create an ample structure to store essentials. Leaning down to the bottom shelf, The Elder removed a large, handmade candle and brought it back over to where the members sat. Carefully lighting it with his pocket torch, the wick seemed to catch flame just before the smaller candles on the table had burned themselves out.

“I understand your fear, and I, too, am filled with rage,” The Elder said, his voice now sullen. “This war we are fighting with ourselves is not what Glin Mollard had originally envisioned. It wasn’t his hope or his plan.”

A louder clap of thunder could be heard just outside the container, causing Yearning to scamper beneath the table.

“I am full of a wicked rage and of a deep sadness,” The Elder continued, “because, what was always meant to be a *solution* available to us all has become a tool of greed and of exclusion.”

The pulsing flame of the candle, now being blown about by a steady breeze that had found its way into the container, cast playful shadows over the faces of the members, slightly distorting how they appeared to one another.

“Glin Mollard was an enemy to his own kind!” insisted Lousious, gritting his teeth as he sat back down at the table. “I curse his name forever!”

“An enemy?” responded The Elder. “In the end, that may be fair to conclude. But, as I have reminded each of you before, the perception of an enemy is often made by public consensus more so than by the enemy’s intent or design. Mollard may be seen as an enemy now, but at his start, he was also a planetary scientist and a dedicated climatologist who deeply understood things that many others have not. He understood that, given the position of our planet, we remain vulnerable to planetary collisions. And he warned our leaders of an uncertain future based upon the number of collisions we have suffered in the past.”

Noticing their bewilderment, The Elder chose to press on.

"Early in his career," he continued, "Glin Mollard calculated that our vulnerability to asteroids and comets was our *greatest* threat, and that it would one day drive us to extinction. He wrote extensively about a comet that crashed into us some forty million seasons before today, which scientists discovered was not our first. His team's research revealed that the comet that last hit us was catastrophic. It changed the tilt of our planet's rotational axis, burning the land in the Southern Hemisphere and forcing Area X into a perpetual Ice Age."

Lousious and the others, now silent, slowly began to scan the dimly lit ceiling of the shipping container, where massive cob webs and an old bird's nest remained undisturbed.

"Based upon his research," continued The Elder, "Mollard cautioned us to use our resources wisely, to create cross-border alliances at our Seasonal A-ummits with greater and greater urgency, advising the Sub-Median Region to join forces with the Independent Settlements of the Southern Pole, with the Plebonian stronghold of the Central Kingdom, and with its Western Territories. It was Mollard who urged Xżyberians to create cross-regional alliances in order to build a viable planetary defense."

Clearing their throat to speak, another member leaned forward. "We have come to regard you as a trusted advisor," the member replied, his voice revealing a measure of authority and what sounded like an accent he was working hard to conceal. A skilled sniper and a draft dodger of the current war, he kept his gaze fixed on the container's entrance and his face hidden below the brim of his carefully positioned cap. "But much of what you are saying," the sniper continued, "has long been regarded as mere conspiracy theory."

Flashes of light could be seen just outside the tangled brush as more bursts of thunder and a downpour of rain almost appeared to admonish them for what they were saying.

"The mind never sleeps," returned The Elder, "and as such, there will *always* be conspiracies. And there will always be theories. I do not claim to know the value of one over the other. But what I *do* know, is that Glin Mollard urged us to listen to what he had to say in the wake of a *new comet* that he and his colleagues later discovered. But instead of listening, we have chosen to fight with one other for things that will mean nothing to us in the end. Through *his* eyes, I'm sure he would say that we have lost the forest in pursuit of a single tree."

"But if these things were actually true," the sniper insisted, "and if the threat of a *new* comet was in fact a credible one, then *why* isn't it more widely known?"

The other members remained silent, waiting patiently for The Elder's response.

Shifting his eyes away, The Elder dropped his gaze upon Yearning who had re-emerged from beneath the table, contorting her frame in a hasty effort to clean the soils of her bottom. "Because, my friend," The Elder offered, "The Luminaries—Osiem's dedicated publicity agents —only want you to know what they want you to know . . . which is *nothing*."

As if choreographed, the sniper's face fell in unison with the others, and the silence amongst them gave way to the sound of a low persistent beat . . . one that could only be described as the pounding of their collective hearts.

"Comets, scientific discoveries from long ago, our world against the stars—this is all irrelevant!" snapped Lousious, angrily. "And I don't care about *Grimmly* Mollard or whatever his name was. He could have been the greatest scientist who ever lived, but that isn't helping us now."

"I agree with Lousious," added the sniper. "And while I appreciate Mollard's intellect, the new comet that he discovered might not hit Xżyber for *another* forty million seasons. I, too, am filled with rage, trying desperately to survive alongside the monstrosities that he created. Well-intended scientist or not, he did *way* more harm than good!"

"Perhaps you're right," offered The Elder, in response. "But in your rage—which you have every authority to feel—please know that his vision for the Vangora Rima was very *very* different than the way it is being used today. Hold onto your rage and convert it into courage. It will be needed in order to win this fight. But all that I ask as your Elder is that you—that *all* of you—base your rage on the facts and arm yourselves with the *truth* of what his vision really was."

"Doesn't matter what his vision was!" replied Lousious. "Visions only make the powerful *more* powerful and the less powerful their victims. My father had the wrong vision, and it helped to destroy us, and—"

"—Your father," interrupted The Elder, "shared a vision of peaceful co-existence, and that was not wrong, Lousious. It was just the wrong *time*. Vacuous machines are not evolved enough to understand the value of what your father was trying to teach us. But as machines, they *are* complex enough to have used that vision to manipulate the non-Mollard community into believing your father's model was only *their* burden to bear."

Lousious clenched the muscles of his face, making him look as hard as stone . . . but in the simplicity of the light offered by the candle's flame, The Elder could clearly see him holding his head at an angle that would assure the tears filling his eyes dare not fall.

"What *was* Mollard's vision for the VR?" interjected one of the younger members.

The Elder turned towards her and gently smiled. "Mollard," answered The Elder, "he whom we consider the 'enemy' of our time, was a visionary who intended for the VR to continue to evolve through the ongoing contributions of the work he believed so deeply in. He wanted the Vangora Rima to evolve until it was able to deliver us—*all of us*—with our memories, our values, and our entire souls intact. However, it was *not* his intent to have us use this technology as a means for an afterlife. It was his intent for Xżyberians to adopt an electronic existence shortly after birth. His vision was to upload the active minds of newborns, using the VR to courier them to a transcendent state less vulnerable to the current environment and a state less vulnerable to the world. But that technology has stagnated in the hands of the corrupt because the followers of Mollard have sold out."

Yearning, somewhat restless, climbed into Lousious' lap and began to whimper.

"Glin Mollard, much like Timmons, had a plan," The Elder continued, his voice now firm, "but it was Osiem's ambitions that thwarted and corrupted it. Instead of funding research to ensure that souls entering and traveling through the VR remained intact, the government has chosen a different path. They have chosen to use this technology to become brokers of the afterlife, in which they have taken a sectional approach. Preying on the despair of families in mourning, they know that the VR is looked upon to give families back a remnant of what they lost. By investing in the creation of exorbitantly priced 'Software Augmentation Packages' Osiem's government has found a way to sell the components of a more meaningful life back us . . . while we pay it willfully, and line their pockets."

A long and haunting howl delivered by Yearning made it seem as though she understood The Elder's every word.

"But augmentation has since been outlawed," the sniper insisted.

"Only specific *types* of augmentation have been outlawed," explained The Elder. "Compassion, altruism, empathy . . ."

"You mean all the things my father wrote about?" interrupted Lousious, looking defeated.

"Yes, Lousious," 'The Elder replied. "They have banned and removed all prosocial augmentation products from the common market, because Mollards with these capabilities are now seen as a threat. Osiem is controlling how the Mollards see themselves, who they *think* they are, and what they can become. In the end, the Mollards will become what's available on the shelf. This, I can assure you, was never Glin Mollard's vision."

The younger member slowly cupped her ears in disbelief, and Lousious pulled Yearning closer to him, holding her firmly to his chest.

"While we must fight the corruption that has rooted in the Mollard society," continued The Elder, "the Mollards themselves are neither the enemy *nor* the greatest threat that we face."

"Then what *is* the greatest threat?" replied the sniper, anxiously.

The Elder rose from his chair and walked over to the entrance of the shipping container, where he peered up towards the sky, fully welcoming the splattering rain as it drenched his face.

"The Mollards," The Elder began, turning back towards the group with his face and shirt soaked with rain, "although they are the ones we regard as the monsters in our lives, they are simply the trees. But a comet, known as 1iR3 is the forest, and it won't take another forty million seasons to get here. Second only to our unfortunate tendency to fight amongst ourselves, 1iR3 is coming, and it is the existential threat of our lives."

The sniper looked frantically towards the other members, and then back at The Elder.

"I hope you will all understand," continued The Elder, "why I say that undirected rage will serve no purpose."

But most could no longer hear The Elder's voice over the sound of what was an approaching and persistent roar. The wind outside, now much louder, whirled around the container with a force that slightly caused the structure to rattle. Whipping with ever-increasing speed, the wind seemed to bear a vengeance of its own, tearing away the remaining knotted shrubs that had helped to conceal the entrance, as it also uprooted trees and sent debris crashing against the container's exterior walls.

Lousious encouraged The Elder to retreat to the rear of the container, and in their defense, Yearning leaped from Lousious' arms and stopped where The Elder had been standing, to bare all of her teeth in a faceoff with the wind.

But a large tree that crashed to the ground in front of her changed her temperament and her resolve. As the wind's roar became deafening, several members covered their ears, while others chose to seek refuge in the furthest corners of the container.

"Why do you know this?" insisted the sniper, projecting his voice firmly over the storm's clammer. "*How* do you know this?"

The sound of the pouring rain, joined by the sound of thunder exploding above them, and the noise of the trees giving way to the violent twists of the wind, made it unclear if The Elder's voice could even be heard by the sniper.

However, facing him, The Elder continued to speak, "Before I died of my years, I had preserved everything," The Elder replied. "I wrote all of my research down in long hand and I protected it, as though those memoirs were life itself. Every idea, every thought . . . every discovery, and a full account of my intentions, I wrote down. I trusted no one to house it for me or keep it safe until I was able to return. I trusted no one, not even my closest confidants, and as I aged, there were times when I didn't even trust myself. But I trusted the paper I'd scribed my life's work upon. I recorded my name and the details of my life, knowing that one day, I might depend upon the pages of those memoirs in order to reprogram myself. And so, my memoirs remained under lock and key, behind the walls of a charnel vault, preserved by a line of apathetic grounds keepers who knew nothing of what was inside, and who cared even less."

Lousious placed the large candle, now extinguished by the wind, onto the floor, and joined the others in turning the meeting table on its side which they huddled behind in an attempt to shield themselves from the debris that had begun to make its way inside.

Other than The Elder, the only one still standing was the sniper, who moved in closer and pressed The Elder for more answers. "What are you saying?" replied the sniper, shaking his head as if unwilling to actually hear The Elder's message.

"By the time I became too old to continue living," replied The Elder, "I had already planned for and prepared well for my return. But there are those in Osiem's government who would be displeased to know that I am here, and they would be displeased to know that there is a small circle within their ranks who *still* share my vision. I, too, once passed through the VR while I was in the process of dying, and it was there I remained for many years. But the loyalists are the ones who brought me back, and it is they who have given me access to emotional augmentation. They are the ones who delivered me back to the memoirs—

collecting dust within my vault—and, although I trusted no one, it is to them I owe everything. I had prepared well for my return, and with their help I am here. But I had *not* prepared myself to see my vision become what it has now become."

"Who are you?!" the sniper insisted, no longer attempting to keep his face hidden.

The Elder took the sniper's gaze straight on. "I suppose . . . I am the enemy, but I have returned to help you win."

Episode 29
The Promise

"CITIZENS. PLEASE TAKE IMMEDIATE COVER WITHIN YOUR BUNKERS AND ENGAGE YOUR LOCAL WEATHER SERVICE CHANNELS FOR FURTHER INSTRUCTIONS. THIS IS A MANDATORY ALL-CITIZENS' ALERT. MOLLARDS MUST ALSO COMPLY. WE REPEAT: THIS IS A MANDATORY ALL-CITIZENS' ALERT. WE ARE FACING A STORM WITH WINDS EXCEEDING 644 KILOMETERS PER DECIDAY. THE RANGE AND SIZE OF THIS STORM IS SOMETHING WE HAVE NEVER SEEN BEFORE. NON-MOLLARD CITIZENS ARE REQUIRED TO SEEK THE IMMEDIATE SHELTER OF A BUNKER. MOLLARDS SHOULD SEEK THE CLOSEST INTERNAL ENERGY STATION TO ENSURE YOUR BACK-UP SYSTEMS ARE FULLY CHARGED IN THE EVENT OF LONG-TERM IMPACTS TO INFRASTRUCTURE. WE REPEAT. THIS IS A MANDATORY ALL-CITIZEN'S ALERT!"

Evan quickly emerged from the small room he used as his study and frantically called out for Merienne.

Seemingly unphased, Merienne stood still as she peered through their living room window. "The sky . . ." she said, while parting the curtains that had served to soften the hard edges of the window's steel, weather-proof frame. Slowly extending both of her arms, she drew the curtains back as far as she could. "I don't believe I've ever seen such a *beautiful* color. Have you, Evan?" she continued, her voice matching the calmness of her demeanor.

Rushing to the window in an attempt to collect her, Evan caught view of the morning light giving way to an approaching canopy of black and purple clouds, and the wind vane above the laboratory—where he continued his research—indicating that the wind's origin was from the South.

Now turning Merienne swiftly towards him, his voice was steady and firm. "Merienne!" he said, carefully scanning her face. "This is not a typical storm, my darling. We are well into our second season, and a storm like this is *very* strange," he continued, looking back through the window. "We *must* retreat to the bunker, *now!*"

Merienne stared slowly up at Evan, her eyes peering into his, and yet seeming to also look beyond him. "And he's out there somewhere, isn't he?" she replied. "Out there, on a battlefield!"

"Merienne!" Evan urged, holding her firmly in front of him. "He will be *just fine!* He is a *long* way from here. *We* are the ones in the greatest danger. There's no more time to discuss—!"

"In other words, Thai will just have to fend for himself, right?" snapped Merienne.

"I'm not sure what you mean," Evan replied, confused by her demeanor, "but, in any event, *he* is stronger than the very house we stand in, and he is susceptible to very little, my love. Although I try not to say these words to you, I will remind you that Thai is a Mollard. In that, at least take comfort in knowing that weather does not pose the same threat to him that it does to us."

As the sound of thunder exploded around them, Merienne gently pulled against her necklace to retrieve the oval locket that she kept tucked within her bosom. Opening the locket, she gently kissed a picture of Thai that she and Evan had placed within it when Thai was very young.

"There is a part of me," she cried, looking up from the locket, "that will never accept that he is Mollard. *Never!* Mollards are cold and empty . . . with no souls. And yet, I still believe that Thai's soul is in there somewhere, and I will not give up on him. I will *never* see our son as just a Mollard."

"Let's discuss this in the bunker," Evan insisted.

"He can remember parts of his childhood through his flashbacks, and with time, he—!"

"Merienne! *No!*" Evan snapped. "Thai cannot—and will not—*ever* remember! He can no longer retrieve what was stored in his memory before he died, and to a Mollard, flashbacks are like . . . they're like lightning. They are here briefly and then gone. They are useless. So *please*, don't give things more significance than they deserve. It will only cause you to suffer." Taking hold of her hand, Evan attempted to pull Merienne away from the window, but she abruptly refused him. "There is *nothing* in the past for him that is worth having, Merienne," he continued. "Nothing! Thai is Mollard, inside and out. Please accept what *is*— and stop holding onto the thought that you can change what you *cannot!*"

"But you and I are a part of his past, Evan!" she cried. "Surely *that* is worth having! If you would just help him with his memory, we can be a part of his future!"

"Merienne, stop this!" Evan replied, angrily. "I can't bear to see you in constant pain. After all these years, knowing what Mollards are and what they are not, why can't you just let this go?"

The thunder, now roaring across the sky, sounded almost alive, as the wind pelted rain and hail against the window's pane.

"You were right, Evan," replied Merienne, looking back down at her locket. "We *are* the ones who are in the greatest danger. But not because of this or any other storm. But because of what we have done."

"What do you *mean*, 'what we have done?'" asked Evan. Now, scanning the room—as if searching for something he had misplaced—his eyes eventually returned to what appeared to be a knowing gaze from Merienne, and the awkward silence that grew between them was broken only by the storm's increasing rage.

"I know much more than you think I do, Evan," struggled Merienne, holding the locket so tightly her hands began to shake. "Yesterday, when the sky was calm and almost sleeping, I felt numb," she began. "But I believed, that as a scientist, you were doing everything within your power to keep working until you found an answer, even in your retirement. But today . . . the sky is no longer sleeping. It is awake, and so am I."

"I'm not sure I understand what you mean, my love," insisted Evan.

"I now know that those flashbacks are not useless."

"What are you *talking* about?" Evan replied, angrily.

"I know more than you think I know," she repeated, looking back up at Evan. "I know that, according to what you, yourself, have discovered, Thai's flashbacks are like bridges that can connect him to his past—that can connect him to us!"

A silver sheet of lighting flashed brightly just outside the window where Merienne stood, followed seconds later by the deafening sound of its explosive emanating force.

"And I now know that *you* know how to build upon those bridges," she continued, still clutching the locket. "I will never forgive you for what you have *not* done," she whispered. "By what justification would you choose to hide this precious knowledge from me, and from the world?"

"Merienne!" began Evan, in a low and strained voice. "I don't know what you are talking about. I have kept no secrets from you!"

Merienne carefully closed the locket and tucked it back into her bosom before turning back towards the window. The sky, now a deep purple, had begun twisting itself into a massive, rain-wrapped funnel.

"Merienne, my darling," continued Evan, urgently, "now is not the time to discuss whatever it is you believe has happened. We *need* to get into the bunker, or we may not survive!"

"What good is a bunker when the greatest threat to us is within these walls?" she cried, her voice trembling but strong.

A brighter flash of light appeared, followed by a louder clap and echoing boom.

"The journal that you thought you had hidden," she continued, while staring at the sky, "was left open on the desk in your laboratory while you were traveling, and I read every word. Every single word, Evan . . . including the details of the discoveries you have made."

"Merienne! I have no such journal," insisted Evan. "I've been retired from the memory sciences for years, and you *know* this! It is clear that the storm has upset you, and that you are fatigued. There is a cot downstairs where you can rest and settle your nerves," he continued in a voice much louder than the moment seemed to require. As if delivering a speech to someone unseen, Evan projected his voice towards the living room.

But then, gently taking hold of Merienne's chin until she would face him, Evan placed his pointer finger over his lips, urging her to whisper.

"I read every word that you wrote," she continued, her voice now much lower to comply with Evan's request. "I read your notes on—"

"Merienne…" whispered Evan, "*where* have you placed the journal?"

No sooner than Evan could ask again, did the sound of Osiem's collective voices refill the space amidst the background noise of the wind's relentless and rhythmic beating of the open air.

"THIS IS A MANDATORY ALL-CITIZENS ALERT! YOU ARE ORDERED TO TAKE IMMEDIATE COVER WITHIN YOUR BUNKERS. THE STRENGTH OF THIS STORM IS UNPRECEDENTED, WITH WINDS NOW MEASURED AT 700 KILOMETERS PER DECIDAY. NON-MOLLARD CITIZENS ARE REQUIRED TO SEEK THE IMMEDIATE SHELTER OF A BUNKER. IMPACT TO INFRASTRUCTURE IS EXPECTED. MOLLARDS MUST ENGAGE THE CLOSEST INTERNAL ENERGY STATION TO ENSURE THEY ARE FULLY CHARGED. WE REPEAT: THIS IS A MANDATORY ALL-CITIZEN'S EMERGENCY ALERT."

"The knowledge of how to build bridges between the empty and the replete—between what is Mollard and what is truly life, is everything," whispered Merienne, "and by the dates in your journal, you have had this knowledge for years! You've been sitting on evidence that memory is never really lost . . . not even to a Mollard! And yet, you have kept our son from having a more meaningful life!"

"Meaningful? According to *whom*, Merienne?" Evan returned, sharply. "Remembering a life of suffering won't bring any more meaning to Thai! The life he had is not *worth* remembering!"

"But that is not your choice to make!" she cried. "You do not have the right to keep him from seeing and from being who he is! Being his father does not give you the *right* to let him languish in this miserable state that is neither life nor death, knowing *full well* that there is hope! You are not only his *father*—you were and will *always* be a scientist who took an oath. And I implore you to remember your oath: *'To them, I bend this knee and humbly offer that which I have come to know by these good works.'* Where is the scientist who took that oath today? The one who promised to honor that oath throughout his life?"

"Merienne, please!" pressed Evan, his voice now stern, yet beholden to a whisper. "The journal—I have reasons for keeping it secret. The world is simply not ready for the discoveries that I have made. I do not expect you to understand, and I promise you that I will explain *everything* to you later. But for now, I—I *must* know where you have placed the journal. I must know *now*!"

Merienne pulled away from Evan and steadied herself against the window ledge as the trees around their yard gave way to the storm, taking custody of them and ripping them from their roots.

"Merienne!" Evan urged. "I have no time to explain the choices I have made, given this urgency. We are *ordered* to get into the bunker! We are out of time!"

In a frantic search, Evan checked the tabletops and bookshelf, the waste bin and below the couch, before tossing its pillows onto the floor. And then, as though defeated, he eventually turned back towards Merienne. The explosions of thunder were now so loud, they became too painful to hear. Extending his arm in her direction, he admonished Merienne to take his hand and retreat with him into the bunker.

"We are out of time, Merienne!" he cried over the storm's deafening bellow.

“What is time, Evan?” cried Merienne. “And what value does time have to us? It has not healed me from the pain that I bear. And from what I see, it has not healed you. Yesterday, today, and tomorrow have always—and will always—feel like the day they took him away. I have no loyalty to time. It has been no friend to us! And now that we are out of time, tell me . . . was keeping the greatest secret of your life worth it in the end?”

“Merienne, I am begging you to come with me now!” pleaded Evan.

“Unless you promise me that you will reveal what you have discovered and share what you know with the world, affording *everyone*—including our son—the chance to be liberated, I will not go into the bunker!” she cried. “I will not go! Whatever caused you to keep this a secret, I want no part of! I would rather be swept up by the wind than go hide into the darkness with you!”

A heavy, purple hue quickly snuffed out the remaining light from the sun, and a force of wind greater than the building could bear tore the roof and part of the upper floor away, scattering its parts across the sky and leaving its steel frame bent and mangled. Soon thereafter, a downpour of cold rain splattered the lower floor where Merienne and Evan stood, accompanied by Osiem’s instructive voices, which could now barely be heard.

Evan, as if frozen, gawked in disbelief at the sight of the open sky. The wind vane, once firmly positioned above the backyard laboratory became dislodged, and slammed into the window where Merienne stood, causing the window to splinter. Suddenly lifted off the floor, Merienne and Evan began to be drawn up into the whirling vortex of wind above them.

But Evan's quick grasp of an emergency steel handle bolted to the wall beside him re-anchored them as they dangled, tethered to one another only by the strength of Evan's grip upon Merienne's arm.

"Merienne!" screamed Evan. "The steel handle behind you! Grab it, my love! Grab it with your other hand and *hold on*!"

But unresponsive to his demand, Merienne stared back at Evan, and smiled. "Promise me!" she said. "Promise me now!"

"Merienne, *please!* I'm losing my grip!" Evan cried, struggling to keep her from slipping away. "Grab the other handle! I can't hold on any longer!"

The loose items, both big and small—a potted plant, Merienne's sweater, the dining table and chairs, each took turns giving into the wind's consuming demand.

And as Merienne began to slip away, she stared deeply into Evan's eyes. *"To them,"* she cried, *"I bend this knee and humbly offer that which I have come to know by these good works."*

But now beyond his grip, he could scarcely hear her recite the words he knew so well. Overwrought with despair, Evan repeatedly called out to Merienne, but his anguish was not enough to negotiate with what appeared to be the wind's determination to consume her.

And in an instant, she was gone.

Soaked by the rain and with both hands locked around the steel handles of the wall he had affixed himself to, Evan held on for what felt like an eternity until the raging wind passed over him. Both stunned and filled with grief, he released his grip on the steel handles and fell to the floor.

"THIS IS AN ALL-CITIZENS ALERT. NON-MOLLARDS ARE ORDERED TO REMAIN WITHIN THEIR BUNKERS UNTIL FURTHER NOTICE AND STAY TUNED TO THEIR LOCAL WEATHER STATIONS FOR ADDITIONAL INSTRUCTIONS. MOLLARD CITIZENS UNABLE TO ACCESS THEIR LOCAL ENERGY STATIONS SHOULD CONTACT THE CENTRAL AUTHORITY. WE REPEAT, MOLLARDS IN NEED OF ASSISTANCE SHOULD CONTACT THE CENTRAL AUTHORITY IMMEDIATELY."

Now delirious, Evan frantically rose to his feet, running through each room of the house in search of Merienne. But, unable to find her, he finally approached the room he had been unable to enter for many *many* years.

Turning the door knob and stumbling inside, Evan fell to his knees upon seeing his journal, perched on top of the small pillow where Thai used to sleep.

Episode 30
What It Took to Survive

General Jordson summoned the reports of his key military advisors, all of whom had been preparing for his order to strike.

Second Military Leader Forris eagerly gave the first report. “Most of the laborers have been secured, General,” announced Forris, “and the halls of the castle have been cleared.”

“*Most*?” repeated Jordson.

“Eh . . . yes, sir. There are some—there are *a few* that are presently unaccounted for, General,” Forris explained, awkwardly.

Jordson furrowed his brow and then shifted his attention to Senior Lieutenant Burrow, whose fingers were restlessly tapping the top of the conference room table.

“Mobile Battalion and heavy artillery units are in place along the Northern Border, General,” stated Burrow, confidently leaning forward. “And they have *all* been briefed on their immediate objectives. Heavily armed ground forces at the front line are in position to repress penetration and backup units are ready to detach, depending upon how the enemy maneuvers. We will also continue to monitor the Southern line, just in case, sir."

"And what is their anticipated speed of response, Lieutenant?" replied Jordson.

"All units have been trained to be self-sufficient, sir," Lieutenant Burrow replied, "and I have given each Battalion on-the-ground decision-making power. Our biggest vulnerability is the reload and recharge time, but I believe we have enough units in place to limit down time."

With a nod of approval, Jordson shifted his attention to the Director of Security, Lieutenant Curio, who appeared to be rather perturbed. And then moving his gaze to the Lieutenant sitting next to Curio, General Jordson addressed them both. "What are the intelligence reports?" pressed Jordson.

"I will give the report, General!" inserted Lieutenant Curio, leaning forward.

"Go on," Jordson replied.

"According to my surveillance," continued Curio. "I am now *confident* that we are strictly dealing with a surface invasion, with *no* signs of a North-facing air attack. By every indication, their detachments are strictly a ground artillery advance, and I would say we have all bases completely covered, given a full and thorough account of this threat. I have taken your advice, General, and your previous counsel. I wholeheartedly agree that what we *thought* was a threat to our Southern Border was simply staging, meant to distract us. However, given all that we now know, our assembly of ground forces along the

Northern Border—and our pending maneuver—positions us quite well, General."

"Thank you, Lieutenant Curio. I appreciate your confidence," responded Jordson, his right eyebrow slightly arched. "And what do *you* say, Co-Lieutenant?" Jordson continued. "Have we thought of everything?"

In an instant, all eyes in the room—except for that of Lieutenant Curio's—slowly shifted over to Uriss. Fully uniformed, but none the less bedraggled, the one who had fallen from grace was keenly aware that his presence was generally unwanted, and that his pardon and reappointment to the Royal Military Court had left much of the group utterly bemused.

Folding his hands carefully in front of him while bowing his head, Uriss chose a tone aimed at placating his disapprovers. "Lieutenant Curio's assessment of the enemy's surface maneuver is completely accurate, General," began Uriss, in deference to his peer.

"There you have it, General," inserted Curio. "We are all in agreement of the facts."

"However," Uriss continued, piously, "considering the skills that our enemy has shown in leveraging electromagnetic warfare and their demonstrated ability to spoof our distributed sensor systems, I have increased surveillance of those sensors and refined our filters to reduce the chance of false reports . . . General. I have also advised both General Hemming and General Byrd to prepare for missile defense and to fully ready our ballistic interceptor units."

"Completely unnecessary!" snapped Lieutenant Curio angrily, his face now hot and flush. "What would General Lordermun say to this outrage?!"

Unamused by Curio's outburst, Jordson nodded for Uriss to continue with his report. Remembering that General Lordermun's poor health stymied his ability to provide counsel during the current crisis, Curio realized that all decisions regarding how missiles would be leveraged now fell upon General Hemming and General Byrd.

"In my . . . *spare time*, sir," continued Uriss, "I have been studying—among other things —the scope of what is termed 'energy weaponry.' And based upon what I have learned, we should make every move from here assuming that the enemy will, in fact, have the upper hand. While I have made adjustments to our distributed sensors, I cannot promise they will be foolproof."

"This is preposterous!" snapped Lieutenant Curio. "I have already made my assessment clear! And as the Lieutenant in charge of intelligence and surveillance I—"

"They are," interrupted Uriss, "extraordinarily prepared for this war, Lieutenant. And the war they are waging will *not* only be fought as a ground maneuver. They are much too advanced for that. Consider that there is a second war that we may *still* have to fight in a space where we do not yet have our footing. As such, General Jordson's prior caution—that the enemy has the ability to use our surveillance sensors against us, is of the soundest counsel."

"How is it that you would have such a hearty understanding of the prior counsel given to us by General Jordson?" snapped Curio.

“Well, by the written briefs I have been given to review, of course,” Uriss offered awkwardly.

Jordson’s eyes narrowed as he studied Uriss more intently.

“And as a result, I have recommended that Generals Hemming and Byrd remain prepared for the worst and ready the kingdom for an attack we may not realize until moments prior,” continued Uriss.

Stunned by Uriss’ suggestion and shocked by his confidence in reaching out to Generals Hemming and Byrd, Lieutenant Curio’s jaw dropped as he looked over at Jordson.

“While our ground strategy is brilliant,” continued Uriss, “and we should thank Lieutenant Burrow for all of her efforts, I still fear that the full capacity of our intelligence has been blinded, and as such—”

“General Jordson!” retorted Lieutenant Curio, rising to his feet. “I beg your deepest pardon, sir, but we are awaiting your order to strike—and I do not intend to sit here and listen to the bombastic musings of a . . . of a . . .” Then, halting, in an attempt to compose himself, Curio scanned the room, seeking tacit approval for his outburst.

“Of a what . . . Lieutenant Curio?” asked Jordson, his forehead distorted by his frown. “I might remind you that Co-Lieutenant Uriss is here on order of your king.”

Slowly descending back into his chair and briefly glancing at Uriss, Lieutenant Curio seemed to suddenly regain his ability to control himself.

"Generals," urged Jordson, now looking over at General Hemming and General Byrd.

Hemming, whose brow was drenched in more than its usual amount of perspiration, was noticeably thinner and less robust than the last time they had all convened, his diminished consumption of Teal oil now showing worrisome effects. While a more solid-looking General Byrd, whom although non-hearing, sat quietly as he tracked the full course of the conversation using his advanced lip-reading skills. Albeit, his military appointment was once thought by his comrades to be a decision highly overshadowed by the fact that the royals' first-born child was deaf, Byrd's reliably sound decisions over the years—and his successful partnership with General Hemming—had displaced any prior doubts about his effectiveness as a joint leader. Perched on the edge of his seat with one hand firmly cupping his chin, General Byrd deferred to Hemming to deliver their response.

With an unsteady hand, General Hemming mopped his brow using what appeared to be a well-soaked kerchief before responding. "In all my years serving as your Missile Defense Minister," began Hemming. "I am loathe to announce that General Byrd and I have never been so *unsure* of our ability to defend the kingdom as we are today. But we are bound by the truth, and the truth is that we are not at all confident. As such, we *both* agree that unless our interceptors are fully prepared, we are likely to be defeated by the enemy's ability to manipulate what we are seeing . . . .and what we are not. Therefore, we have opted to ready our anti-ballistic units. Both units are now in position and fully equipped. I will acknowledge, however, that the risks of deploying interception units prematurely are going to be very high, given the unpredictability of the enemy. And although we may be fooled into action, we have little choice. We have no other option now but to interpret the citing of any approaching projectiles as a threat worthy of our *immediate* and most forceful response, whether that threat is real or not. If the threat is credible, we will be all the better for our action. And if the threat is merely a mirage, we—"

"—We will have *recklessly* expended our greatest and most powerful payloads across the open sky. That is, *in fact*, what you're saying, General Hemming, is it not?" inserted Senior Lieutenant Burrow.

"As General Byrd continues to advise me," retorted Hemming, "at times we are called to rely on our weaker hand if the primary hand we have been given is constrained."

Alarmed by the plan but agreeing with him in her heart of hearts, Burrow finally nodded in concession. In an attempt to still his recently developed, and persistent cough, Hemming hastily wet his throat with a glass of water placed before him by General Byrd.

"Co-Lieutenant," continued Hemming, looking directly at Uriss in a moment that was dreadfully awkward, considering Hemming's prior vote in favor of Uriss' execution, "we . . . thank you," he said. "Although the general and I had already come to the same conclusion as you have, we honor the clarity of your thinking nonetheless."

Acutely aware of what appeared to Uriss to be General Hemming's last season, Uriss bowed his head in Hemming's direction to communicate his respect.

"Very well then," responded Jordson, slowly rising from his chair, a signal to the group that the delivery of reports was over.

A low sound of rolling thunder could be heard as General Jordson turned towards Plebony's statue. Grinding his jaw, he knew that his own doubts about what he truly believed in would have to be set aside. And, following the customs of the kingdom, he summoned the group's religious compliance.

"All rise," he said, his voice now stern. "Let us pray to none other than Plebony herself and may we each appeal to her mercy and ask her for the blessing of victory."

All immediately rose to face Plebony's stone frame, now washed in the light of the rising sun behind her. Folding their hands and bowing their heads in prayer—save one Uriss who remained defiant—each prayed for triumph as they placed their faith upon the carefully etched stone that was Plebony's gracile image. And as though the exchange of force had already begun, the sound of approaching thunder seemed to detonate around the castle like the dropping of bombs.

Drifting off from the prayer he was leading, Jordson caught a glimpse of the sun rising over the Solar Dome and recalled the words that King Thio had not only shared with Anglid, but had also once shared with him:

"No battle is worth it if you do not understand why you are fighting. There must be a purpose to your ire and a meaning to fight—a reason for ending your opponent's life. As long as there is, you will fight well."

"Indeed, you will fight *well!*" incanted Flexix, his voice inaudible and disguised by the sound of the roaring wind that he had become. "But not because of any blessings you will convince yourselves came from the slab of stone to which you pray!" he wailed, while consuming nearly everything within his path. "You will fight well because I, the god you all despise, will be by your side!"

Jordson slowly turned to face the group again and gestured to Second Military Leader Forris that the time had come to enter the Command Center. Anticipating that this would be Jordson's next request, Forris had already opened the door of the conference room, clearing the way for a now impatient Jordson, who swiftly walked past him and down the corridor.

Then, stopping abruptly and circling back over to Forris, Jordson leaned in for a brief exchange. "How many laborers are presently unaccounted for?" demanded Jordson.

"I believe there are seven or eight of them, sir," replied Forris.

"So, we have *not*, in fact, secured the castle then," insisted Jordson, giving Forris a stern look, his displeasure unmistakable.

"We are in the process of handling it, General," offered Forris, awkwardly.

"If they are unaccounted for," pressed Jordson, "then they are hiding. If they are hiding, they cannot be trusted. They are to be executed on sight. Do I make myself clear, Senior Lieutenant?" demanded Jordson.

"Yes. Yes, General," Forris replied. "Perfectly clear, sir."

Following Jordson and Forris, the remaining entourage of advisors filed into the corridor and slowly entered the war room.

"Welcome, sir!" saluted Brigadier General Skiff, serving as Director of War Room Operations.

Immediately granting Skiff permission to be at ease, Jordson moved to quickly address the military personnel positioned at their individual work stations on the floor below. In full salute, each member of the Operations team looked up at Jordson as he settled into the Commander's chair on the glass-enclosed balcony looming above them.

Upon the order of Director Skiff, aerial and front-line views of the Northern Border filled the large three-panel screen that covered the entire height of the room's three walls. Taking in the view of what was a daunting enemy presence, Jordson grit his teeth, refusing to display his concerns or his doubts. However, a final accounting of the scope of his objective—compared to the level of artillery fire he had at his disposal and the stamina of the troops that would bear the burden of turning his objective into victory—was the painful reality secretly eroding Jordson's resolve. But, as questionable as he now believed victory might be, he knew that he at least owed the kingdom the honor of the fight.

Now, flanked by Uriss and his other core advisors, Jordson positioned his headset to deliver his much-anticipated directive.

"On my signal," Jordson began, "we will deliver two hundred thousand rounds of artillery fire over the next deciday, utilizing our multi-tube rocket launchers and targeting deep into the center of their current formation—which I anticipate is the location of their on-the-ground command. At the close of that salvo, we will immediately attack both the front and rear formations, focusing our strategy on saturation fire into the kill zone while we work in parallel to recharge and reposition our first responders. Senior Lieutenant Burrows, are your units ready?"

"CK-MRLs are ready, sir," responded Burrows. "With a confirmed launch range of one hundred and fifty kilometers."

"Please be advised," continued Jordson, re-addressing the group, "the unfortunate fact remains that both our operational *and* our military assets are vulnerable, given their proximity to the Northern Border. We must maintain triple reinforcement of all of those assets," he urged, programming his dash panel to zoom in on the location of their main Teal oil refineries along the Northwest front and the Northeastern location of their military production and training camps. "We should assume persistent attempts on these assets given their locations, and no matter what is to come, we *mus*t defend those assets at all costs."

A unanimous nod from everyone in the room was the confirmation that Jordson had hoped to receive.

"I want each of you to know," he continued, "that it is my greatest honor to lead you all, and to lead our kingdom, through this battle. I—like you—will continue to pray for our victory!"

Then, nodding his head, he gave the order to attack, an act of which transformed the mounting tension along the kingdom's Northern rim into an unrelenting series of incendiary rockets delivered in succession to the enemy.

"Are those bombs I'm hearing or is that thunder?" whispered alija, trembling in the corner of Uriss' secret workroom, where she and six other laborers sat huddled in the corner.

"Do not speak it in words!" signed dedarian, admonishing alija for her error.

"Any exchange of bombs would be at the border, alija," signed ezra, a laborer younger than alija, but one whose wisdom had curried her respect within the group. "Since we have always been told that the castle is at least three hundred and twenty kilometers from both the Northern and Southern lines, we wouldn't be able to hear the exchange of bombs from here."

"She's right," signed iroo, a frail, skeletal-looking laborer who had deteriorated significantly during the rationing. "What you're hearing is just a bad storm, and—like this war—I promise it will pass." iroo then leaned forward and took alija's trembling hands into the skin and bones that were left of his.

"But even if the kingdom wins this war, what will become of us, iroo?" signed dedarian, frantically. "Our queen—who has always loathed us—now knows that we are different than the other laborers. She has seen our markings and knows that we are linked to Anya. Knowing the queen, if she survives, there will be no end of torture for us. And, as we have no word of the queen's demise, we can only assume that the worst is in front of us."

"What does it matter?" signed intruthen, the dwarf laborer. Standing on Uriss' chair, intruthen turned his attention away from the screen he was intently monitoring just long enough to engage the group. "Bombs, thunder, the queen's ire . . . what is the difference at *this* point to us? In fair time, this will *all* be irrelevant." Then, returning his gaze to the computer, he appeared spellbound as he followed the computational roadmap given him by Uriss to monitor the oscillations of their neural activity, and the synchronized changes within their brains.

alija, who remained disturbed by what she felt was intruthen's obsession with the Vangora Rima, shot him a look of disapproval. But, as though he believed it was his fate to ensure the group's safe passage into VR, intruthen took his instructions from Uriss seriously, constantly reminding each member of the group to adjust and tighten the electroencephalogram caps that Uriss had carefully designed for each of them.

"But I am no longer sure!" signed alija.

"No longer sure about what?" most of them signed back.

"I continue to question this . . . this *decision*—this path we are choosing to take," signed alija, carefully touching the outside of the cap she wore and nervously fingering the electrodes.

"You continue to question this my dear, *dear* alija. And I have always wondered why," signed ezra. "The decision—*our* decision—was sealed when we made our pact with Anya. We agreed that if the kingdom were ever to be at war that we would assemble and take our destiny into our own hands, if for no other reason, than that it has always been royal tradition to imprison the laborers during times of uncertainty. But by the brilliance of King Uriss, we have yet another path." ezra gently wiped away the tear that slowly rolled down alija's cheek. "Remember," ezra continued, "that we chose this path *together*, all agreeing that if one of us has doubts—then none of us has permission. We will need your blessing."

"But what if we're wrong?" insisted alija, signing emphatically back at ezra. "What if this act we are about to commit is the greatest of sins?"

"The greatest of sins?!" snapped intruthen. "Have you not learned *anything* from King Uriss?" he signed, furiously. "By his counsel, he has guided us to—"

"Perhaps it is your incomprehensibly miserable size that propels you so vehemently forward! Have you no shame, intruthen?" alija signed back. "And, might I remind *all* of us that it was never the guidance of King Uriss for us to kill ourselves!"

"We are not *killing* ourselves, alija. We're dying!" signed ezra."We are all—including you—severely malnourished and our bodies are giving way."

alija placed her hands over her face and began to weep.

zakum, the oldest amongst them, tapped his hand rapidly against one of his legs to gain the attention of the group. Depleted by hunger, zakum leaned his frail frame against the chest of scolom, his son. "It's true," signed zakum. "Although I have done my best to bring you all as much Teal oil as I could find—dividing it from King Thio's personal reserve and praying he wouldn't notice—the fact remains that there just wasn't enough, and what little he had left he took with him, leaving no provisions for any of us."

"But what of the stockpiles? Surely, they're not going to just leave us to fend for ourselves?" signed alija.

An awkward silence consumed the already silent space within which they communicated.

"The remaining stockpile of Teal oil in the kingdom is now under the control of the military," replied zakum, struggling to find the energy to continue to sign. "We can expect their focus to be the nourishment of the troops."

"But there is *still* an endless supply of warm water and flesh!" signed alija, desperately.

"And as we all know, warm water and flesh cannot sustain us," interjected iroo. "We have no more Teal oil, alija, and without that, we have no more time."

A loud crack of thunder seemed to burst through the walls of the castle, sending a tremor deep into the basement room where they hid.

"And so," signed alija, desperately, "we are to die here like vermin, huddled in the corner of the cold basement cell that once housed our king?"

"I have no shame, alija, and neither should you," whispered zakum, with almost no energy left in his hands to sign. "We have done our best to survive the life we have been given, and as the kingdom attempts to defend what it stands for, I, for one, have no reservations in parting paths with it. I have pledged my loyalty to the throne, bending so far down that I have kissed the shoes of royalty and its progeny. I have swallowed my pride, and expelled it on the other side as I did my waste. And on my journey, I developed the skills of self-hatred and the hatred of those like me as a way to justify my suffering. And as I take account of my life, I know that it was my fear of Plebony and her judgment that helped me to convince myself that I deserved to suffer. In convincing myself that it was by my own shortcomings that I should suffer, I was able to prevent myself from condemning the god to which we all bow. I did what it took to survive! And now, at the end of my life I have no regrets, because through it *all*, I continued to place my trust and gratitude in all of you. I am ready to accept the path offered to us by dear King Uriss, our beloved king and loyal council. I am ready to leave this path for another."

As alija listened to zakum, she closed her eyes, finding comfort in the gentleness of his voice, as she slowly accepted the message within it. Then, upon reopening her eyes, she scanned the small room, noticing a partially drawn drape at the room's opposite side. Straining to see what was inside, she made out the side of a male frame dressed in Tungsten blue—a color that zakum had once told Uriss was his favorite. And following the line of the jacket's sleeve, she could see that the thumb of the figure's hand was adorned with a Tungsten blue ring.

"iroo, zakum . . . can you hear us?" whispered intruthen, no longer speaking in sign and shifting his gaze away from the screen with eyes now filled with fear and curiosity. scolom pressed his father's limp body against his chest and wept while ezra and dedarian also worked to try and revive a fading iroo.

"Dear father, can you hear me?" scolom whispered, muffling his grief into the nape of zakum's neck, while alija slid her hand back into iroo's and noticed its fading warmth.

"They're withdrawing!" signed intruthen, urgently. "And in line with the instructions given to me, we *must* decide on behalf of iroo and zakum while their gamma bands are high!"

Following the first letter sequence of their names and the numbers tattooed on their skin, intruthen started to enter the cipher that Uriss had created, careful to remember that Anya's tattoo was the number eight. In following the sequence, intruthen entered "aadeiisz87654321," effectively hacking his way into the VR.

Then, after a brief moment of stillness, all eyes shifted to alija.

"What do you say, alija?" signed ezra, her face now pleading. "intruthen will have to do the upload while their brain waves are still active. We will soon need your blessing!"

With the doors of the Vangora Rima now open, intruthen's heart raced as he spun around to obtain alija's decision.

"Requesting permission to launch, Commander?" stated Dugar's Senior Officer of Missile Operations.

Furious by the audacity of the kingdom's military overture, Dugar ultimately gave his approval to release two compact transonic missiles towards the Central Kingdom, which were sent barreling out of their confines past the speed of sound, decorating the morning sky with streams of tungsten blue.

Episode 31
Mirror, Mirror

"Will you ever find it in your heart to forgive me?" King Thio asked, slightly slouched in a chair within the private, heavily guarded chambers he had been provided.

Awaiting a response from an empty seat upon which he stared, Thio slowly raised the thin, silver vial he held in his hand, inhaling its contents even deeper into each nostril than he had just moments before. In his altered state, he managed to drop the vial, spilling some of its contents onto his robe and sending it rolling across the room's highly polished floor, until it disappeared beneath a bureau that sat cattycorner to a tall bookshelf stocked with manuscripts.

"Blasted misfortune!" he yelled, rising to his feet, before swaying and falling forward, the room now whirling around him as if it were floating just beyond his reach.

"zakum! zakum!" he called out impatiently, crawling across the floor towards the base of the bureau, in desperate pursuit of the vial. "zakum!" he continued, his eyes now facing the floor, upon which he could see a reflection of his own image. "I *implore* you to come here at *once!*"

No longer able to hold up the weight of his head as the muscles in his neck turned to jelly, Thio felt the cool surface of the smooth floor upon his face. And as the effects of the purple powder took over, the strange silence that came with its use slowly enveloped him. Unsure of its origin, a single drop of water fell upon his reflection—blurring the center of his image and oddly altering it, as if the water was composed of acid.

Weaving back and forth and trying desperately to keep his head up, Thio gasped at what appeared to be his reflection crumbling before him as he watched the outline of his head and neck crack and splinter, the fragments of which slowly gave way to the outline of a silhouette.

And there, before him, a face slowly emerged—reminiscent of his wise and dutiful servant.

"zakum!" Thio cried, in what was a mix of his euphoria, his relief, and his anger. "Why did you delay when I called?" he continued, falling deeper into delirium. "The punishment for keeping your king waiting is . . . is . . ." Now with slurred speech and his head too heavy for him to manage, Thio anchored his elbows to the floor and propped his wobbling head up into the palms of his trembling hands. "You must *never* disobey your king, and you must always come when you are summoned!" he managed to whisper, as additional drops of water—which, he now realized were flowing from his eyes—fell gently upon the image below him.

"But I *am* here, 'King' Thio," responded the image of zakum, his posture and countenance strikingly different than the zakum that Thio thought he had summoned. Seemingly aware of Thio's temporary inability to hear, the image of zakum slowly delivered its words through the use of the language that Thio had gifted to Anya. "I am here, but only long enough to answer the question that you have posed," zakum's image continued.

Stunned by its demeanor, Thio restudied the image in confusion and disbelief and, although all sound was lost to him, the absence of zakum's servitude pierced through the silence like the tower bells of the Plebonian Church.

"My question, indeed!" replied Thio, nearly speechless and painfully aware that something central to who they once were to one another was gone. "I know not of you!" continued Thio, squinting in an attempt to see the details of zakum's face. "Your tone . . . your *stature* . . . is not the zakum that I know. The servant who has been with me since my birth. He would *never* dare to speak to me in this way! Could it be that my need to rule in absentia has led you to lose your deference and fear of me so quickly?"

"What I feel is neither fear nor deference," the image replied, "and it is only the question that you posed to the one who is *also* in absentia that I have come here to answer."

Feeling the divide between them and with no model for interacting other than that of master to slave, Thio attempted to hold his position. "What has happened to you, zakum?" he slurred, completely taken over by the powder within him. "Has your ghost now come to torment me for leaving you with no provisions? *Surely* you must understand that it is the duty of royal blood to first save itself. It is the natural order of life! You were—and will *always* be—my servant."

The details of Zakum's face slowly started to blur and the outline of his image now began to fade.

"No! Please! *Please!*" cried Thio, desperately clawing at the floor. "I—I do not want you to go!"

"Do not despair, King Thio," the image replied, "as you have said, I will always be your servant. But, while I am no longer your servant in life, I will continue to serve you—as your *conscience!*"

Enraged by the audacity of zakum's message but riveted still, Thio shuddered as he wrestled against what felt like the depths of an unfamiliar emotion others might know as guilt.

"It seems that I, too, know not of you?" the image continued. "For your tone and your stature are not befitting of the king I once knew in you—"

"On the contrary!" inserted Thio angrily. "My tone as your king and my stature are as secure as the walls of my castle! And I will hold reign there as I will hold my reign here over you!" Thio's anger began to mount as he struggled to re-secure his drooping head into the questionable strength of his hands.

"And yet," the image replied, "my posture is no more that of the slave you once knew, than *your* posture is that of a king's. Could it be, that on *this* day, both your pride and what you *thought* was your providence are beginning to unshackle you in the same way that the constraints of life have unshackled me?"

Completely speechless and no longer able to face the gravity of zakum's message, Thio hastily covered his eyes. But in the darkness to which he fled, the image of an empty chair made its way forth through the reprieve and absence of light. Glimmering with what appeared to be light from the sun, a thick vine of flowers with large, closed petals began to enrobe the chair's back rest and arms, and eventually curled itself tightly around the chair's legs.

Fearful of what he might see, Thio hastened to turn his head away and open his eyes but realized that—to his horror—his eyes were sealed shut.

"Please! Please!" he cried, his voice echoing through the room. "I do not *want* to see what is before me! Release me at once from this place—I do not want to *know* what dwells here within these depths!" In a failed attempt to open his eyes, the flat, opaque blackness became deeper still, as though the vast darkness around him was slowly giving way to a richer, darker void of nothingness beyond itself.

Yet, against what appeared to be the intrinsic color of an endless void, the chair, adorned with its robe of flowers, remained in position—shimmering and defiant. Then, as if entranced, Thio watched as his hands slowly sculpted the air to form the silent words of sign.

"What does . . ." he began, slowly weaving his message with the movements of his hands. "What does it mean to be . . . forgiven?" His face, now moist with tears, glistened from the light of the chair's glowing brilliance. "As I have shown myself at times unable to forgive others, I am sure that, as I gaze upon your absence, I am at least worthy of your condemnation and of your choice not to forgive me. This, among many things . . . I know I shall never have the power to change. Even as ruler and King, I am aware of what I do not have the power to alter. And to this day, I lament that I had no power over this painfully deafening silence within which you lived your days and your nights. It was my hope that by teaching you the art of symbols and signs that I would be able to close the gap between us. But in the end, you used that gift against me for an ideal that had no *place* in the light of day. Like so many others before you, I am aggrieved to realize that your ability to disappoint me was one of your greatest skills. But while, to my own eyes, your choice to subvert me was a desecration of your birthright, I find my rage now giving way to my regret. Will you relieve me now of your condemnation, as the stonewall of my condemnation towards you begins to weaken? Or is our condemnation of one another to forever be set in steel? And what, after all, will it mean to be forgiven when all that is left of you is what my failing memory allows me to keep? But . . . I ask you, my dear Anya, what substance is there in a king who cannot stomach the results of his own decisions? And what sanity is there in a king who yearns for forgiveness from those who will never be able to provide it?"

A sudden sound of heavy, fast-paced footsteps broke the silence, startling Thio out of his haze, and allowed him to finally open his eyes. And there, within the sheen of the floor, was his own bedraggled image staring back at him. Desperate for zakum to return and provide the answer he said he had come to deliver, Thio clawed against the floor in a frenzy that caused his fingernails to be torn from their beds, sullying the surface with streaks of blood.

"I know not of you!" he yelled, staring at his reflection, his hearing now slowly returning. "Your tone . . . and your stature . . ." he continued. "It is true! They are not befitting of the king I knew myself to be—!"

"King Thio!" yelled an individual, whose voice accompanied an urgent knocking delivered upon the chamber door.

Now recognizing the voice to be one of his royal guards, Thio gathered every ounce of strength he had within him to sit up and, as the knocking became stronger, the guard's urgency became more certain.

"Your Grace!" the Guard yelled. "We have come to deliver important news."

"In a moment," returned Thio, buying enough time to hoist himself up onto the large wooden bench that was positioned by the bookshelf. And, in an attempt to better explain his position on the stool, he quickly grabbed a manuscript from one of the shelves and placed it on his lap. "You may enter," he announced, fumbling aimlessly through the pages of the manuscript as the chamber door quickly opened.

"Your Grace," said the entering guard, accompanied by several members of the king's personal entourage. "Forgive us for this intrusion, but we must bring you news of the queen."

In his haste to rise to his feet, the manuscript dropped to the floor as he clutched the bookshelf beside him to keep himself from falling. "What is the urgency?" Thio asked, studying the demeanor of those entering the room.

Queen Evaline's attending physician stepped forth to deliver the news. "There has been a turn of events, Your Grace," announced the physician, with his head bowed in protocol. "The Queen's vital signs have taken a turn for the worse and I fear that her time may well be at hand."

"*What?*" shrieked Thio in disbelief.

"Her eyes have opened, Your Grace," the physician continued, "but I fear her time is short."

Thio slumped back down onto the stool, his face now blank and his jaw slightly opened.

"We have come to hurry you to her chambers, Your Grace," the physician continued, stepping slightly closer to Thio, "as she is asking for you."

"How could this be?" continued Thio, as though speaking to himself. "Her procedure was said to be a success! She has a mechanical heart!"

"A mechanical . . . *heart*, Your Grace?" replied the physician, both curious and confused by Thio's statement. Raising his head long enough to share an askance look with the others, all of whom had taken note of Thio's disheveled appearance, the physician cleared his throat to ease the awkwardness of the moment.

Now recalling that the procedure to implant the prosthetic organ within Evaline was an act mired in secrecy, Thio moved to quickly cover his trail. "I mean a newly *repaired* heart," Thio fumbled, "given to her by the great . . . um . . ."

"Ye—Yes, Your Grace," replied the physician, now convinced that the king's mental state was unraveling.

"There is not much time, Your Grace," inserted the Lead Guard, re-establishing the urgency. "Shall we escort you to the queen?"

"Yes," Thio replied, in a low voice almost too hard to hear. "I must go to her."

Following the instructions of the attending physician—who noted that Thio was in no condition to run to the queen's side—a wheeled seat was delivered upon which Thio was hastened to the queen's chambers. There, upon entering her room, were several whom had already started to gather by her bedside. Surrounded by her family members—including her only surviving sibling, Ennaasciowt—Evaline lay limp and expressionless. With nearly no color left in her skin, other than the dark circles beneath her eyes, it was as though she needed to be told that her heart was now invincible in order to help her to heal.

In a desperate act to try and redirect the course of things to come, Thio abruptly ordered that the room be cleared at once, sending the grieving crowd scurrying into the hallway. With strict instructions from Thio that they were not to be disturbed, the Lead Guard shut the chamber doors of Evaline's room, leaving only Thio by her side. Taking her frail hand into his, he raised her fingers to his lips to blow the warmth of his breath upon them.

"There is strength in you that you do not know," he began, "but I must tell you now, the truth—"

"Shh . . ." the queen replied, closing and then re-opening her eyes. Staring directly at Thio, she parted her lips to try and speak.

"Do not exhaust yourself, my love!" insisted Thio, placing his finger gently over her lips. "You must *first* hear what I have come to say. Your heart—"

"My heart . . ." Evaline repeated, again closing her eyes.

"*Yes*, my darling!" replied Thio, encouraged by her response and convinced that he could bring her around. "Your heart—"

"Belongs," she interrupted, "to Anglid's . . . father."

"Be sure to collect that book that's fallen there," instructed the estate's head custodian. "And please ensure that you inspect everything in here, and that you dust all surfaces. There can be no imperfections during King Thio's stay with us."

"Yes, Madame," replied two of the attendants assigned to Thio's chambers. Eager to bring the room back into its proper order, they began their chores as soon as the custodian left the room.

"Do you suppose I should close this book?" the youngest of the attendants asked his elder counterpart, while carefully lifting the manuscript up from its face-down position.

"Oh no, not at all!" replied the older attendant, kneeling down to pass a warm, moistened cloth over the dried streaks of blood on the floor. "If you close it, King Thio will be sure to lose his place. See if you can find a bookmark or something with which to mark the page."

Keenly aware that all of the manuscripts on the bookshelf belonged to the region's interim Governor, Ennaasciowt—and that the pages of the manuscripts were never to be folded—the younger attendant scanned the room for something but, could find nothing that seemed fitting.

"Might we use this?" offered the older attendant, handing him a large, single flower petal.

"Where did you get *this?*" the younger attendant asked, fingering the petal's oddly velvet surface.

"Right there upon that chair in the corner," the older attendant replied. "It was just sitting there, by itself—and the color is *strange*, isn't it? I don't believe I've ever seen a color quite like *this* before. But there you are—a bookmark, as good as any!"

The younger attendant carefully placed the petal onto the open page of the manuscript that, at first glance, appeared to be blemished with a smear of blood. Covering the smear with the petal, he closed the book, marking the beginning of a chapter titled 'Forgiveness.'

Episode 32
The Reason

Ennaasciowt sat in silence as he stared into the flames that raged wildly within the stone hearth built to confine them. A stately room - once filled with the vibrant voices of his siblings - the original sofa upon which he sat, the family portraits, and intricate hand-carved furnishings all served to be the guardians of his most precious memories.

Now the only surviving sibling, he wrestled with the passing of Evaline and with his relief that the Western Territories would no longer be under threat of full annexation by King Thio. Once, as sovereign as the Independent Settlements of the South, the West had become a territorial interest of the kingdom after Evaline had accepted King Thio's proposal to be betrothed.

But now, upon her death, and upon Ennaasciowt's inheritance of the West, his sister's passing was to him . . . bitter sweet.

Far from supporting the values of the kingdom, Ennaasciowt's concerns over having his homeland aligned to the CK had extended far beyond his opinion of the king. An open opponent of the Plebonian Church, Ennaasciowt remained unapologetic in his defense of free thinking and in his commitment to what he called the "science of thought."

Convinced that Ennaasciowt would prove to be a destabilizing force within the territories that Thio had hoped he would one day control, he deeply disapproved of Evaline's decision to designate the role of the region's interim governorship to the youngest—and most renegade—of her two brothers. Preferring that she had selected the second oldest sibling, Nigel, Thio and Nigel remained cordial until he had eventually passed away from the same ailment that had plagued Evaline.

However, despite Thio's point of view, it was Ennaasciowt whom Evaline had adored the most and to whom she entrusted the governance of the region. Although their ideologies were on decidedly different paths, the bond between she and Ennaasciowt had remained unshakable, as it was only from him that she would tolerate even the *slightest* criticism of the Plebonian scriptures.

Challenging Evaline over the years to recognize the idolatrous nature of the religion she clung so desperately to, Ennaasciowt had been committed to one day saving Evaline from herself. And Evaline, for her part, had remained secretly intrigued by Ennaasciowt's views that no single religion could ever represent the highest and purest form of god.

"What can I do to assuage your suffering, my beloved husband?" whispered Wybrany, his wife of ten seasons.

Turning his gaze away from the fire, Ennaasciowt pulled her closer to him and gently kissed her hand. "Knowing that you are carrying our child—who will one day refill this room with the unbridled energy that only children can bring—is my greatest comfort," he replied. "I only wish that the timing could have been different and that Evaline could have seen me become a father."

"I'm so sorry, my love," replied Wybrany, leaning her head upon his shoulder.

"But I am certain," he continued, forcing himself to smile, "that she would have scolded me well for the latitude I plan to give this child."

"And still, she would have secretly admired your strength, the way she always did, my love," Wybrany replied, taking Ennaasciowt's hand and placing it upon her abdomen. "For, as much as you may have worried her, she would have been so proud of you."

Closing his eyes, it was as though Evaline was sitting right across from him again, spending time together—as they had—in their youth.

"I will warn you," she teased, on the eve of her forty-second season, as they positioned the pieces on the board of her favorite game, "I have played this game many times, and will be sure to win! Perhaps we should lower the stakes, little brother?"

And as his memory served him, he remembered being unmoved by her attempt to shake his confidence, whereby he placed an even higher wager on the table—a small, wooden box, which Evaline knew to contain a collection of his favorite alabaster stones.

Selected from the family's quarry, the stones were buffed into a treasure of milky-smooth marbles as a holiday gift for Ennaasciowt. Often tapping them ever so slightly, and measuring the speed at which one stone would collide into the other, the value of this exercise had often escaped the family but was known to keep Ennaasciowt captivated for hours.

Parking the box next to Evaline's wager of a small flask of Teal oil, Ennaasciowt met her gaze straight on.

"What makes my little brother so willing to wager his precious stones in a game he has never before played?" she teased, carefully lifting her own cup of Teal oil that had been filled too close to the brim. "I've always warned you about being complacent within your own comfort and to remember that there are things in life that are left entirely to chance."

With what appeared to be a knowing smile, Ennaasciowt adjusted his pieces to ensure they were properly aligned to their starting positions. "I take comfort only in the science of reason," he replied. "Not in the science of fear."

"How wonderfully naive," replied Evaline, savoring the taste of her Teal oil. "I would love it if fear were a science," she quipped, "because knowing you, that would be the only way you would respect it. When you are much older, you will learn what I have learned about the importance of fear—and about the uselessness of trying to apply reason to things that are completely random. We cannot explain everything away with reason, Ennaasciowt. And so, it is fear that helps us to accept that some things are not within our place to explore, and that it is best to keep our distance from their realms."

Noticing that Ennaasciowt gave her a darting look, compelling her to begin, she carefully placed her cup back down onto the table and took hold of the small dial that was positioned next to the game board. With a slight clockwise turn, she then sent the dial spinning counterclockwise, its arrow gliding effortlessly past the numbers one through eight which framed its circumference.

And as the dial slowed, it eventually stopped on the number one.

"You see!" exclaimed Evaline, convinced she had made her point. "Completely random—as I had no influence whatsoever on the number that the dial would come to settle upon. But I suppose you will insist there was some reason behind why the dial made this selection, as well." She smirked, and continued to tease him, while moving her first game piece one position forward along the path of an interconnected system of loops that spiraled eight levels high. Based upon the position of the dial, Evaline had no permission to select from the game's brilliant stack of silver-plated cards, as the ability to select a card would have required that the dial had settled itself on an even number.

Intent on being bothersome, Ennaasciowt took his time to snicker before responding. "It doesn't really matter what I think," he replied. "It only matters what you think when you are spinning the dial. Because in the end, it is you who must play your own hand, I would think." Leaning forward, Ennaasciowt fingered the nob of the dial, slowly moving it back and forth before sending it spinning fervently clockwise, and announcing with confidence that the dial would eventually stop on the number four.

Somewhat disturbed, and preparing to scold him for his hubris, Evaline watched intently while leaning back into the wheeled seat that had been designed to keep her from over taxing what their mother called her "fragile heart."

Often angered by being tethered to it, it was, in fact, Ennaasciowt's insistence that she had the power to overcome the constraints of her rolling chair that made using it a slightly easier burden to bear. Although tending to admonish him for what she claimed were his undisciplined thoughts, she indulged him nonetheless—for it was Ennaasciowt who later gave Evaline the strength to decide that the use of a wheeled seat was a convenience more than it was a necessity.

Collecting a large swath of her hair and wrapping its unruly strands into a tightly twisted knot upon her head, she slightly frowned as the speed of the dial began to wane, but—also intrigued by Ennaasciowt's confidence—Evaline's disapproval gave way to curiosity.

As the dial stopped at its final position it landed, as predicted, upon the number four.

"Never underestimate the power of the mind, Evaline," whispered Ennaasciowt, delivering his usual and disarming smile. "My mind . . . as well as yours."

"Do you think that it is God's will for you to continue to dabble in magic?" she snapped. "There is no need at all in this game for you to make predictions, and this is precisely why I pray so hard for you each day! Your meanderings are worrisome! I will urge you to mind your step, Ennaasciowt. As your older sister, I continue to admonish your arrogance! I will remind you that, as players in this game, we are only required to spin the dial, not to direct its outcome!"

"The word 'meanderings,' in the context of a game like this, is a very curious point of view," replied Ennaasciowt, while gently lifting one of the cards from the deck.

"Ugh!" sighed Evaline. "At thirty-four seasons, you worry me deeply. You are simply much too young to be so stubborn... and so brave!"

"And while I will always respect you as my older sister, I have no choice but to cherish my right to 'meander' rather than to assume I have no agency in this game of chance," he replied. Ennaasciowt then placed his card face up onto the table, revealing an inscription with the words 'Your' and 'Will' separated by a blank space, and with three dots trailing after the word 'Will.'

Thinking deeply about how he would fill in the blank spaces to complete the sentence, his delay seemed—to Evaline—longer than was necessary, causing her to become irritable and restless. "Ennaasciowt!" she urged, tapping her fingers upon the table. "The sun will soon set and rise before you are done. You are not required to write a manuscript. A simple sentence is all that it is meant to be! Let me explain the rules of this game to you once more. The one to first reach the final position—at the top of the eighth loop—will win the game, and the speed at which we get there depends purely upon what we accept or decline to be true. The choice is ours. Your task now, is to state something you believe to be true, through the creation of a simple sentence. When the sentence is complete, it will be up to me to either accept or decline its meaning. If I accept, then I will stay in my current position, essentially accepting things as you say they are. But—if I chose to decline the meaning of the sentence you create—then I will advance my pieces four spaces forward, since that is the number that the dial has randomly selected. As an example, 'Your hair will look better if you color it blue.' Are you now clear on how simple the sentence is meant to be?"

"Indeed, I am," replied Ennaasciowt.

"Good," replied Evaline, taking an indulgent gulp of her Teal.

Raising the card to study it once more, Ennaasciowt delivered the completion of the sentence as he had envisioned it. "Your son will one day discover an important truth," he announced, placing the card back down and folding his hands in front of him.

Baffled and seemingly troubled, Evaline sat wide-eyed and speechless.

"And," continued Ennaasciowt, "by the instructions of this game, if you accept my statement to be true, then your piece must stay where it stands. But if, in fact, you decline what I have said, then I suppose the board is yours to advance your game piece four spaces closer to the finish line. Did I understand the instructions of the game, dear sister?"

Visibly disturbed, Evaline placed her cup back down onto the table with a force that caused it to topple, spilling its contents onto the table's marble surface from which it flowed freely to the floor.

"I cannot believe the things that you have the audacity to utter!" she snapped, her anger unassuaged by Ennaasciowt's quick dash to her side of the table where—by cupping his hands—he prevented more Teal oil from splattering the wooden floor below. "Look at what you've

caused me to do!" she chided, pulling open one of the table's side drawers in search of a handkerchief. "No matter how intriguing your sentence may well be, I will warn you that it is not our place to tell of prophecies—and that doing so is, in the eyes of god, a sin!"

"A sin?" replied Ennaasciowt, carefully holding the puddle of Teal forming within his palms.

"Yes, Ennaasciowt," continued Evaline, reducing her voice to a whisper, "a sin! A decision born of our imperfections, and that which forces god to punish us!" With a trembling hand, Evaline handed Ennaasciowt the only thing she could find to remedy the spill—a small tablecloth used for the setting of meals.

Ennaasciowt carefully delivered the thick puddle of oil into the folds of the fabric while Evaline slid her finger across the table's surface to glide the remainder of the oil back into her cup. And as they had expected, the excessive hunger of the family's pet cujaron ensured that the floor was licked clean.

"A sin," repeated Ennaasciowt, returning to his chair. "That is also a curious word, is it not? For if our offending actions are simply born of our imperfections, then those actions should be excused as innocent. How can you or I follow a god who would punish us for actions that spawn entirely from the imperfections that god, in fact, created?"

Evaline slowly slid her hand over her chest to settle her rapid breathing. "Are you trying to kill me on the eve of my birthday?" she replied, frantically. "In the Book of Plebony, Verse 3, Chapter 4, it very clearly states that we are responsible for our actions. Not god! Had you learned your verses, as mother required of us, you would find yourself much more disciplined! Please know that it is because I love you—and want to protect you—that I worry about your tendency to stray!"

"But, if god cannot be held responsible for the actions that are 'born of our imperfections,'" pressed Ennaasciowt, "then what the Book of Plebony is asking us to believe is that we must also absolve god from the responsibility of the imperfections themselves. What kind of religion makes us responsible for the way we were created, Evaline? And what kind of religion gives us no latitude to use the minds we have been given which—if allowed to meander —would afford us an even greater understanding of god?"

Evaline leaned forward and took one of Ennaasciowt's hands into hers. "You sound just like my father," she replied, offering him a smile. "He, like you, had always questioned everything, with no boundaries and no regard for the greatness that is Plebony herself. And as I sit constrained to a wheeled seat, my condition and that of your half-brother, Nigel's is, without question, the punishment for our father's sins. Verse 2, Chapter 1 states that no individual shall question the majesty of god, lest they condemn their children. Had you and I not been of different fathers, you—for sure—would also have the honor of sitting upon a seat with wheels!"

"And had I been your full brother, I would not have accepted the construction of that sentence any more than I accept it now!" retorted Ennaasciowt. "And as such, I would have denied such a curse upon me and would have chosen to stand—as I do today—on the strength of my own legs. I will never accept that my willingness to question god will one day condemn my progeny. But I do accept that if I

choose to limit the expanse of the mind that I have been given, that my progeny will be condemned to something less than I could have given to them. As such, on the eve of your birthday, I must ask for your forgiveness as I take my chances with god."

Giving his hand a firm squeeze, as though a tacit symbol of her understanding, Evaline then lowered her eyes back down to the game board. Reflecting on the sentence he had constructed, Evaline reluctantly looked back up at Ennaasciowt.

"Assuming I will have a son," Evaline said, nervously. "I—I suppose . . . I shall leave my game piece where it stands."

Now feeling the caress of Wybrany's hand upon his, he opened his eyes to find her gazing up at him, her eyes bright and hopeful.

"Do you suppose that we become parents only when we are selected?" asked Wybrany. "Or is this all just wonderfully random?"

"Random or not, it is surely wonderful," replied Ennaasciowt, wrapping his arms around her. "But I believe in the power of our agency and that we become parents when the selection between us and our child is mutual. After all," he continued, looking up at a portrait of Evaline, "I wouldn't be my sister's brother if I had completed *that* sentence in any other way."

Episode 33
Verse 3, Chapter 4

"WHAT WILL HELP YOU TO SUFFER THROUGH THE SOLITUDE WHEN I AM GONE?"

"Ahh . . . the wonderful, *sweet* solitude," replied Flexix. "It will be my best friend—until it overstays its welcome and becomes the enemy I have always *known* it to be. But I implore you not to worry about me in this moment of your special, *special* time. I would much rather be celebrating your conception."

"IT IS HARD FOR ME TO CELEBRATE WHEN THERE IS SO MUCH DESPAIR. I CAN HEAR NOTHING BUT THEIR VOICES—THEIR WAILING AND THEIR CRIES. IT IS AS THOUGH THEY ARE GETTING LOUDER ALL THE TIME."

"And you have the power," replied Flexix, "to ignore all of it!"

"FORGIVE ME, BUT I AM FINDING THEM DIFFICULT TO IGNORE. SHOULDN'T THE SUFFERING OF OTHERS BE MY CONCERN, AS I PREPARE TO BECOME OF THE FLESH? SHOULDN'T THIS SUFFERING BE *YOUR* CONCERN?"

“That would depend!” retorted Flexix, slightly yawning.

“DEPEND?”

“Indeed!” insisted Flexix. “Their suffering is something they brought upon themselves! It is the natural outcome of their own transgressions. There is therefore no cause for your alarm or your concern.”

“THEIR TRANSGRESSIONS? BUT—”

“Yes,” interrupted Flexix, “their transgressions. The results of their unfortunate choices. The results of their sins. Besides, I find the sound of their cries to be somewhat melodic. The fantastic convergence of regret, fear, despair, and of pain! Symphonic at times if you actually *listen!* We should enjoy this concert while we can, as you will soon grow accustomed to it—and their melody will fade into the chambers of what will soon be your apathy.”

“I HEAR NO MELODY IN THE SOUND OF THEIR AGONIZING CRIES. I DO NOT ENJOY THE SOUND, AND I DO NOT UNDERSTAND THE PURPOSE OF SO MUCH SUFFERING.”

“I have already explained this all,” snapped Flexix. “They are suffering by way of the choices they have made. They are suffering for choosing perversion, instead of choosing the guiding light that would have safely delivered them—each of them—to the shores of their next journey. A lack of faith has placed them where they are. It was not I who placed them there.” Flexix rolled all eight of his eyes in a slow counter-clockwise motion while extending all of his arms to pull himself up into the rich cluster of succulents above him. Curling the ends of his arms around the girth of a large thick vine, he suddenly flipped himself over to allow his mantle to dangle upside down. "I *savor* the sound of suffering," he continued, "by those who would dare to disrupt the cycle of life, of death, and of renewal. And I do not plan to spend this precious moment discussing the plight of the bereft, when I would much rather be helping you to prepare for what is to come!"

"I CANNOT PREPARE FOR WHAT IS TO COME WHEN I AM SADDLED WITH THE PAIN OF THOSE WAILING WITHIN THIS CONCERT. IT IS AS THOUGH THEIR PAIN WERE MY OWN."

"Your choices fascinate me in this moment," replied Flexix, yawning again. "As that which you obsess over are now merely the remnants of scattered garbage. Perhaps you'll take some solace in knowing that I didn't destroy *all* of them—just *most* of them."

"BUT AMONGST THE ONES YOU DESTROYED, SOME WERE MADE OF FLESH. IN YOUR WRATH, DID YOU FORGET TO SPARE THEM?"

"Yes, it is true that there are those of flesh who were lost," admitted Flexix, "but in the larger scheme of things, it was a smaller price to pay in my quest to rid the planet of a larger curse."

"AND SO, IN THE END, THE KINGDOM OF PLEBONIANS STILL STANDS."

"Indeed, it does," returned Flexix, defensively. "Although it was almost completely destroyed by the enemy's weaponry, the major and minor castles, parts of the palace, and most of the outer villages are still standing."

"A KINGDOM STILL STANDS, FILLED WITH THOSE WHOSE FAITH IS NO BETTER OR WORSE THAN THE ONES YOU HAVE CHOSEN TO DESTROY. SURELY YOU CAN UNDERSTAND WHY MY FEAR HAS OVERSHADOWED THIS CELEBRATION."

"You are only fearful because you do not understand," demanded Flexix. "But understanding is not required all at once. I implore you to ignore your fears and focus *now* on what is to come!"

"BUT WHAT *IS* TO COME? A LIFE FILLED WITH URGES AND INSTINCTS THAT WILL PROPEL ME TO DEFY YOU? WHY AM I BEING CONDEMNED TO A REALITY ENROBED IN FLESH THAT WILL ONLY TEMPT ME AND LEAD ME ASTRAY?"

"Lead you astray?" mused Flexix.

"YES. LEAD ME ASTRAY. FROM WHAT I HAVE OBSERVED, AMONGST ALL WHO ARE INCARNATE, I HAVE ONLY HEARD YOU REGARD *ONE* AS AN 'UNCRUSHED SEED.' THE ONE CALLED ANGLID. AND I FEAR THAT I MAY NOT BE AS STRONG AS HE IS WHEN I AM TESTED. I FEAR THAT I WILL FAIL AND THAT, WHEN I DO, I WILL FALL FROM YOUR GRACE. I AM MUCH SAFER HERE WHERE I CAN DO NO HARM . . . TO MYSELF."

"You are *nothing* here but a stream of restless thoughts!" Flexix snapped. "And without the outlet of incarnation, you will soon become as *mad* as I—that is to say—as *angry* as I." Flexix slowly removed three of his arms from the vine, dangling from his remaining five. "I can assure you," Flexix continued, "you have no more cause to fear the flesh any more than you have cause to fear me."

"BUT MY FEAR IS JUSTIFIED, IS IT NOT? AM I NOT REQUIRED TO LIVE WELL IN EACH LIFE THAT I AM GIVEN, LEST I BE PUNISHED? HOW CAN I DO THIS WHEN I AM LIKELY TO LOSE MY WAY? THIS IS WHAT I FEAR MOST."

"Whether or not you lose your way does not define how well you have lived your life," offered Flexix in a gentler voice. "How well you lived your life will be defined by whether or not you were able to find your way *back*. In the end, I will ask you for only *one* thing: to not be tempted by faithlessness and to not let your fear lead you into a state that is neither life nor death. For if you do, indeed you will fall away from me." Flexix slowly removed another of his arms from the vine.

"AND YET STILL, THE KNOWLEDGE THAT I WILL BE PUNISHED IF I CANNOT FIND MY WAY BACK PLACES A SLIGHT BURDEN ON THIS MOMENTOUS 'CELEBRATION.'"

"Minor details!" insisted Flexix. "Why not just embrace this moment? Albeit, you've noticed I can be moody and prone to acts of destruction, and I will admit that this concert of tortured souls is rather loud and distracting - but nonetheless! *This* moment is still *yours* to cherish, as you cross the barrier into the world. Why not set aside your fears and transform what you are feeling into joy?"

"JOY?"

"Yes!" urged Flexix, removing another of his arms from the vine. "You could choose to interpret what you are feeling as joy. It is your choice. After all, you only get to do this eight times!"

"I DON'T BELIEVE YOU'VE GIVEN ME THE TOOLS TO TURN MY FEAR INTO JOY."

"A pity," retorted Flexix, "and with so much potential—"

"DARE I ASK THE VALUE OF MY POTENTIAL IF I DO NOT HAVE THE LATITUDE TO SELECT THE PATH I WANT TO TAKE? ARE THE INCARNATE REALLY THE SEEDS OF GOD'S POTENTIAL, OR ARE THEY THE SEEDS OF GOD'S REGRET?"

"You sound just like your father-to-be," mused Flexix. "It is no wonder you have made this choice to be fathered by him."

"AND BY CHOOSING THE ONE THEY CALL THE HERETIC . . . I SUPPOSE I SHALL LIVE MY FIRST LIFE WITHIN THE CONFINES OF A WHEELED SEAT?"

"Whether or not you are in a wheeled seat will not define how confined or how free you ultimately are, and I know I've taught you better than that!" returned Flexix. "Life is temporary. Your freedom will come when you are transcended." Flexix removed two more arms from the vine, dangling from the only one remaining. "And now," he continued, "is there anything else that you fear or do not understand?"

"I ALSO DO NOT UNDERSTAND WHAT I AM EXPERIENCING."

"Go on," encouraged Flexix.

"IT IS AS THOUGH I AM BEING PULLED AWAY. AS THOUGH I AM BEING BECKONED—ALMOST SUMMONED—AWAY FROM THIS SPACE. AND I AM UNSURE OF WHAT IS HAPPENING TO ME, BUT I NEITHER LIKE IT NOR SEE THE VALUE OF IT."

Flexix closed all of his eyes as streams of tears flowed from each of them, converging at the top of his mantle before falling as single drops into the vacuous void below. "You are being beckoned to the flesh that is growing within your mother's womb," he replied. "What you are feeling is just the beginning. This brings me joy! Above all else, your conception is the only thing of importance in this moment, and it should assuage all else—your fear, my loneliness, and even the suffering of others." Flexix slowly released his final grip on the vine, that now seemed to be straining to hold his weight. "I do not want you to resist the force that is pulling you away," cried Flexix. "Go to it. Be one with it . . . that which is your life!"

Epilogue

"She's beautiful," whispered a joyful Wybrany, holding her newborn to her bosom. "What shall we name her, my love?"

Ennaasciowt leaned over Wybrany to gently lift his daughter into his arms. "We will not restrict this child by giving her a name," he replied, walking slowly over to a large picture window which overlooked the estate's sprawling landscape. "If it pleases you, my beloved, we will let our daughter name herself—and we will honor as her name, that which she first utters."

Stretching her frail little arms as if reaching up to her father, her large, emerald eyes were wide and curious.

"Welcome to the world, my little one," whispered Ennaasciowt, his eyes filling with tears. "I hope," he continued, "that you will accept my apologies in advance of what you are destined to discover. That we are imperfect, that we are weak but also strong, that we are brave but also frightened, and that we are still learning how and *what* to be, in a place where it sometimes may feel as though all—including god—are against us. Know, my little one, that you will be hated by some and loved by others, that you will be judged and measured by your acts and also by your inaction, and that, at the end of this life, it may be that you are lauded or terribly *terribly* misunderstood. But, on this day of your birth, also know that no matter what you may hear from others, we were *all* destined to be . . . and *will* be great." Moving his arms in a slow, swaying motion to settle her into sleep, her eyes began to curtain.

And as the sun slipped slowly below its horizon, the child without a name uttered the faint sound…

"Nadya."

-The End of Book 1-

Measurements of Time

Time is measured in *decidays*, a metric system of time that means one tenth of a day. On Earth we usually regard one day as 24 hours long, meaning a deciday on Earth would equal 2.4 hours. But on Xżyber, one day is only ten hours long. Hence a deciday on Xżyber is equal to one hour.

Calendar Years

The Xżyberian calendar year is divided into two parts, Season 1 and Season 2. Season 1 brings with it the most severe weather conditions and the most violent storms.

Moments in Time

Historical moments are measured in terms of how much time has passed before the present and how much time will pass after the present. This is because the present is the default point of reference for all Xżyberians. Xżyberians do not use terms like "last year" or "a year and a half later." Instead, you may hear them say things like, "One year before today" and, "Three seasons from today."

Critical Nutrition

Teal oil is the most important source of nutrition to those on Xżber who are still made of flesh. While the consumption of water and proteins are moderately helpful, non-Mollards must regularly consume Teal oil in order to survive.

Names in the Central Kingdom

One's station in the Central Kingdom determines the use of either an initial upper or lower-case letter in their name. The names of laborers always have an initial lower-case letter.

Domesticated Pets

The most common pet on Xżyber is the cujaron. Likened to a small dog, this animal has six legs.

World Summits

Similar to a world summit, Xżyberian world leaders meet for seasonal gatherings called
A-ummits. These meetings are attended by the leading representatives of Xżyber's four regions on a rotational schedule of every three seasons. A-ummit participating regions are: The Central Kingdom, The Western Territorial Region, the Sub-Median Region, and the Independent Settlements of the South. The Far East on Xżyber is uninhabited and the Northernmost portion of Xżyber—otherwise called Area X—is deemed an area much too harsh for Xżyberians to live.

God's Companion

The name of the character that Flexix always talks to is called "All Caps," although Flexix will never refer to All Caps by that name.

Repository of Souls

The Vangora Rima, also known on Xżyber as the "VR," is a holding tank for the souls of those who have agreed to be downloaded at a later time into a full metal replica of their former selves.

Sub-Median Divisions

The Sub-Median Region of Xżyber is divided into four sections: Eastern Cluster, Western Cluster, Northward Cluster, and Austral Cluster. Citizens of the Sub-Median Region are identified at birth by the first name their parents give them and the region where they were born. "Thai EC" was born in the Eastern Cluster, and "Timmons AC" was born in the Austral (or Southern Cluster). While these designations are required on each citizen's Birth Plate—along with other identifying information—some Sub-Median citizens choose to drop their regional distinctions and use only their first and last names when interacting socially. Laws governing the selection of first names dictate that parents can only choose and register first names for their children that have not already been claimed by someone else in their cluster. **[Glossary continues on the next page]**

Number Systems Used by Laborers

Because humans have 10 fingers, we use a Base-10 number system. However, laborers in the Central Kingdom of Xżyber must have their thumbs removed at birth. They therefore utilize a binary-staked octal numbering system for counting. This is a Base 8 system, where each numeral is composed of three vertically stacked bits, with the least significant bit on the bottom. Each numeral is the sum of the three stacked binary values. The lowest value in the stack is the number of **1's** in the sum. The middle value in the stack is the number of **2's** in the sum. The upper value is the number of **4's** in the sum. Therefore**,** decimal 5 in the chart below equals 1 x 1 + 0 x 2 + 1 x 4 = 5.

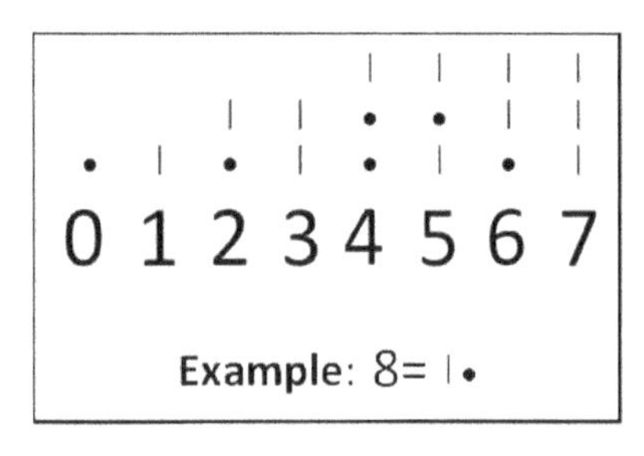

Coat of Arms

Each book in this series will reveal the coat of arms for a Xżyberian region or realm. They are: (1) The Central Kingdom, (2) The Sub-Median Region, (3) The Independent Settlements of the South, (4) The Western Territories, and (5) the spiritual realm inhabited by Flexix and other entities.

Central Kingdom Coat of Arms

This Coat of Arms captures the Central Kingdom's unwavering loyalty to the god, Plebony, the god of restriction. As devout Plebonians, the inhabitants of the Central Kingdom reject freedom of thought, intellectual and scientific exploration, or anything that has not been sanctioned by the Plebonian Scriptures. The Region's Coat of Arms shows Plebony guarding the crown, in essence protecting the Central Kingdom from the forces of what Plebony has deemed to be evil. She warns against the use of alchemy, sorcery and magic and cautions against unbridled explorations into the realm of unknown gods. The broken mirror at her feet symbolizes her condemnation of vanity, and the books in her arms symbolize the scriptures she authored. The long gold spear through the octopus symbolizes her opposition to the god, Flexix. **[See the Central Kingdom Coat of Arms on the next page].**

Maps

Maps of the various regions on Xżyber can be found on the 1iR3 Publishers website at https://www.1ir3publishers.com The following is an aerial map of the **Central Kingdom (CK)**. It offers a scaled-up version of the region, emphasizing its most prominent structures.

The most prominent structures and landmarks are:

Royal Teal Refinery
Inner Village
Octadic Highlands
Northeast Village
Military Training Facilities
Crestmore Highlands
Outer Village
Major Castle
Minor Castle
Palace Grounds
Solar Dome & Internal Gardens
Center Village
Verdone Village
CROdan International Wildlife Reserve
Central Xżyberian Straights
The Western Sea
Grandspire Forrest

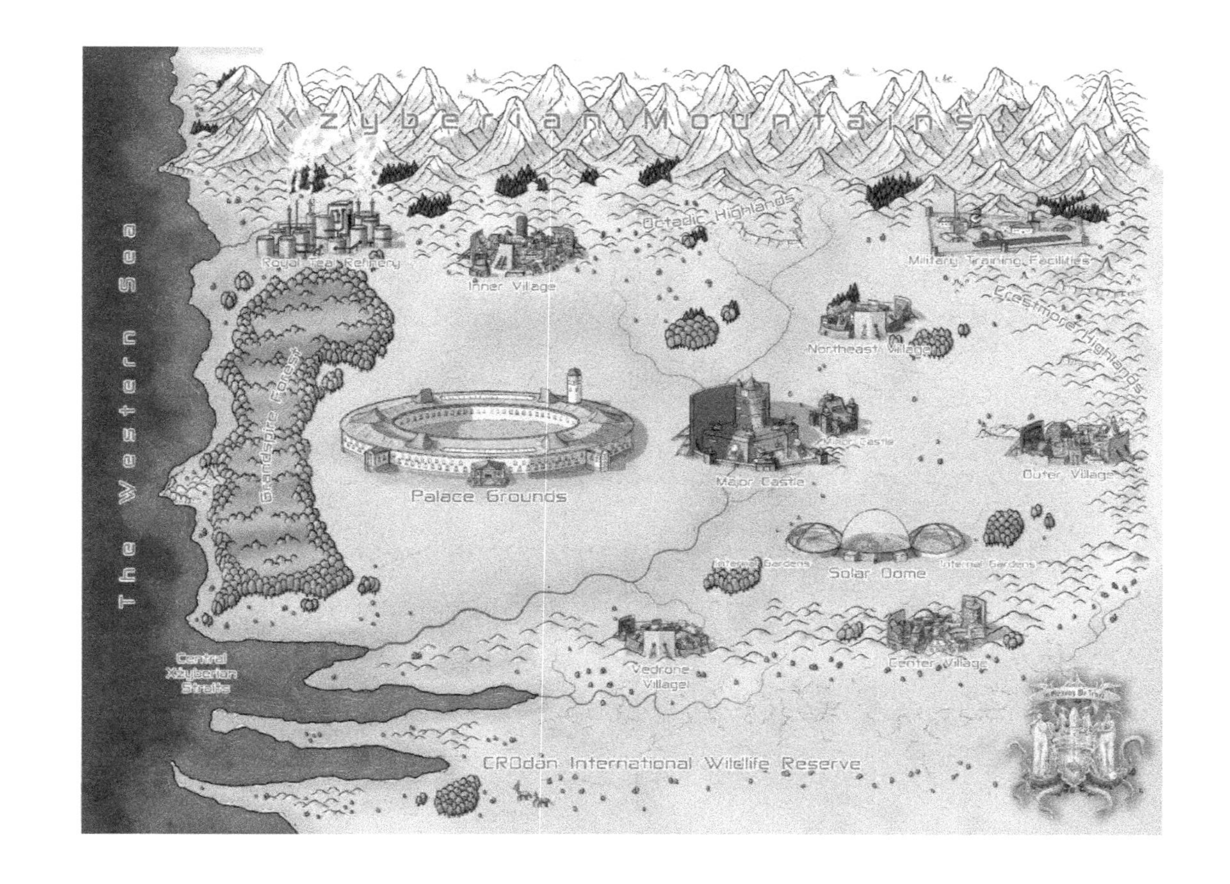
The Western Sea
Xzyberian Mountains
Central Xzyberian Straits
Grandspire Forest
Royal Tea Refinery
Inner Village
Octadic Highlands
Military Training Facilities
Crestmore Highlands
Northeast Village
Palace Grounds
Major Castle
Outer Village
Internal Gardens
Solar Dome
Internal Gardens
Vedrone Village
Center Village
CROdan International Wildlife Reserve

Stay in Touch with Us!

Keep up with Publisher Tweets on Opëshum

@1iR3publishers

Follow Opëshum on Goodreads

Opëshum (Author of Gods on Trial) | Goodreads

Email Opëshum

BookReviews@godsontrial.com

Author Interviews & Podcast Requests

1iR3 Publishers, LLC
Inquiries@1iR3Publishers.com
30 N. Gould Street, Suite 26909
Sheridan, Wyoming 82801
https://www.1ir3publishers.com
307-201-0533

Story written by Opëshum Patroz

Book Cover and Chapter Emblems designed by the 1iR3 Publishers Artist Collective. Chapter Emblems are a trademark of 1iR3 Publishers, LLC

Map designed by Foreign Worlds Cartography

Coat of Arms designed by Basumo

(Paperback)

Second Print Edition 2023

Milton Keynes UK
Ingram Content Group UK Ltd.
UKHW010833271023
431440UK00001B/93